DRAWN TO DEATH

by
MALCOLM HAMER

Grosvenor House
Publishing Limited

All rights reserved
Copyright © Malcolm Hamer, 2020

The right of Malcolm Hamer to be identified as the author of this
work has been asserted in accordance with Section 78
of the Copyright, Designs and Patents Act 1988

The book cover is copyright to Malcolm Hamer

This book is published by
Grosvenor House Publishing Ltd
Link House
140 The Broadway, Tolworth, Surrey, KT6 7HT.
www.grosvenorhousepublishing.co.uk

This book is sold subject to the conditions that it shall not, by way of
trade or otherwise, be lent, resold, hired out or otherwise circulated
without the author's or publisher's prior consent in any form of binding or
cover other than that in which it is published and
without a similar condition including this condition being imposed
on the subsequent purchaser.

This book is a work of fiction. Any resemblance to
people or events, past or present, is purely coincidental.

A CIP record for this book
is available from the British Library

ISBN 978-1-83975-036-6

Malcolm Hamer's novels include the Chris Ludlow golf mysteries:

Sudden Death

A Deadly Lie

Death Trap

Shadows on the Green

Dead on Line

Drawn to Death

His other novels are:

Predator

Patriotic Games

All are available as e-books

His non-fiction includes:

The Family Welcome Guide - over 20 editions, written with his wife, Jill Foster

The Ryder Cup – The Players

The Guinness Continental Europe Golf Course Guide

His website is: www.GolfandSportsThrillers.com

Malcolm Hamer – CV

MALCOLM HAMER has been working in the sports business for several decades. He founded his agency in the early 1970s and his clients, past and present, include Gareth Edwards, Phil Bennett and Gerald Davies; Denis Law and Trevor Brooking; Johnny Miller; Jonah Barrington; John Snow and Barry Richards; and Muhammad Ali.

His writing encompassed The Family Welcome Guide, and then a series of novels, all with sporting backgrounds.

Dedication

To Jill
With love

CHAPTER 1

It had been one of those near-perfect days that live long in the memory: a bright and gentle day in early summer, and a round of golf with my younger brother, Max, at one of my favourite courses in Surrey.

When I returned home, I stowed away my golf clubs in one of the hall cupboards, stretched my arms lazily and smiled contentedly. I'd even managed to win the money for once, by dint of a birdie on the final hole. A very rare outcome, since Max is one of those irritating people who can play any sport with a carefree skill that defies analysis. As I once said to him, rather peevishly and undoubtedly after yet another defeat on the golf course or tennis court or squash court: 'if I invented a game today, you'd beat me at it tomorrow.'

At six o'clock on a balmy spring evening I was looking forward to a stroll to a local pub for a beer or two and then a meal in a nearby restaurant which had two great merits; it served tasty and unpretentious food and some of its tables overlooked the river in Putney, in south-west London.

I could hear Max in the guest bedroom as he put away the few belongings he had brought for a weekend visit. I heard a ring on the front doorbell, which was immediately followed by a loud rap on the knocker, a demonstration of impatience which always annoys me.

My flat is on the ground floor of a large Victorian house. One of its advantages is that my front door opens directly on to the garden, but this makes me an easy prey for casual callers: charity collectors, double-glazing salesmen, Jehovah's Witnesses, and men selling 'fresh fish from Grimsby'. I hoped above all that it wasn't someone soliciting support for one of the candidates in the forthcoming local elections. All I wanted to do was to get to the pub as soon as possible and enjoy a well-earned drink or two with Max.

With a determination to get rid of the caller as quickly as possible, but without being unnecessarily brusque, I opened the door just over halfway and looked questioningly at a tall and bulky man in jeans and a grubby, grey sweat-shirt; a hood, which seems to be obligatory with such misbegotten garments, half-covered his shaven skull. Tattoos, patterned in red and black, covered every available area of his flesh and even snaked up over most of his neck. His shirt stretched to breaking point across his upper body and heavily-muscled arms. I guessed that his favourite hobby wasn't ballroom dancing; he was clearly a body-builder – and proud of it. I certainly didn't care much for what I saw, nor did I fancy taking him on in an arm-wrestling contest, especially when I looked at his slab-like, expressionless face. Standing to one side and slightly smaller (but not much), his companion was clad in baggy towelling shorts and a T-shirt. His tattoos seemed to be even denser and more prolific, since they covered his legs as well as his arms.

This was when my enjoyable day went seriously awry, as the smaller man reached into the pocket of his shorts, produced a gun and levelled it at my chest. It was far too late to slam the door. I recognised the gun as a Glock automatic, but that knowledge didn't make me feel any more optimistic about my immediate future.

It was clearly a misunderstanding of some kind; people living in the genteel surroundings of Putney are not normally threatened by men with hand-guns.

'What's the problem?' I asked. A rather pathetic reaction in the circumstances.

'You are', said the man with the gun. Mr Big then stepped forward, grabbed me by the front of my shirt, stuck his formidably large and rough hand over my mouth and forced me backwards into the hallway. My nostrils registered a strong whiff of stale tobacco, which, however, didn't mask the odour of stale sweat.

The smaller man, and I realized that he seemed small only in comparison to his companion in intimidation, followed us in and shut the door quietly. 'OK,' he said, 'you're Chris Ludlow, eh?' I nodded. He tapped the other intruder on the arm. 'Let him go. You know what to do if he makes a noise.'

'Who the bloody hell are you?' I asked, not unreasonably.

'You don't need to know,' said the smaller man and I noticed that the accent seemed to come from somewhere in the middle of Europe. 'All you need to know is that we're here to talk about a book.'

'I don't lend my books out.' I hoped that a bit of levity might help.

It didn't. At a nod from the smaller thug, Mr Big grabbed me by the throat and forced me against the nearest wall, almost dislodging one of my favourite sporting prints in the process. It showed the great bare-knuckle fighter, 'Bendigo' William Thompson, on guard and ready to do battle. If only he could have walked through the door and helped me out.

'This isn't a joke. You've got a book by some tosser called Derek Headlam and my boss don't want to see it in print. In fact, he wants the book destroyed. Every copy. That'd be in your best interests, see.'

I nodded and the number two thug released his grip on my throat. 'I'll think about it,' I said, wheezing from the pressure that had been applied to my windpipe. He was a big, strong lad, all right.

Ruefully I thought back to my plans for the evening. The gunman sneered at me. 'So, you think about it, uh?'

I could see that he was serious. I took a few moments to curse my brother Max, who had originally brought a dead artist called Derek Headlam into my life, along with his confounded book. And where the hell was he when I needed him?

My involvement with the world of so-called celebrities and their books had begun in a minor way a few months before when I had attended the opening of a new golf course. It had been designed by Calvin Blair, for whom I worked on an *ad hoc* basis. The work had tailed off while he was finalising his proposals for several new projects in Europe and Calvin was uneasily aware that I had time on my hands. It worried him, since, although he maintains a façade of being a bluff no-nonsense Northerner, he is a generous and fair-minded man. It was at the official opening of the course that I met Dan Fairfax.

He had played in the same four-ball team as Calvin and when they had finished their round I was introduced to him. We gravitated to the verandah and

Calvin ordered up some glasses of beer. Covertly I studied Fairfax. In his mid-40s, he had a fleshy, slightly florid face and was just a shade below average height, but with a muscular physique. He represented every club professional's dream customer, since he had all the latest equipment: the deep-faced driver, a couple of hybrid clubs, the specialist wedges, and the designer clothing to complement the clubs. However, as Calvin told me later and he is a stern critic, Fairfax had the game to go with the gear; he was a competent golfer off his handicap of six.

As we sipped our beers, I tried to make the conversational running by enquiring about Fairfax's business. In my experience such a question usually results in a fairly non-committal response: accountant, banker, engineer, lawyer, and so on. But Fairfax unleashed a barrage of information.

'I started in the City on the bottom rung of the ladder, Chris. A dogsbody at a stock-broking firm, and I worked my way up, got into trading and ended up as a foreign exchange dealer. You know how tough that is, old son. Made plenty and then set up on my own. Investing in various business ventures. You know, pubs and wine bars, films and telly, computer games, some betting shops. I'm an entrepreneur, in the real sense of the word, and I enjoy it. And now I've got a talent agency, too. We look after a few footballers, some golfers, you know the form.'

He paused for breath and Calvin seized his chance. 'Do you need any help, Dan? Chris is at a loose end at present and he knows his sport, I can vouch for that.'

Fairfax looked warily at me. 'Well...'

'I've still got work to do here, Calvin,' I said quickly, gesturing at the wide expanses of fairways beyond the verandah. 'There are bound to be teething troubles.' I really was not attracted by the thought of Dan Fairfax as an employer.

But Fairfax took the initiative and insisted that I should call him and make an appointment for a chat sometime during the following week. His attention was then caught by another of his acquaintances and he yelled over my shoulder. 'Hey, Alan, great to see you. How's everything?'

With a wave, he moved off and I said to Calvin, 'I'll go to see him of course, but I'm not sure we'll ever be on the same wave-length.'

'I'm told he's a good operator and generous if people produce the goods. At worst the work will tide you over until another of my course designs is approved.'

A couple of weeks later I met Fairfax at his office, a mews house just off Kensington High Street and he offered me a very modest retainer to work on various projects that his 'main man', Simon, was too busy to handle.

'I'm a fair man, Chris,' Fairfax said, as we tucked into some pasta at a nearby restaurant, 'and I'll put some commission your way if and when any of these deals take off. All right, old son?'

Although the retainer didn't even cover the mortgage payments on my flat, it was welcome. The projects were varied enough to keep me interested and encompassed the import and distribution of a range of sporting goods which were made in Taiwan, the conversion of a huge public house in Chiswick to an infants' nursery, and the placing of some 'kiss and tell' memoirs by a 'celebrity', who was celebrated only for her inept contributions to a number of reality television shows.

I made a good start and, more important, earned some much-needed commission from Fairfax by selling the serial rights in the memoirs to one of the tabloid newspapers. Although I had a very limited knowledge of that market, I was fortunate to have a 'friend at court' at *The Daily News*. Toby Greenslade was the paper's golf correspondent, even if he was rarely seen near the fairways and practice grounds of professional tournaments. His portly form was usually espied in the sponsor's tent, his elbow propped proprietarily on the bar, a glass of champagne within easy reach.

'You learn far more about golf at the bar than you do skulking among the spectators', was Toby's oft-expressed opinion.

His recommendation of the salacious life story of Mitzi Moorcock – though hardly a life story since she was not yet thirty years of age – carried the day; and Dan Fairfax's 'main man', Simon, sold the publishing rights on the back of the *Daily News* deal.

I tried to spend as little time in the offices of Fairfax's Gold Medal Management as possible, since I had been allotted a desk that was crammed into a small space in the reception area. It was much more comfortable to work in my own office at home. But on this particular day I needed to look at some information in the files about the sports equipment market.

When I arrived in the office Lindy, who was Simon's assistant, was perched on the edge of her desk, one long and shapely leg folded over the other, and in the middle of a seemingly interminable telephone conversation with a friend. I registered some sharp intakes of breath, a screech of laughter and several 'Oh my Gods'.

My own phone then rang and it was my brother, Max. 'How's the agent to the stars today?' he asked with a laugh.

'In need of a game of golf,' I replied. 'How's your no doubt invaluable work?' Max was doing some undefined work for a think-tank in Cambridge. He had left that august university with a first in mathematics; a brilliant career in either academic or business circles seemed to beckon. But since then much of his work seemed to have been curiously unexplained; especially the two years he spent in Northern Ireland.

'Demanding. Interesting. But I'm not sure it'll lead anywhere. How's the lovely Jane?'

Max was referring to my current girlfriend, who was separated from her husband, a lawyer in the City of London. 'Demanding. Interesting. And having problems.'

'With you, no doubt.'

'No, Max, with her husband. He won't let go.'

'Neither would I. She's lovely, not to say rather special.'

'Er. . . yes.' Unwilling to say anything more, I paused.

Max said, 'I met someone recently who needs some help with a book. So I recommended you.'

'Thanks. I assume he's got best-selling potential.'

'Who knows. I met him in a pub. A nice lad called Tim Headlam. Very bright.'

'I suppose he's written the great British novel,' I replied cynically.

'No, it's something about art. And he's not the writer.'

'I know very little about art.'

'It's all right, Chris, it's about the seedy side of the business, art fraud and all that kind of thing. Right up your street. I told Tim that you've got all the right media contacts and that you're just the man to help him.'

'Thanks, Max.' I said drily.

'He'll be in the Red Lion in Earl's Court at half-twelve. Tall, archetypal student, long hair, jeans. You'll like him. Must go. Cheerio, see you soon.'

When Headlam finally arrived at just before one o'clock I had to admit that Max's brief description of him was spot-on. The ripped jeans, bedraggled sweater, and even more bedraggled hair firmly type-cast him as a young man enjoying further education. I waved at him from my corner table and he ambled towards me.

'Very sorry to be late, Chris,' he said in a pleasant, well-modulated voice. He deposited his motor-cycle helmet on the table. 'The old bike packed up on the way. It's OK now.'

I bought him the soft drink for which he asked and, after the usual polite conversational processes, Headlam said, 'Your brother Max told me that you might be able to help me.'

'With your book.'

'Well, it's not mine really. It's by my uncle, Derek Headlam. Have you heard of him?'

'No, I'm sorry. I can't say that I have.'

'An interesting man. Killed in a hit-and-run accident in Rome six or seven years ago.'

Alarm bells were ringing insistently in my head. An unkown artist who died nearly a decade ago. How could a book by him be of any interest to a publisher? But I merely said, 'It's a long time ago, Tim. Remember that publishers have a perspective that stretches to about a week.'

Headlam slurped some of his fruit juice. 'Let me give you some of the background. My father died about three months ago and I helped my mother sort out his things.' I nodded sympathetically and he continued. 'The old boy was some sort of bureaucrat. He was a strait-laced but very kind man, and I was on tenterhooks just in case we found something awful, something that would upset Mother.'

'Such as?'

'Oh, you know the sort of thing. Love letters from a mistress, a collection of porn, something unsavoury like that.'

'And?'

'Nothing untoward, thank heavens, and I was so glad because I liked the old boy.'

I asked Headlam to pause for a moment while I fetched two more drinks from the bar. He decided to have 'just one glass of wine' and I came back with some Viognier. I sipped mine and it was excellent. 'And I suppose you found your uncle's manuscript tucked away in a drawer.'

'Exactly.' Headlam glugged half his glass of wine, smacked his lips and nodded his appreciation. 'Amongst all the papers, bank and financial statements, all that palaver, there was a file with a manuscript inside. Dog-eared, coffee and wine stains here and there, lots of hand-written alterations, but 300-odd pages of it. The memoirs of Uncle Derek.'

'And you've obviously read them thoroughly.'

'Oh yes, and with great interest. As Max probably told you my subject is the history of art. I'm doing some post-graduate research.'

I nodded and decided to get down to basics. 'Why would these memoirs be of any interest to a publisher?'

'Because Derek claims to have forged thousands of drawings, by great artists from Michelangelo through to Hockney. Nothing was beyond him.'

'Claims to have done them?' I said without bothering to disguise my disbelief. 'Why didn't he end up in prison?'

'Because he was a brilliant copier of other artists' work.' Headlam finished his wine in a gulp. 'And he never claimed that any of his drawings were genuine, he always let a so-called expert give his judgement, make the attribution. To a potential buyer he'd say "I've come across this drawing and I think it could be a Manet, but what do you think?". That was his approach.'

'It's still fraud.'

'Agreed and many reputable art dealers connived in the fraud. But let me give you one particular example of how good Uncle Derek was, and this also has a bearing on how this book might be of interest to a publisher. He was a friend of Anthony Blunt.'

'A close friend?'

'Well, I don't know if they were lovers. But I do know that Blunt was the foremost authority on the work of Poussin, and Derek tells how he offered one of his drawings to Blunt and with his usual diffidence asked the expert whether he thought it might be by Poussin. And the old bugger agreed that it was, and bought it.'

'OK, your uncle was a brilliant forger, but maybe a fantasist as well?'

'He undoubtedly exaggerated how prolific he was, but his works are certainly in many of the best museums and art galleries in the world. There are drawings, supposedly by Raphael, in the Getty Museum and another, by Francesco del Cossa, has been in the Pierpont Morgan Library in New York since the sixties. Admittedly, some doubts about its provenance were aired, but there are many more of Derek's works in the leading museums and galleries.'

'The connection with Blunt is interesting,' I said, 'but all that Cambridge spy business has rather been done to death, hasn't it? Novels, plays, documentaries, dozens of books analysing what Burgess and Maclean and Philby got up to.'

Headlam was silent for a few moments and then delved into his back-pack and handed me a thick padded envelope. 'Please read the manuscript. It isn't just about Uncle Derek's series of Old Master copies, it's more spectacular than that. It's about a conspiracy to foist forged art on the public on a large scale, the influential people behind it, and why Uncle Derek was probably murdered.'

It was my turn to be silent and then I said quietly, 'Murdered? That sounds far-fetched.'

Headlam looked at his watch and got up from the table. 'Forgive me, Chris, but I must be off in a minute or two.' He reached into his back-pack again and handed me an envelope. 'But before I go please read this letter that Uncle Derek left for my father and then you'll understand.'

The letter was written in pencil on a scrap of lined paper, probably torn from an old notebook, and was only just legible. After a bit of news the final sentence read: 'Please keep my memories safe, or to be rather affected, keep my memoirs safe. You'll think me daft, but I fear for my life. I like my so-called business partners, but I don't trust them. As for all those bastards in the art world, there are dozens who'd like to see me dead. If anything happens to me, get this story out into the open as soon as you can.'

I looked up uncertainly at Tim, who said, 'Look at the date on the letter, Chris. Uncle Derek died a week later in a so-called accident. That's quite a coincidence, isn't it?'

'What sort of accident?'

'A hit-and-run just after midnight in a back-street in Rome. Derek had just left his favourite bar.'

'Any witnesses?'

'None. Just to re-assure you, that's a copy I've given you. The original's hidden away in my room in Oxford.'

'OK, I'll make some more copies and try to work out if the book has any commercial value.'

'I don't care about the money,' Tim said firmly. 'I just want Uncle Derek's story to be made public.'

'I'll do my best.' As Headlam turned to leave, I said, 'One more thing. Who owns the copyright?'

'Ah, yes. Uncle Derek died intestate and his only relative was my father. So, I suppose that my mother is now the owner.'

'And is she content to have the book published?'

'Yes, she's as keen as I am.' Tim lumbered towards the door, waved and was gone.

CHAPTER 2

Over the course of the next two days I read through the Headlam manuscript. The typing was as erratic as the spelling, but did not spoil the accounts of his various artistic coups, as he foisted his 'Old Master' copies on many of the most knowledgeable experts and prominent museums and galleries in the world. His encounters with the notorious spy, Anthony Blunt, were also narrated with panache. Despite the reservations I had expressed to Tim Headlam, I became optimistic that a newspaper serialisation was a distinct possibility, since Blunt and his associates exercised a continuing grip on the public's imagination; and newspaper editors reflect this eagerness to read stories about spies and toffs.

My old friend, Toby Greenslade, the golf correspondent of *The Daily News* and its unofficial wine expert, was the obvious person to contact for some advice on the matter. We arranged to meet in one of his favourite wine bars in Chelsea on the following evening.

'Don't be late,' Toby admonished me. 'I will have been in a meeting with that odious and semi-literate scrote of a sports editor. So, I shall be more than ready for a decent drink.' Toby, needless to say, is always ready for a drink, decent or otherwise.

I was nearly late. A few minutes before I was due to leave my flat my girlfriend, Jane, telephoned me. I had met her at a party a few months previously and she had appealed to me immediately; she was lively, intelligent and very attractive. As the evening had worn on and the wine made its presence felt, she became more and more confiding and eventually confessed that she was on the rebound from a failed marriage.

'The problem with my husband,' she said, 'is that he wants to watch over every aspect of my life. His brand of attentiveness, I suppose one would call it if one were being kind, was lovely when we first met and were married, but then it turned into a sort of obsessive wish to control every minute of my day.'

'So, what happened?'

'Since I didn't want to be treated like a pet poodle, I left him.'

It wasn't difficult for me to take an interest in such an agreeable woman's problems and an enjoyable and relaxed affair did not take long to blossom. But it also brought problems in its wake, since Jane's husband would not let her go and was emphatic that he would not contemplate a divorce.

I heard an unusual shrillness in Jane's voice as she said, 'Chris, I think Hugo is having me followed.'

I said nothing since I found the idea to be ridiculous. Hugo is a solicitor with a firm in the City of London and clearly has a very considerable income, but the thought of his putting a gumshoe on his wife's tail didn't ring true.

'You know that he's taking me to Covent Garden tomorrow?'

'Yes, *Turandot* isn't it?'

'That's right. Well, what worries me is that he said something about a new dress, and that he hoped I'd be wearing it.'

'So?'

'How would he know about a new dress? I've only just bought it.'

I sighed. 'Jane, I'm sure it's just a coincidence. He was probably teasing you. After all, you do buy lots of new clothes, so it's very much a joke a husband would make. Don't worry about such things.' Before she could launch into any more of her fervid imaginings, I swiftly said, 'I'm really sorry, but I'll have to call you tomorrow. I'm running late for a meeting. Must go.' I blew a pretend kiss down the telephone and ended the conversation with some relief.

Instead of walking to the wine bar I elected to take a taxi in order not to keep Toby waiting too long.

Toby likes the place because, he once told me, it harks back to the Sixties, when he and the world were young. To my untutored eyes it certainly seems like a throwback; the sawn-off ends of wine barrels with famous vineyards stamped on them march across the walls, with empty bottles of equally famous wines arrayed above. A variety of wooden tables, most of which look at least thirty years old, are scattered around the room; a few alcoves lurk at the rear. A long bar takes up one side of the room and Toby had assumed his well-practised pose thereon, with his pudgy hand grasping a brimming glass of champagne. It didn't brim for long, as he drained it, smacked his lips and filled two flutes.

'Quite a nice drop,' he said contentedly, 'even if it's only the house brand.'

'You're drinking the house fizz, Toby?' I said in mock horror.

'Expenses are a bit tight at the moment, dear boy. Even though we are not yet even in the middle of summer my intellectually-challenged editor can think only of football. He's about to spend pots of money to sign up a former professional player who, I'm told on good authority, has to have help to sign his own name. Well, he probably puts a cross instead of a signature. And he will, of course, be headlined as "our brilliant new columnist". I pity the poor bloody journalist who has to drag the material out of him every week. It'll be the usual rubbish, of course. Everything will be "amazing" or "incredible" or "brilliant" and he'll report how so-and-so was "gutted" when his team lost.'

'It's all of a piece with the girlie pictures on the front page, isn't it?'

'Yes, those ladies of easy virtue.'

'You're being a bit hypocritical, Toby, aren't you? You've done some ghost-writing in your time, I seem to remember.'

'That's quite different, dear boy. That was helping a golfer to distil the essence of his career, and in a book designed to be read by intelligent human beings. Not the rubbish that passes for writing in most of the newspapers these days.'

I interrupted Toby before he could start yet another diatribe on his favourite subject and said quickly, 'Coincidentally, I want to talk to you about a book. It's a rather specialised subject, but I hope you can suggest where I might try to sell the serialisation rights.'

I gave him a brief summary of the work and he at once made the obvious point that *The Daily News* would not be interested. 'Far too cultural for our readers,' he opined. 'Far too highbrow for most of our editors, too. You'll have to approach one of the broadsheets. I happen to know the features editor at *The Courier* and he might help us.'

'Us?'

'Yes, us, because from what you've said about the book you'll need an experienced and skilful editor. And here he is before your very eyes. As I often say, Chris, I may be a hack but I can hack with the best of them.'

'That's very true.' I grinned at Toby as he poured more fizz into our glasses.

'And since we're discussing some interesting projects,' Toby said, 'I'm working on something that's becoming rather intriguing, to put it mildly.' He looked up as a burst of laughter erupted from four girls at a nearby table. 'I wish I were twenty years younger,' he said wistfully.

'You'd need to be forty years younger to tackle one of those young ladies,' I replied.

'Cheeky young pup. Anyway, for once my lickspittle slime of a sports editor came up with an idea. It's not new of course, but it is of perennial interest. His dutiful sporting hacks are to do some research into drug abuse in some of the major sports. Including golf.'

'That shouldn't take you long. Some recreational drugs, presumably. Some of the younger players undoubtedly smoke some pot, but not over-much. And maybe some of the more misguided ones have moved on to cocaine. But performance-enhancing drugs? What's the point? Golf doesn't lend itself to such things. Not like athletics or boxing, where you need big muscles and stamina.'

'That's what I thought, Chris. Those drug-addled athletes are beyond the pale. I wonder how far back we'd have to go for an Olympic Games which was not corrupted by drugs?'

'I suppose steroid abuse on a major scale began in the 1950s. Look at all those Russian shot-putters, the female ones, I mean. Well, that's the wrong adjective, they looked like hybrid humans manufactured in laboratories. Even their photos frighten me. Heaven alone knows what they were like close-up and personal. I'd hazard a guess that the last clean Olympics were in London in 1948. They were fairly innocent days, I would imagine.'

'Yes. The likes of Arthur Wint and Bob Mathias and Fanny Blankers-Koen were undoubtedly true-blue amateurs.'

'Your eyes have gone all misty and romantic, Toby. I didn't know you had it in you.'

'Oh well, they were proper athletes, they didn't cheat.'

'I still think there won't be much to say about drugs in golf. The game isn't so much about strength, it's about timing, about tempo, about split-second reactions as the clubhead rips into the back of the ball.'

'Up to a point, Lord Copper. But steroids allow a runner, for instance, to train harder and longer. The drugs stave off exhaustion, and so build strength and stamina. And this principle can apply in golf, since a player can practise for longer periods without strain. This helps him considerably and he can also build his strength in the gym more easily, and that brings with it more physical confidence.'

I nodded my thanks as Toby poured the last few drops from the champagne bottle into our glasses and then ordered another. 'Have you unearthed any evidence of drug abuse on the golf tour?'

'Yes, very much so. In fact, after I've contributed to the *Daily News* series, I'm going to expand the whole subject into book form. "Caddie Confidential" is the title. The inside story of what goes on behind the scenes of professional golf.'

'I like the title, very snappy.'

'Well, it's derivative of course, but thank you anyway.'

'But aren't caddies meant to be like doctors or priests? Whatever happens between a caddie and his pro must remain confidential. The sanctity of the confessional and all that. Heavens above, the things I could tell you about Jack Mason. And, if I did, he'd come after me with a shotgun.'

I had carried Jack Mason's bag on the professional tour for several years. A good-natured man, he had allowed me to work for him on a part-time basis; and my employer at that time in the City, Andrew Buccleuth, had been similarly generous in allowing me time off for the tournaments that really mattered. Jack was a superb golfer, though with a mercurial temperament, and I'd had a fascinating and enjoyable time with him.

'You're right, so I won't be naming names.'

I shook my head in disbelief. 'But, Toby, it'll be pretty anodyne stuff if you don't name names, won't it? That's the whole point about scandal, that it attaches itself to certain people in the public eye and we can all have a good laugh at their antics, and make self-righteous remarks about their depravity.' I paused, as for once Toby was silent. 'Mind you, anyone with a bit of knowledge of golf will probably be able to work out who the villains are.'

'That's right, so it shouldn't pose a problem.' Toby leaned closer, though nobody could have heard a word amid the growing hubbub generated by the early evening, after-work crowd. 'Except that I've already been warned off.'

'By whom?'

'Presumably by the connections of one of the golfers who is. . . er. . . under discussion. It was of course an anonymous phone call.'

'Which golfer? Which caddie?' I asked eagerly.

'Between you and me and the nearest bottle of Viognier the caddie is Andy Massey.'

'So, he's lifting the lid on Gary Peters? That can't be so, Toby, he's Mister Clean.'

That was a reasonably accurate description of Gary Peters's public image. In his early thirties, he is a very accomplished golfer, who has won over a dozen tournaments in the past five years, has represented Europe in the Ryder Cup and is tipped as a future winner of one of golf's 'majors'. In addition, he has a charming wife, Annette, who was once a model and now has her own newspaper column. He has, of course, 'two wonderful children', and is an active supporter of several charities.

We spent some time in discussing how professional sportsmen, especially golfers, were able to exploit their fame and earn lots of money by way of endorsements and other promotional activities. The second bottle went the way of the first and Toby waved at the barman and ordered two glasses of Viognier, 'just to see us home safely'. He then said, 'Peters is quite a slim young man, isn't he.'

'Yes, but tall and very fit.'

Toby grimaced slightly. 'However, if you look more closely you'll see that he's a lot more muscular these days. And you will notice how he keeps up with the long hitters. In the past he didn't, he used to be thirty yards or more behind.'

'Peters changed to a different manufacturer for his clubs and balls a couple of years back, didn't he? That's probably helped. And, like so many of them , he's become a gym-rat. So, he's much stronger.'

'Suspiciously so, according to Andy.'

My eyes opened wide in surprise. 'Surely he's not on steroids?'

'Apparently so. Like those cheating bastards who masquerade as athletes, he's realized that steroids can help build muscle and strength.'

'By pumping iron for longer periods in the gym . . .'

'And also being able to spend even more time pumping balls down the practice range.'

CHAPTER 3

On the following day I telephoned the owner of Gold Medal Management, Dan Fairfax, to tell him of my plans to market Derek Headlam's book, since I felt that it was ethical to put the business through his agency. His reaction was predictable.

'Old Master drawings, art fraud? Do me a favour, Chris, what's that gonna bring in? Pennies, that's what. I'm lining up a million quid contract for Sally Shears with ITV, that's the business we're in.'

'The serial rights may be worth a lot of money,' I protested.

'What, ten or twenty grand?'

'Maybe more.'

'Right, get on with it, old son, but don't waste too much time on it. Your priority should be that golf resort in Cyprus. That should be right up your street, what with all the people you know in the golf business, and the money men you know in the City.'

'OK, Dan, but is Calvin definitely on board as the designer of the course?' Calvin Blair, apart from being a good friend, is one of the best golf architects in the business.

'Yeah, Chris, we're talking about it, discussing the terms, getting down to the nitty-gritty.'

It was undeniable that Fairfax had a point about the Headlam book, and he was after all the man who owned the agency which employed me. Nevertheless, the more I thought about it the more I was convinced, against all the evidence, that it had great potential.

However, the copy I had sent to *The Courier* came back within days with a terse note from the Features Editor, David Minshall. The crucial paragraph read as follows: 'In our estimation, Mr Headlam's memoir would not appeal greatly to our readers. Much of the material is obscure and in particular the stories about Anthony Blunt are either old hat or do not ring true. My art correspondent, Jolyon Fairbrother, who is very well-regarded in the art world, went further and designated Mr Headlam's accounts of his various coups as the fanciful ravings of a man with an enormous grudge against an art establishment which never afforded him the recognition he craved.'

It was, to put it mildly, a pointed and comprehensive rejection.

The other newspapers to which I had sent the book reacted in much the same, though milder, ways and I transferred my hopes to the publishing companies. If I managed to do a deal I might well gain enough credibility with the 'Fourth Estate' to have a sporting chance of unloading the serial rights.

I discussed the notion briefly with Toby, who warned me that most publishers were obsessed with the 'celebrity culture'. 'Their favourite reading is the TV listings and the gossip columns. That's where they find their authors,' he boomed magisterially down the telephone. 'Anyway, good luck.'

I scanned the book reviews to uncover publishers with an interest in the art world and also looked on the shelves of a couple of large bookshops. As a result I jotted down the names of half a dozen likely candidates. I was about to leave the second bookshop I'd visited when a display of non-fiction books on a table near the door caught my eye. One title in particular stood out. It was entitled 'The Man Who Conned the Art World' and a quick look inside told me that, thank heavens, it wasn't about Derek Headlam. I had never heard of the publisher, but I bought the book.

When I looked at it on my return home, I found that it told the story of an obscure Dutch artist who had, in the 1950s and 1960s, forged several hundred drawings and paintings purporting to be the work of many artistic luminaries, including Chagal, Munch, and Toulouse-Lautrec. The publisher, Galbraith, was added to my list and that afternoon I despatched a summary of Headlam's book and a few extracts to six lucky publishers. With a half-formed notion in my head about 'niche marketing' I also included a copy of the complete manuscript in the package I sent to Galbraith.

Saturday dawned crisp and clear, with a promise of reasonably warm weather and I decided to drive over to my golf club and join the early morning roll-up. This is an informal group of a dozen or so members who play a Stableford competition on most Saturdays. If you fancy a game, you can turn up and join in the fun. I played reasonably well, thoroughly enjoyed myself in the company of a computer engineer and a landscape gardener, and finished in third place. I profited to the tune of ten pounds and spent several times that amount at the bar.

As I was about to leave, coverage of the European Tour's tournament in Spain began on the club's television. I waited until the leader board was shown and saw that Gary Peters was lying in a tie for fourth place.

I wanted to get home since my flat needed some attention and, in particular, it was overdue a thorough clean-up. Although I know the basics of such routine domestic toil, since my mother had over the years tried hard to drill them into my head, the bulk of such work had in the past been undertaken by my friend and neighbour, Mrs Bradshaw, who lived in an upstairs apartment. She treated me like a rather incompetent son and gave my home what she termed 'a complete dusting' once a week. And it certainly was thorough. However, two weeks ago she had fallen and broken her arm. For a lady in her mid-70s this was a severe setback. Although she maintained her vigorous approach to life, I knew that she had been shocked by the accident. Her attitude was that such things could not and should not happen to someone like her.

Towards the end of the afternoon, after some desultory housework, I decided to see how she was coping, though I had no fears that it would be anything other than with competence and good humour.

I walked upstairs, rang the doorbell and heard Mrs Bradshaw moving towards her front door.

'Who's there?' she asked.

This was unusual since she invariably flung open the door with alacrity. 'It's Chris,' I replied. 'Are you OK?'

The door then opened quickly and Mrs Bradshaw, her arm in a sling, said, 'Sorry, Chris, I'm so glad it's you and not one of my confounded relatives from

Woking and its hinterland . They're always popping in. They've become real pests.'

'Oh, surely they're just concerned about you, they want to help.'

'Perhaps so. Anyway, come in. I'll make us some tea.'

She led me into her spacious kitchen. When I offered to make the tea, I was told sharply that she wasn't yet an incompetent invalid and could manage very well on her own, thank you.

Suitably chastened, I took a chair at the square wooden table and watched as she assembled some mugs and plates, a selection of biscuits and then a pot of tea. 'Now then, Chris, what's happening in your world?' she asked brightly.

'Oh, bits and pieces, as always.' I then gave her a brief account of the Derek Headlam book and its problems.

'But that's fascinating,' she said. 'People love stories of fraud and double-dealing, and you've got the extra dimension of the world of spies and all their subterfuges and treachery. That's quite an appealing package, I would've thought. By the way, dear old Henry had some occasional contacts with Blunt when he worked at the Home Office. And he wasn't exactly complimentary about the fellow.'

Mrs Bradshaw's husband had died about ten years before and still loomed large in her memory.

'Not many people were complimentary,' I replied drily. 'Anyway, what about you? Do I gather that you're being harassed by your nearest and dearest?'

She frowned and was silent for a few moments. 'Oh, I don't know, Chris. Perhaps I'm just becoming a mean-spirited old lady, but I sense some sort of undercurrent in their concern for me.'

'In what way?'

'One of the nephews, Charles, and his very pushy wife, mentioned some sheltered accommodation near their home at Woking. "We can keep an eye on you, my dear, look after everything for you," she said, the patronising... no, I mustn't use bad language.'

I looked hard at her, since Mrs Bradshaw was one of the most equable people I knew and she was clearly upset. 'You think they're trying to take you over, so to speak.'

'Yes, I do. Charles is an accountant and I am betting that the long-term plan is to secure power of attorney and get control of all my assets. But, as I said, maybe I'm becoming a very silly and suspicious old lady.'

'You'll never be that,' I said firmly.

'Thank you, Chris. Now, how's that lovely lady of yours? Jane, isn't it?'

Jane was in the fortunate position of being able to rent a spacious apartment near the river in Chiswick, while her estranged husband, Hugo, retained the house in Ealing.

We met that evening at a brasserie near her home. Although the food was middling, the views of the river were enchanting, especially when the rays of the setting sun played on the water.

Towards the end of the meal Jane said, without any preamble, 'Hugo wants to take me on holiday to the Seychelles later in the year. What do you think?'

'Well, I've never been there but I'm told it's a lovely place,' I said, playing for time.

'No, Chris,' and the exasperation was already clear in her voice, 'that's not what I mean. I don't need a travel critique. Would you be put out, upset, devastated, if I went with him? Perhaps we can do points out of ten, with one meaning you couldn't care less and ten being that you're suicidal.'

I drank deeply from my glass of Corbiéres and tried to give Jane my best concerned look. 'That's not easy because I'm very fond of you, but I don't want you to make difficult choices for my sake, and you should concentrate in your present circumstances on doing the best thing for yourself.' Even I was well aware that my response was pure waffle, and I also knew that it was far from what she had hoped to hear.

She scowled at me and then softened it to a look of resignation. 'What a scabbily diplomatic answer, Chris. But, just to re-assure you that your mistress, lover, good chum, or however you regard me, and how would I know, isn't going to consort with her former husband, I've turned him down, because I know that within days he'll revert to his usual control freak mode.'

I had clearly failed Jane's test and merely said, 'Fine. The decision can only be yours.'

Although we returned to her apartment and made love, it seemed to be a rather desultory performance.

CHAPTER 4

I had taken Fairfax's comments to heart about my working priorities and on Monday trawled through the many contacts I had made during my days as a stockbroker in the City of London.

First of all and out of courtesy I called my former employer, Andrew Buccleuth, who had run a very successful firm of stockbrokers. After the so-called 'Big Bang' of the mid-1980s, it had, like so many similar companies, inevitably been taken over by a major international bank. However, he had managed to stay at the helm of his firm and, even more important from my point of view, he was still besotted with the game of golf.

After the usual greetings and enquiries about health and happiness, Andrew launched into his favourite subject with gusto. 'I've just bought a couple of those hybrid clubs, Chris. Marvellous. Perfect for an old hacker like me, so easy to use. But I suppose you're still hitting those two- and three-irons, eh?'

'Well, trying to,' I said modestly. 'And the reason I rang, Andrew, is to ask your advice about another golfing matter. We need some investors for a big golf project in Cyprus. A resort, you know the kind of thing. It will have two courses, an hotel, and. . .'

'Lots of villas and apartments along the fairways. Penina, with bells on, eh?'

'Exactly,' I agreed, 'and we need some capital. Rather a lot, as you can imagine.'

'Well, let me see, I can certainly think of one man who'd fit the bill very neatly. Old Roley Jenkins. Roland to give you his proper first name. A property developer, owns hotels in Spain and Portugal, and mad on the game. It's right up his street. I'll email his details to you.'

After we had agreed that a game of golf was long overdue, we ended the conversation. I added some other property companies to my list of possible investors, the owner of one of the largest golf equipment manufacturers in the world, a large wine and spirits company, one or two other firms and several wealthy individuals, who were keen participants on the pro-am golf circuit.

As I was pondering the best way to approach the difficult business of raising several hundred million pounds, my telephone buzzed and I heard the gruff tones of one of Fleet Street's finest rumbling down the line. 'Greenslade, under-paid and under-appreciated hack, speaking.'

'Was Sunday a particularly heavy day, Toby? You sound a little bit constricted.'

'No more than usual, dear boy. Just lunch with a few chums, but it did go on a bit.'

'Midday to midnight?'

'Erm, well, not a bad guess. Anyway, you no doubt saw that Gary Peters finished tied for second yesterday.'

'Yes, and was unlucky with a ruling from one of the officials, I believe.'

'He grounded his club in what he didn't realize was a hazard.'

'It can happen.'

'But what shouldn't happen is that a professional golfer calls the rules official an ignorant bastard.'

'Ah, so the steroids are kicking in, are they? Increasingly aggressive behaviour patterns and so on.'

'It seems so, and it won't do his public image much good, will it?'

'But it's all grist to your literary mill, Toby.'

'Perhaps. But I thought you might like to observe Mister Peters at close quarters. He will of course be at Shere Forest this week for the British Classic. It's your old stamping ground, so to speak* and your old boss Jack Mason will be making an appearance. And no doubt Calvin Blair will be on hand. I take it that you're still doing some work with him.'

'Intermittently, yes.'

'So, let's go on Friday.'

I was well aware that book publishers are hardly renowned for the rapidity of their reactions to a proposal, especially when it comes from an unknown source. Which is what I was; I was neither a literary agent, nor a well-known writer, nor a celebrity with a scandalous story to tell. I had resigned myself to waiting for several weeks before following up my initial approaches.

Early on Thursday evening the prospect of having a pint or two of beer before dinner was an appealing one. I was assessing the relative merits of a pleasant pub on the edge of Wimbledon Common, or those of a very popular hostelry in Wandsworth and, when my telephone rang, I almost ignored it. Then the thought occurred that it might be Jane or my brother or Toby and I picked up

---

*See 'Shadows on the Green'

the receiver. It wasn't any of them, since I heard a quiet but distinctively American voice announce that he was Grant Jezzard, of the publisher, Galbraith.

To say that I was surprised would have been an under-statement, especially when my caller said, without any preamble, 'I love that book proposal of yours. It's right up our street and I do know a little about Derek Headlam's activities. But I wasn't aware that he was involved with that old bugger Blunt.'

Taken aback by his forthright manner, I managed to say, 'Well, that's very encouraging, Mister Jezzard. Can we meet soon to discuss the project?'

'Are you doing anything now? You live in Putney, I see, and our offices and my house are not far away on the darker fringes of Chelsea. Let's meet in that wine bar in the New King's Road. The Burnished Barrel. You probably know it.'

I did know it and was familiar with its over-priced wine list, since it was yet another of Toby's favoured watering holes; occasionally, if not covering a golf tournament, he would lure me there for a Sunday lunchtime drink.

Grant Jezzard told me that he was tall, and had a beard and a pony-tail. Oh well, he sounded pleasant enough, nevertheless. 'I'll be carrying the company's catalogue,' he said. I told him that I would have a copy of 'Private Eye'.

Although my ear for accents is not particularly acute I thought he sounded like a Californian; the timbre of his voice was light and unaffected, and I warmed to its clearly humorous undertones.

I could hardly believe my luck as I hurried down Putney Hill and along the New King's Road. This man was not behaving like a publisher; he was straightforward and enthusiastic. What was the catch? I told myself sternly not to be cynical, and to take the man at face-value. Or perhaps he was hoping to buy the rights to the book for a token sum. I then tried to work out how much money I could sensibly demand as an advance against future sales. Five thousand pounds seemed to be a good number, so I decided to ask for double that figure and hope to get lucky.

The rustic tables and chairs of the Burnished Barrel were already well-populated with drinkers when I arrived at just after half-past six. I paused in the doorway and looked around and a tall man waved to me from a table in a corner of the bar. As he stood up to greet me, I could see that he was tall, several inches over six feet, and had the beard and the pony-tail. He was wearing jeans and a dark-red polo shirt. A bottle of wine was sitting in an ice-bucket on the table.

We shook hands and he waved at the bottle. 'Chenin blanc. I hope that's to your taste.' We clinked glasses, wished each other well and drank.

'I hope you don't mind my transatlantic directness,' Jezzard said. 'I prefer to be up front and get on with things. So, as I told you, I really like the concept of the book and enjoyed the material you sent me. Of course, we'll need a good editor because Headlam's grammar and spelling are eccentric, to put it mildly. Do you agree?'

'Yes, and I might have the right man for you. A journalist friend. Toby Greenslade.'

'The golf writer. Yes, he's wasted on *The Daily News* in my opinion.'

'He'd like that comment.'

Jezzard smiled and drank some more wine. 'I've no doubt you have a figure in mind for the advance . . .' I started to speak, but he held up the palms of his hands to silence me. 'Whatever that figure is, I'm going to pre-empt you, Chris, and I hope that my offer will find favour with you. It's twenty-five thousand pounds. How does that grab you?'

It grabbed my attention very well, as my grin certainly told Jezzard, who promised to send a contract to me within a couple of days. 'It's our standard agreement,' he said, 'and not bloated by convoluted legalese. So I hope it will be acceptable to you and I'm looking forward to working with you.'

When I returned home I tried to contact Tim Headlam to pass on the good news. There was no reply and I left him a telephone message which was deliberately vague; I merely said that I'd had a promising meeting with a London publisher and would tell him more during the following week.

CHAPTER 5

On the following morning, as I drove westwards in my ageing Porsche towards Shere Forest Golf Club, I felt full of optimism and enthusiasm. Apart from the sale of the Headlam book, I was about to re-enter a milieu which had always fascinated me: professional golf. It would be fun to observe it at close quarters again, to immerse myself in its rituals and its many dramas.

Shere Forest is now one of the finest inland courses in Britain, a tribute to the expertise of my old friend and occasional employer, Calvin Blair, who a few years earlier had, against the odds, extended and modernised it with both skill and a sympathetic regard for its traditions.

At the entrance I tendered the press pass which Toby had provided and headed for the first tee. It was just before midday and I knew that the golfer whose bag I had once carried on the European Tour was about to tee off. Jack Mason was standing next to the starter and was looking as relaxed as ever. He saw me and waved me over. His huge hand enveloped mine as we greeted each other. 'What are you doing here, Chris?'

'Just here for fun, Jack. Especially the fun of seeing your immaculate golf swing.'

'It wasn't too bad yesterday. Two under, but the wind is a little stronger today. Have you seen Toby?'

'Not yet, but I haven't been to the sponsor's tent yet, or, rather, the bar in the sponsor's tent.'

Jack laughed. 'I don't know how he gets away with it. And he tells me he's gathering material for an article about caddies. I would've thought that would be of very limited interest.' He grinned at his present caddie, a fit-looking but solemn young man whom I hadn't met before. 'As long as he keeps his mouth shut, knows all the yardages and hands over the right club, that's all a caddie has to do, isn't that right, Marlon?'

Marlon grinned weakly as he handed Jack his driver for the first shot of the day.

'Play well, Jack,' I said. His drive was a beauty, long and straight and into the perfect position for a mid-iron to the green. I noticed yet again how balanced Jack's swing was, how steady was its tempo. It was a model for any golfer to try to emulate.

On the way to the sponsor's tent I could not resist a look inside the huge exhibition facility, where manufacturers of all sorts of golf equipment were housed. They were selling dreams: golf balls that would go thirty yards further off the tee: clubs with 'sweet spots' that were so prominent that the player could not possibly hit a bad shot; putters that were infallibly accurate from any distance. In addition, there were the golf holiday companies which would provide the perfect golfing break anywhere in the world. More dreams.

There were several companies which were developing golf courses and their attendant villas and apartments in the sunnier parts of Europe and I took brochures from their eager salesmen. My heart sank a little at the thought that I was about enter their world and attempt to compete with them, that is if Dan Fairfax's venture in Cyprus ever got beyond the drawing board.

To my surprise there was no sign of Toby in the sponsor's tent and I decided to head for the practice ground. It was always instructive to watch as Europe's finest golfers went through their exhaustive drills prior to their rounds. It reminded me anew of just how much dedication went into becoming a leading player.

A further surprise awaited me since Toby was standing on the edge of the practice area and seemed to be watching the proceedings with great interest. I flashed my press pass at one of the stewards and joined him.

'What are you doing here, Toby?' I asked. 'The sponsor's bar is already open.'

'Very funny,' he growled. 'I'm just watching Gary Peters over there and marvelling at his power and control.'

'That sounds like a rather loaded remark.'

'Possibly. You know his caddie, I expect. Andy Massey.'

I did. Massey had been on the circuit for at least a decade and was acknowledged as a highly competent and well-organised caddie. He was quite tall, sported a goatee beard and quite long hair. His slight stoop and long, skinny arms gave him an almost academic appearance. But the obligatory shorts and sleeveless tunic with the sponsor's name and logo upon it rather spoiled the illusion.

I then took a close look at Gary Peters, who was hitting one of his irons powerfully down the range. He looked the perfect build for a golfer: a shade under six feet tall, with broad shoulders and well-muscled arms.

'Any more revelations?' I asked Toby quietly. 'I must admit that Peters looks to have gained quite a bit of muscle since last I saw him.'

'Yes, and Andy tells me that his temper, or perhaps I should say his temperament, is not getting any better. He's less and less communicative, according to Andy. The gym, the practice range, the golf course and his hotel room are the limits of his universe.'

'You mean that he's taking his profession seriously. And rightly so since success brings in its train vast rewards. He wants to be a winner.'

'Your old friend Jack Mason is a winner, but he's always been aware of the wider world. He has a sense of proportion. That lovely writer on another sport summed it up: "what does he know of cricket who only cricket knows?".'

'Fair comment, but Jack possesses so much natural talent that he can get away with a more Corinthian approach. But we're in the 'nineties now and, as another writer said, "the times they are a-changing". And Peters is one of the new breed. Totally dedicated.'

Toby grunted. 'Yes, and perhaps willing to go to any lengths to succeed.' He gestured towards Peters. 'They're off to the putting green now. Let's take a closer look and you'll see that he's more like a weight-lifter than a golfer.'

We intercepted Peters and Massey as they walked quickly away from the range towards the practice putting green. 'Greenslade of *The Daily News*,' Toby began. 'Gary, how do you rate your chances today after your excellent opening round?' Peters was two shots behind the leader.

'It's bloody stupid to make predictions,' he replied. He had a low-pitched voice with an indeterminate Midlands accent. 'I'll do my best, that's all I've got to say.' Massey winced and made sure that Peters didn't see the apologetic shrug he aimed in Toby's direction. Meanwhile Peters was striding quickly towards the putting green and he snapped at Massey, 'Let's have the putter, Andy.'

During this short exchange I took a close look at Peters and was impressed by his physique. Both his forearms and what I could see of his biceps below his golf shirt looked very powerful.

Toby and I watched as Peters went through his putting drills; he was timing his stroke perfectly and many of his putts were running remorselessly into the centre of the cup. 'I see what you mean, Toby, about the weight-lifter's physique. And he's not exactly media-friendly, is he.'

I then joined the solid throng of spectators by the first tee and watched the next few golfers hit their opening drives. They all seemed to have compact and efficient methods, without much hint of individuality or indeed of the eccentricities which might have been seen a decade or more ago. Then I joined Toby for one drink, courtesy of the sponsor, and left it at that, despite my bibulous friend's encouragement to 'have one more for the swing of the door'. I was able to tell him of my success in placing the Derek Headlam book and he jotted down the details and promised to try to secure some coverage in the weekend edition of his newspaper. 'As you know, Chris, it's not really the kind of thing that *The News* bothers with, it's not knockers and knickers, but if we get lucky art fraud and spies might steal a few lines. I'll do my best anyway.'

As I headed for home, with the uplifting sound of Fauré's Requiem coming soothingly through the car's speakers, I reflected on Toby's suspicions of Gary Peters.

A physique like his and such sullen behaviour were often clear signs of the use of performance enhancing drugs, probably the usual ones, anabolic steroids or possibly human growth hormones. But I was still troubled by the reasoning behind the use of illegal drugs; power is certainly required to play good golf at the professional level, but so is finesse and clear thinking; and perhaps the latter quality is the most important of all.

I arrived home in the middle of the afternoon when many of the parking spaces at the front and side of the building tend to be vacant and was able to claim a spot quite close to my front door.

There were a few messages on my telephone, including one from Tim Headlam in which he expressed his delight that I had made so much progress with his uncle's book. He was getting ahead of himself since the deal had not yet been finalised, but I liked his enthusiasm. I made myself a cup of tea and then settled myself in front of my computer and looked at emails, one of which was from Tim and repeated his telephone message. Ah, the joys of modern-day communication, I reflected cynically, or should one say over-communication.

Next I looked at the mail which was strewn by my front door and found a bulkier than normal envelope carrying the name 'Galbraith Publications' on the front. I tore it open and found two copies of a contract and a letter asking me to ensure that the owner of the copyright signed both copies and returned one to the company. So, Jezzard was as good as his word, and he had added a hand-written note to the bottom of his letter: 'I would like to meet Mr Headlam in the very near future, please. At my office? Early next week?'

I called Jezzard and his enthusiasm for the book was undimmed. 'I think we've got a winner here, Chris. A great story. Art fraud and fakery on a grand scale, a major conspiracy to foist the fakes onto the international market, spies, and in Mister Blunt's case a spy in high places. Wonderful stuff. My goodness, even your wonderful Queen is part of the story.'

'Perhaps I should ask you to double the advance you offered,' I said lightly.

'My bosses in Boston have already read me the riot act about the twenty-five grand. But don't worry, the book will earn many times the advance, I promise you.' It was then agreed that I would arrange for Tim Headlam to meet him at his house in Chelsea during the following week for an early evening drink.

'And I've been calling in favours from the press,' Jezzard said. 'We should get some coverage over the weekend. Oh, and you and Tim will meet my assistant, Mandy. She's a bright girl, you'll like her.'

Over the course of the weekend I bought most of the broadsheet newspapers and several of them had news items about the book, even if they were mostly brief. The headlines were variations on a theme, one of the more concise being in Toby's paper, *The Daily News*. It read: 'Queen's art expert Blunt and the fraudsters.'

The Courier gave it a reasonable amount of space with the headline: 'Blunt and the art fakers'. The report read: 'The full scale and extent of fraud in the world of art will shortly be exposed when a book by a little-known faker called Derek Headlam is published. A homosexual and close friend of the disgraced spy, Anthony Blunt, Headlam claims to have faked thousands of Old Master drawings and great numbers of paintings by the likes of Utrillo, Chagall, Picasso and Hockney. The book will be published by Galbraith Publications.'

One of the financial journals had the provocative headline, 'Art Fraud Set to Rock the Market; Stormy Times Ahead When Faker's Book Published.'

Grant Jezzard had certainly demonstrated his professional acumen and it wasn't long before Toby telephoned me.

CHAPTER 6

On the Tuesday evening of the following week, I arrived at the mews where Grant Jezzard lived and worked. It was a few minutes before 7 o'clock, the time at which the three of us were due to meet. I paused under the archway which marked the entrance in order to await the arrival of Tim Headlam. I looked down the length of the street, an archetypal mews whose narrow, two-storied houses stretched away on either side. They were a mixed bag. Some had been renovated and sported bay windows and roof gardens, and several ambitious owners had turned two of the buildings into double-fronted houses with integral garages. I wondered if they had yet installed the underground gyms and swimming pools. Gentrification was certainly on the march, if a little slowly, even in 'the outer reaches of Chelsea' as Jezzard had described it.

However, the street was still rather dilapidated compared to those over-priced oases for the rich and the privileged further to the east in Kensington and Knightsbridge. For example, the corner on which I was standing housed a car repair shop, and the two houses next to it were undeveloped. Some of the wood on their windows and doors was rotting and the paintwork looked as if it hadn't been touched for several decades. No doubt they would soon be snapped up and lovingly renovated by a young 'upwardly mobile' couple with a nose for a bargain.

I glanced at my watch and then walked out of the mews to see if there was any sign of Tim Headlam, since our meeting should have begun a few minutes earlier. I am, as both my brother Max and my friend Toby frequently point out, neurotic about time-keeping; I prefer to arrive a quarter of an hour early and wait around rather than be even a couple of minutes late. There was no sign of Headlam and I decided to locate Jezzard's home, which was roughly in the middle of the street. It had a tired, even shabby, appearance and I assumed that he was renting it. I could not discern any signs of activity, mainly because the shutters on the windows were shut tight. His office, which occupied the ground floor of the house opposite, was similarly quiet.

I walked back to the mews entrance and waited impatiently for Headlam. Finally, I heard the yammering sound of a motor-bike and, to my relief, there he was, yelling his apologies as he jumped off the bike and removed his helmet.

'Sorry, Chris, bloody awful traffic near London, even on a bike I got held up. Not to worry, eh, I'm here and looking forward to meeting my publisher. Great stuff, I'm so excited.'

I led him down the mews and he parked his machine alongside the garage doors of Jezzard's house. The bell on the door didn't seem to work and I bashed on the solid brass knocker a couple of times. There was no reply.

'That's odd,' I said. 'Let's try his office over the road. Maybe his assistant, Mandy, is there and can help us.'

The bell on the office door did work and, just after I'd pressed it and heard it jangle inside, there was a shout from the other end of the street. It emanated from a tall, slim girl in tight jeans and an even tighter T-shirt; long blonde hair added to her attractions. Headlam took a long look and then grinned. 'That must be Mandy,' he said, 'and I'm already looking forward to working with her.'

'Gin and tonic mixes well, Tim, but not business and pleasure,' I said with a mock primness that nevertheless made me feel middle-aged.

Headlam laughed. 'Of course, you've never strayed from the straight and narrow, eh, Chris.'

I shrugged as Mandy arrived and shook hands with us. 'I'm a bit late. So sorry.' Her dark eyes sparkled in her oval-shaped face and she had one of those breathy, low-pitched voices. Very appealing. 'I thought you and Grant would be well down the first bottle by now.' She looked puzzled. 'Is he not in?'

'No answer,' I explained. 'And we were a bit late.'

'Oh, but he must be there,' Mandy replied. 'He told me he'd be in the house all day. He wanted to work on the manuscript and mustn't be disturbed under any circumstances. Maybe he was in the loo.'

She walked briskly across the road and hammered on the door. After a pause, she frowned and said, 'I'll get one of the house keys. He leaves a set in the office.'

While she went in search of the keys I looked again at the house, particularly for any gaps in the shutters through which I might peer. To no avail since they really were tightly closed. This seemed odd to me, but the thought occurred that Jezzard might be the sort of man who, when concentrating on a demanding task, would expunge as much of the outside world as he could.

As Mandy unlocked the door and threw it open, a sense of foreboding made my skin prickle slightly. The suggestion of death is distinctive and I sensed something that reminded me of death.

Mandy bustled ahead of me into the room. 'I'll open the shutters,' she said, and it was then that I stepped in front of her.

'Stay by the door, Mandy, just turn on the lights. And Tim, you stay with her. There's something wrong.'

There certainly was. As the lights clicked on, a scene of devastation faced us. Tables and chairs had been turned over, drawers pulled out and emptied, and many of Jezzard's books littered the floor.

I heard Mandy's cry of anguish and I started to look around for Grant Jezzard. The stairs to the upper floor formed a small annexe in the right hand corner of the room and that is where I found him. He was sprawled across his desk, as if he had fallen asleep while reading a very dull manuscript. His pony-tail made him clearly identifiable and I was glad of that since I did not have to move his head and arms out of the profuse pool of blood that had spread across his desk, down one of its sides and on to the carpet. I could see a thick gash in one side of his neck. It was sickeningly clear that he had been murdered in a particularly savage way.

I turned away, sickened by the thought of such brutality. 'Don't come any further, Mandy, Tim. I'm sorry but Grant is dead. Let's lock the door and call the police.'

Mandy tried to move into the room but Headlam grabbed her and ushered her out of the house. She was whimpering and I felt like doing the same; Headlam had gone white in the face, which was filming with sweat.

'And I got back to the flat just before one o'clock the following morning,' I said to Toby, who was sitting opposite me at a corner table in a bistro in Fulham. It was a quiet night and I surveyed the few tables which were occupied. In the opposite corner a woman, who looked to be in her late 30s, was sitting opposite a cadaverous man who was probably at least ten years older. There was something about their body language that suggested that it was a first date. Or maybe a blind date, since they seemed both tentative and unduly attentive towards each other. Three young men sat nearby and were busy discussing football, with a particular concentration on how well England might fare in the forthcoming European Nations Tournament. At a table near the door a middle-aged couple sat in glum silence; obviously they had been married for many years and, I thought cynically, had run out of conversation.

The police who arrived at the scene of the murder on the previous evening had been sympathetic, especially towards Mandy, but had gone over every detail of our grisly experience before repeating the same questions several times more. It was wearing and very dispiriting. When we were eventually released I was about to insist that Tim Headlam stayed the night in my flat, since a trip back to Oxford in the early hours on a motor-bike certainly seemed an unappealing prospect. But he had already made his own arrangements; Mandy had offered him the use of her sofa.

Toby grinned when I told him. 'The lad is quick off the mark, eh. Oh, to be young again. No doubt poor Mandy needed comforting, so he didn't occupy the sofa for very long.'

He toyed half-heartedly with the last few strands of his spaghetti carbonara. For my part I had hardly touched my chicken salad, since the after-effects of

Jezzard's murder were still very much with me. The wine tasted like vinegar. I felt sick both in body and mind.

'To ask the obvious question, what was the motive? Do you have any ideas, Chris?'

'Not really. The cops asked all the usual things. Did Grant have any enemies? Well, obviously. Was he in debt? Drug user? Was he a homosexual? Apparently Mandy poured scorn on all those ideas. And as I kept telling them, I'd only met him once, to do a deal on a book, so I wasn't going to be much help.'

'As a matter of interest does he have any family over here, or over there for that matter?'

'Mandy said that his ex-wife lives in Boston and they have no children.'

'Maybe that's just as well.' Toby pushed aside his plate and took a good draught of wine from his glass. 'But I don't understand about the contract for Headlam's book. You say that someone from Jezzard's parent company in Boston called you and cancelled it.'

'Yes, quick off the mark, wasn't he?'

'But the agreement has been made, how can they do that?'

'True, but the contract hasn't actually been signed. That's what Tim was about to do, on behalf of his mother, who's the copyright owner. But this American publisher pointed out, forcefully I should add, that without Jezzard the project wasn't worth a bent nickel, as he put it. Without his specialized knowledge of the market and his contacts the book had no chance. No Grant, no book.'

'So, back to square one.'

'Unfortunately, yes. But I can't see another publisher touching the book, can you?'

Toby frowned. 'Not if he thinks he'll get his throat cut, no.'

Neither of us spoke for a minute or two, beyond ordering some coffee and then I said, 'I wonder if we should change the emphasis of the book. So far, it's the story of a man with a remarkable talent, a man who can fake drawings and paintings by some of the world's greatest artists. It's a wonderful story, it's amusing, but it's also old hat, because there've been many hundreds of these fraudsters, especially in the last few decades. They litter and distort the history of art. So, I'm suggesting that we concentrate on the other side of Headlam's story.'

'His fellow conspirators?'

'Exactly. The art world is a consolidation of vested interests. There are the dealers who sell the works of art and trip lightly over any awkward questions of authenticity. Then there are the owners of the fakes who want to go on believing that they own genuine works by important artists and, above all, are determined to protect the value of their investment.'

Toby nodded. 'It makes you wonder just how many fakes there are out there, doesn't it.'

'Yes, and there are some interesting numbers in Derek Headlam's book. Astonishing numbers. Picasso, for instance, created thousands of works . . .'

'. . . So there must be tens of thousands of fakes.'

'And Salvador Dali, "that odious popinjay, with a much greater talent for self-publicity than art" as Headlam puts it, colluded in the production of drawings almost on an industrial scale. He'd sit all day at his desk and sign hundreds of blank canvasses and paper sheets on which other artists would fake his work. He didn't give a damn as long as he got his share of the money.'

Toby shook his head in disbelief and I continued. 'So what really interests me about Headlam's book is his claim that he was involved in an international conspiracy to foist fakes on the art market, on a major scale, and that it involved a number of highly-placed people, persons of repute.'

'Persons of repute are usually the worst offenders,' Toby stated wearily. 'Of course I realize, Chris, that the art world has more than its fair share of fraudsters and con-men. It's like the world of finance, isn't it, the rewards are so staggeringly high, but I have to say that I get very nervous and even more sceptical whenever I hear the expression "international conspiracy". It usually turns out to be neither, and this one sounds very far-fetched.'

'Well, I'll have to do some more digging, won't I, because I think the really intriguing story is the one behind Headlam's story.'

CHAPTER 7

On the following morning I had to join Dan Fairfax at a meeting with some potential investors in the Cyprus golf resort. I found Fairfax's blend of street-wise bonhomie and hard-headed entrepreneurial posturing wearisome, but it seemed to work very well on his two targets, who promised to go away and 'analyse the nuts and bolts' of the proposed financing of the project and then give us their considered decisions within a couple of weeks.

After they'd left, Fairfax asked his assistant to bring in some more coffee and said, 'What's your mate, Greenslade, up to? He seems to be making waves about steroid abuse in golf. Bloody nonsense, if you ask me.'

I shrugged. 'He's been told by his editor to do a report for *The News*. The paper's doing a series on drugs in sport and that means all the major sports. Including golf.'

'I was told there's more to it than that and he's going to follow up the article with a book.'

'Who told you that?'

'Peters's agent, Lofty Lazenby.'

Lazenby had played the amateur golf circuit in his youth, with financial support from his father, who owned a chain of car dealerships in the south of England. He had seen an opening as a business manager for golfers and had a small stable of clients, not only in golf but in other sports including tennis and motor racing. He also had very good contacts amongst the golf administrators and was known as a tough negotiator.

'Is Peters on steroids?' I asked mischievously.

Fairfax glared at me. 'Of course he's bloody not. But Greenslade's just like all those journos. Anything for a good story.'

'Not at all, Toby's fair and honest.'

'Oh yeah?' Fairfax sneered, and then slurped some of his coffee. 'A word from the wise, Chris. Lofty and me, we do quite a bit of business together. Peters is one of the up-and-comers in golf and I may get him on to the team with that cosmetics company. So, when I do, we earn a share of Lofty's commission, and it's big money. But that won't happen if there's any bad publicity. By the way, where the hell did Toby get his information? Or rather, his disinformation.'

'I've no idea, he doesn't confide in me, we're just friends who have a few drinks together now and again.'

'Peters's caddie, perhaps?'

'I doubt it, Dan, caddies don't shoot off their mouths about their golfers. It's not in their best interests, is it?'

Fairfax grunted and said, 'There's another thing you should know about Peters. I'm talking to Lofty about his client representing our Cyprus resort. He'll be in the world's top ten golfers soon. He's young, he's just the job.'

'Are you sure that's a good idea? He's hardly the liveliest personality I've seen in the game. In fact, he was virtually monosyllabic when I last met him.'

'He's a family man, with a lovely wife and kids, exactly the sort of people our resort will be aimed at. Young prosperous families. He'll be ideal.' Fairfax finished his coffee and I sipped a little of the muddy fluid. 'So, Chris, if you'd have a word with Greenslade. Me and Lofty would appreciate it if he'd lay off Gary Peters. OK?'

When I returned home in the early evening I decided to take another critical look at Headlam's book. Although he had not named the people who were supposedly implicated in the art fraud conspiracy, I was hopeful that some clues to their identities would become apparent.

Anthony Blunt was much to the fore in the early part of the book, but was clearly never going to be a part of the conspiracy later described by Headlam. Blunt was used to far grander intrigues; art fraud would undoubtedly be beneath his dignity.

However, my eye was caught by the author's account of a meeting he had with Blunt in his rooms at the Courtauld Institute. They have been drinking gin and tonics for some time and Headlam tells how he is determined to demonstrate how he is more than equal to the 'great art scholar'.

'So, you're still a fan of the Russkies, are you?' I said.

Blunt was looking out of the window, his back to me. 'I believe that Communism is a much fairer system for society,' Blunt said in that irritating upper-class drawl of his.

Just to get him hopping, I said, 'What about all those poor bastards that Stalin killed? I don't suppose they thought it was very fair.'

'Revolutions always entail casualties.'

'That's easy to say when you're not actually in the line of fire. And how many of our agents did you and your Commie mates betray and condemn to death, eh?'

The old bugger spluttered into his G&T and I pressed on. 'And what about your chum Burgess? Another fellow-traveller, just like you. But he couldn't stand the flak, could he, when things got hot he legged it. Serves the bastard right. He was a fucking traitor to his country, Anthony.'

That got him. He turned away from the window, Christ knows what he'd been looking at. I suppose he was demonstrating how little he thought of me, how insignificant I was in his grandiose world. Blunt glared at me and collapsed into an armchair. 'Guy was a great man,' he mumbled.

'Yeah, yeah, years ahead of his time, eh. Like Martin Peters.'

'Martin who?'

I knew there was no point in trying to explain who Peters was, or why Alf Ramsey referred to him like that, so I said, 'Burgess was your friend and you loved him.'

'Yes, I did love him,' the old fool said.

I thought I'd really wind him up then, give his gilded cage a bloody good rattle and said, 'I suppose you're going to come up with that crap about the man who has to choose between his country and his friends, are you?'

'Yes. The quotation is "I hope he'd have the courage to betray his country".'

'Well, your mate Burgess certainly did that.'

'It was E M Forster.'

'What was?'

'The man who wrote that.'

I was getting pissed off with his precious brand of bullshit and said, 'What an arsehole. Friend of yours?'

'Yes, he was an Apostle, like me.'

Blunt was clearly off his trolley. I laughed loudly. 'You're a couple of thousand years out, Anthony, old dear.'

'It was a club. At Cambridge.'

'For bum-bandits, I 'spose, like you.'

'I hardly think one would describe Bertie Russell in such a way.'

There was a little more dialogue and then Headlam describes how they both staggered off to bed. Separate ones, he emphasises. It was an amusing account of how Headlam viewed Blunt, 'the great scholar', with such scant respect and I wasn't surprised that he had hatched a plan to sell a fake Poussin to him or that he had succeeded in doing so.

I could appreciate how Headlam's allusion to Martin Peters, one of the heroes of England's World Cup victory in 1966, was beyond Blunt; and how Blunt's mention of the Apostles, a club at Trinity College, Cambridge, for their intellectual elite, was beyond Headlam's ken. Guy Burgess had, of course, also been an Apostle.

CHAPTER 8

I wanted to shake off the strain of spending much of the day with Dan Fairfax and decided to pour myself a glass of wine, while pondering what to eat for dinner when the doorbell rang. Jane, clad in a dark-blue tracksuit, was standing there, an uncertain smile on her face, which was a little damp and pink.

I kissed her. 'Been for a run?'

'Yes, along the towpath.'

'Lovely. Come in and have a drink. Or a cup of tea. I could run back to Chiswick with you later. It'll do me good.'

'No, Chris, I don't want to go home tonight. I'm a bit worried. I think Hugo is still lurking about. I'm sure that he's watching me.'

I tried to treat the matter lightly and said, 'Well, let him. I'm sure he's not going to harm you, Jane. Stalking you won't get him anywhere, will it? Anyway, where do you think you saw him?'

'I was sitting on my little balcony and I'm sure he was on the other side of the river, on the towpath.'

'You could recognise him at that distance?'

'Just about. Well, I thought I recognised him. His clothes, really.'

I put my arm around her and guided her to a chair. 'Come on, have a glass of wine and then I'll organise a take-away. Relax. I honestly cannot believe that Hugo means you any harm.'

'Chris, you don't know him. He can be violent and I think he really wants to unsettle me. What he's really saying is that, if he can't have me all to himself, he'll try to make it impossible for anyone else to take his place.'

I was beginning to wonder how much importance I should attach to Jane's comments. Was she becoming mildly hysterical about her estranged husband, or were her fears to be taken seriously? Despite myself, I also harked back to one of Toby's remarks about her, that she appeared to be 'a high maintenance item'. Since he had two ex-wives in his *curriculum vitae*, I knew that he had a rather distorted view of the fair sex. His own romantic entanglements had never brought him more than a little transient pleasure; true happiness had eluded him. In other words, I did not give much weight to Toby's opinions about such matters.

Despite these thoughts fluttering through the recesses of my mind, Jane and I spent an enjoyable evening together. A bottle of decent wine and some very tasty dishes from a local Indian restaurant usually provides the basis for fun and relaxation.

Quite early on the following morning we set out to run back to Jane's apartment. The sun was already glinting brightly in a crystal-clear blue sky and, when we reached the river, there was hardly a ripple on its surface. Even in the heart of a huge city I was affected by a real feeling of serenity. Plenty of other runners were out and about, as well as a good number of scullers; we made sure that we gave the cyclists, especially the lycra-clad loonies fantasizing about being in the final stages of the Tour de France, a wide berth. Jane runs well, with an easy rhythm, and it was fun, especially since there was an obvious sense of camaraderie amongst the runners, some of whom exchanged nods, grins and an occasional thumbs-up.

When we reached Jane's home, she made some much-needed tea and I suggested that we should sit on her balcony so that she could point out where she thought she had seen Hugo on the previous evening. All I could see were serried ranks of trees and bushes. Jane pointed vaguely across the water at a small gap in the foliage.

'About there, I think. I'm sure he was wearing one of his checked shirts, a blue one, but I could be wrong.'

'Was he there for long?'

'No, just a minute or two.'

'So, it could have been someone taking a walk before dinner and he just stopped to look at the river. People do that, Jane, it's one of the pleasures of walking along the towpath.'

'Yes, of course. But then I knew you wouldn't take me seriously.'

I saw how her face had tightened and in response I offered to visit her at any time if she felt that Hugo was spying on her. Then I finished my tea and set out back to my flat, this time at a more sedate pace than on the way over with Jane.

At home I did my stretching routine while listening to several inconsequential interviews on the BBC's 'Today' programme and switched to a music station while I pushed and pulled at the weights I kept in the spare bedroom. At the end I felt very tired and a little bit complacent; I still seemed to be in reasonable physical condition, but perhaps not as fit as Jane.

I was looking forward to the soothing properties of a hot shower, when my doorbell rang. Maybe it was the postman, I thought, but instead I found my neighbour, Mrs Bradshaw, on the doorstep. She was holding a large brown envelope and was looking rather stern. She doesn't usually do stern; friendly and jovial is more her style.

Clad in track-suit trousers and a T-shirt, I must have presented a dishevelled appearance and Mrs Bradshaw said, 'Oh, Chris, I'm sorry to disturb you, you've just been out for a run, I see. I'll come back later when you've recovered.'

'No, you won't. Please come on in.' I ushered her inside, careful not to jolt her injured arm. We settled in my kitchen and while I made some coffee, I looked quizzically at her. 'You look a bit ruffled, Mrs Bradshaw, which isn't like you. A problem?'

'Not ruffled, as much as annoyed, even indignant. It's those damned relatives again.' She reached into the envelope with her good hand and pushed a glossy brochure towards me. 'Just look at this rubbish.'

The Golden Acres Retirement Home did not leave any hyperbole untouched in its description of its facilities and services. 'Elegant suites of rooms' specially designed for elderly residents; 'beautiful grounds with immaculate lawns'; '24- hour care available from trained medical staff', and so on. One of its closing exhortations was as follows: 'Leave your cares behind you and enjoy your sunset years at Golden Acres'.

I nearly laughed, but Mrs Bradshaw was looking very serious, so instead I shook my head in disbelief. The thought of her in such an environment was bizarre. 'My nephew Charles sent this nonsense to me, a part of their campaign to take me over. Sunset years indeed, how patronising can you get? He also tells me that there's a vacancy and that he's negotiated a very good deal for me. And that the home is only a few miles from where they live, so they will always be on hand to look after me if the need arises.' She paused for breath.

'So, what will you do?' I smiled in anticipation of Mrs Bradshaw's reply.

'What do you think, Chris? I'm going to tell them in no uncertain terms that I'm happy here in London and have no intention of allowing them to inflict the living death of a retirement home on me.'

I grinned at my delightful and formidable neighbour and raised my cup in a mock salute. 'That should do the trick.'

CHAPTER 9

When Mrs Bradshaw left I had my shower and sat down at my desk in order to give some more thought to what I might do with Derek Headlam's memoirs. Toby had already made the obvious and dispiriting point that the murder of Grant Jezzard would hardly have enhanced the book's appeal to other publishers.

I was more than ever convinced that Headlam's book should be adapted to tell a story with a different emphasis. His account of his life as an art forger was of great interest, but his claims that he was a part of an elaborate conspiracy to create hundreds of fakes and unload them on an unsuspecting art market was of even greater import and was made more intriguing by Headlam's contention that several well-known people were involved in the plot. In addition, Grant Jezzard's murder became an integral and fascinating part of the story.

Unfortunately none of the co-conspirators was named in the memoirs. I would have to try to identify them. The obvious person with whom to start was Charlie Corbett, one of Headlam's lovers who loomed large in his story.

I looked back at one of the many passages about him.

Charlie Corbett was such a handsome young man and intelligent with it, too, though he was a little pretentious about his so-called social status. Who gives a toss what school he'd been to? You've got to live in the present.

I think I met him in some pub in Soho, one of those places where the arty-crafty people gathered with their hangers-on. I say I think so because there were days when I would have my first drink before midday, lurch down the road to Michaela's Club for the afternoon session and then return to the boozer for some more at half-past five. So, you can imagine that my memory of what happened, and when, and who with, can be pretty hazy.

But I was delighted and surprised when we hit it off so well and soon Charlie had moved into my tiny flat in Pimlico. We had such a lot of fun.

And then we moved to Rome after a few months. I hadn't said much to him about my copies. After all, I just did an occasional drawing or painting to make some money. As far as Charlie knew I was a dealer, and a small-time one at that, in minor works of art.

However, one day off we went to the beautiful Villa Medici to see an exhibition. I've still got the catalogue of course. 'Landscapes in European Drawings of 16th Century Rome'. A bit of a mouthful, but works by some of the greatest artists were being shown. Raphael, Giorgione, Titian, Fra Bartolomeo, Breughel and so on. Wonderful stuff.

I decided to wind Charlie up a bit. He looked gorgeous, by the way, in his tight trousers, his silk shirt, with his hair down to his shoulders. There was a drawing by Jan Breughel the Elder, the temples of Venus and Diana at Baiae, it was called. I pointed to it and asked Charlie what he thought of it. 'Very fine,' he said, with that slight drawl that he sometimes affects. 'Typically vigorous Breughel.'

'I see that your expensive education wasn't entirely wasted,' I replied and then read from the catalogue. 'The landscape is not recorded in the authoritative study of the artist's drawings by M Winner. Why d'you think that is, Charlie?'

He shrugged rather indifferently and I whispered in his shell-like. 'Because it's one of mine. I did it in the early 'sixties and flogged it to a London dealer.'

Charlie looked at me in total disbelief, or maybe contempt, for what he saw as a ridiculous lie. 'Oh, come off it, Derek, I've seen some of your copies. Don't get me wrong, love, they're bloody good. . . but you're a dealer. . . just a dealer.'

I grinned at him. 'More than that, luvvie. In fact, I'm surprised there're none of my Giorgiones here. I've done a few in my time. Let's have a look for them.'

How was I to find Corbett? Without any hope of success I looked in the London telephone directory. He was not listed and hardly likely to be since, as Headlam pointed out several times in his book, Corbett had been spoiled all his life; he was a 'kept man' and the telephone would be in the name of his current keeper. Furthermore, there was no reason to think that he lived in London; a more exotic place like Rome or the south of France was just as likely.

I hoped that Toby would be able to help and I called him at his home. Since it was mid-morning I reckoned that I had an even chance of finding him there, before he was lured out for a convivial lunch somewhere in west London.

I was in luck. After a couple of rings Toby picked up the telephone. 'Greenslade, scribe, speaking,' he growled.

'Ludlow, seeker after information,' I countered.

'Do you have the money to pay for it?'

'No. I'm relying on your kindness of heart.' I heard a non-committal grunt. 'I need to find an associate of Derek Headlam's. His boyfriend in the Seventies and early-Eighties. Charlie Corbett. Any ideas?'

'Has he been in the public eye? If he's been a naughty boy, *The News* might have a file on him.'

'Nothing that would interest a paper like *The News*. Headlam accuses him in the book of stealing a car from him, but nothing came of it.'

There was silence from Toby, except for a slurping sound. Coffee, I hoped, at this relatively early hour.

'If Corbett is still on the London scene and if he's still mixed up with the arty crowd, a freelancer called Larry Steinmann might know where he can be found. He covers a lot of ground. Good contacts in the theatre, publishing and so on. We used to know each other well. I'll get his number for you.'

I heard some shuffling of papers and some more slurping. 'That's coffee you're drinking, I hope, Toby.'

'Bloody Mary. Medicinal purposes only.' He gave me Steinmann's number. 'By the way, I have a meeting tomorrow with the Chief Executive of the European Golf Tour.'

'Jeremy Foote?'

'The very same.'

'About?'

'Drugs in golf. And very dismissive he was, but at least he agreed to meet me. To put my mind at rest, as he put it in his rather patrician way. Would you like to join us? As my research assistant, we'll say.'

'Where and when?'

'Foote has a luncheon appointment at the Ritz at half-past twelve and can give me half an hour before that.'

'Fine. I'll see you there at midday'.

CHAPTER 10

The Rivoli Bar at the Ritz Hotel is a wonder to behold with its huge chandeliers, ornate furniture and fanciful decorations. It is flamboyance personified and, as I entered the room, I smiled with pleasure at this remarkable display of Edwardian high camp.

Toby was already ensconced at a table by a window with a glass of wine in front of him. Unusually for him, it wasn't champagne. I nodded at it. 'The fizz not good enough for you, Toby?'

'A bit beyond my means, dear boy. What a place this is, do take a look at the prices. Let's see, how about a bottle of vintage Bollinger and a few grams of Beluga caviar. No change out of five hundred pounds, sir. That's why I'm imbibing a modest glass of white Burgundy. Let's hope the Chief Executive of the European Tour will pick up the bill. By the way, what do we know about Mister Foote? I've met him a few times, but don't know much about his background.'

I had called a few people, including Jack Mason and Andrew Buccleuth, to find out what they knew about Jeremy Foote, but the resulting information was far from startling. 'It's pretty standard stuff,' I told Toby. 'He started out after university at an advertising agency, did various jobs in the sports equipment industry and then joined an agency which handles broadcasting rights for various sporting bodies.'

'Yet another media-tart.'

'Yes, Toby, a bit like you.'

'I like to think of myself as a media professional,' Toby said sharply. 'Was his agency by any chance involved in golf?'

'Yes, and also heavily involved in athletics.'

'Really.' Toby raised his eyebrows theatrically and grinned. 'So he should know plenty about the misuse of drugs in sport.'

'Presumably, but of course he won't admit it. Anyway, here he comes. We'll ask him about athletics later.'

Foote, a tall and stocky man in a dark-grey suit, complemented by a boldly-striped tie, walked towards us. His fleshy face was topped by a thick mantle of grey hair and he was carrying a bulky briefcase.

We stood to greet him and his smile revealed teeth of a startling brightness. 'Toby, very nice to see you again.' He looked at me and shook my hand briefly and I gave him my name.

Foote looked puzzled. 'I know the name from somewhere. Forgive me.'

'Chris is helping me with my research,' Toby said quickly. 'He's in the golf business, he's worked with Calvin Blair, the golf architect for instance.'

'Ah yes, and was a caddie, I seem to recall,' Foote said stiffly.

'Which is why he has some specialist knowledge which is germane to the project on which I'm working,' Toby said quickly.

Foote shrugged, sat down and said, 'I believe that your favourite tipple is champagne, is it not, Toby? A bottle is on its way. As you know, I don't have much time so let's get down to it, shall we.'

'It's simple enough,' Toby replied. 'I'm doing some articles for *The News* about the use, or abuse I should say, of drugs in sport. Specifically in golf. My question to you, Jeremy, and it's a leading one, is this. Is the use of performance-enhancing drugs a problem in golf and, if so, what is the European Tour doing about it?'

The question hung in the air as the waiter arrived with the champagne and poured it into the saucer-shaped glasses that are favoured in the Ritz.

We raised our glasses and Foote spoke. 'And a simple response, Toby. In the Tour's opinion, and mine of course, such drugs are not a problem and, therefore, we don't have any special measures in place to combat it.'

'In your opinion,' Toby replied with thinly veiled sarcasm.

'Yes. Do you have a contrary one?' The timbre of his voice was flinty.

'I certainly do because I have information which would contradict you.'

'Inside information, no doubt,' Foote replied cynically. 'Perhaps from a former caddie, for instance, like Chris?'

'It's from a reliable source, from someone who has nothing to gain from disclosing what he knows.'

I interrupted. 'Just to be clear, Mister Foote, what tests, if any, has the Tour instituted to check on steroid abuse and so on?'

'As I said before,' Foote replied with a weary note in his voice, 'there isn't a discernible problem in our sport, so all we have done is run a pilot scheme. Urine tests. That's all.'

'And?'

'And nothing. We found traces of recreational drugs on a couple of occasions. Marijuana. Not hard drugs like cocaine. So, nothing to be concerned about.'

'But I'm told that if someone is using human growth hormone drugs it won't show up in a urine test,' Toby said. 'Only a blood test will reveal it.'

Foote looked hard at Toby. 'As I have said, there is no evidence that golfers are breaking the rules by using such drugs.'

'Athletics officials used to take the same line years ago and now we know that particular sport is riddled with drug cheats. You must have encountered the problem time and time again when you were involved with that so-called sport,' Toby stated, with venom in his voice.

'I simply helped to sell the television rights in various events,' Foote replied. 'I had no part in the administration of the sport itself.'

'Of course not, but you certainly had an inside track in the sport,' Toby grinned at his unintentional pun, 'and you must have known the extent of the cheating that's been going on for decades.'

The discussion continued for several more minutes as Toby cited various examples of drug abuse in athletics, cycling, tennis and other sports and Foote kept pointing out that such illegal activities had not tainted professional golf. Eventually a waiter arrived and poured the last of the champagne into our glasses. Foote glanced at his watch and told the waiter to put the drinks on his tab, since he was having lunch in the restaurant. 'I must be off in a moment,' Foote said. 'But I have to say, Toby, that I think you're on the wrong track if you think that golf has a problem with drugs. I will emphasise the point again, which is why I have so little to say on the subject.' He glanced at me. 'What about you, Chris, did you encounter any drug abuse during your days as a caddie?'

'Well, I carried for Jack Mason and his only problem was carried in a bottle. Beer, and the stronger the better. But I can understand why some of the younger pros are mis-using steroids in order to put on muscle. Muscle equals power, after all.'

Foote drained his glass and rose to his feet. 'All I can say, Toby, is that I hope you'll be very careful about what you write. I'm concerned about the good name of our great game, and I should warn you that if you libel any of the golfers they'll come after you with a phalanx of lawyers. And so will the Tour, if you attempt to damage its reputation.' He nodded at me, picked up his briefcase and headed for the restaurant on the other side of the hotel.

Toby watched him go and, with more than a hint of disdain in his voice, said, 'What did you make of the Chief Executive, Chris?'

'Strait-laced, wary, rather pompous.'

'Yes, Foote played such a straight bat that you wonder what he's afraid of.'

'I didn't like his warning shot either, Toby.'

'Ah yes, the lawyers. I'm always suspicious of people who use such a threat. I like the character in one of Shakespeare's plays, Henry the Sixth I think it is, who's talking to his friend about what would make a better world and he says "the first thing is, let's kill all the lawyers".'

I laughed and asked Toby what he intended to do next.

'Talk to some of the other caddies, probably,' he replied. 'And I'd like to know where young Gary Peters gets his drugs. Or rather, from whom.'

'Maybe he knows some of the athletes. Come to think of it, his agent looks after a couple of them. There's a distance runner. Ron Rigby, that's his name.'

Toby looked at his empty glass. 'Let's go round the corner, there's a decent pub there, and you don't pay a king's ransom for a glass of wine. By the way, how did you fare with Larry Steinmann?'

'Fine, I'm seeing him later today.'

I met Steinmann outside the door of Michaela's Club, Charlie Corbett's old haunt. Situated in a narrow alley off one of Soho's main streets, it was an unprepossessing location and Steinmann, a very thin man with a shaven head and clad in shabby jeans and an anorak, hardly gave it any added glamour. However, he greeted me warmly with a broad smile. 'Any friend of Toby's...' he said with a laugh. 'How is the old devil?'

I assured him that the old devil was in fine form and Steinmann rang the bell by the front door of the club and then muttered into the entry-phone. 'It's not exactly the Ritz,' he said, as the door buzzed and we started up the stairs, 'but Michaela runs it with panache and there will surely be someone around who'll put us on the trail of Charlie Corbett.'

If the approach to the club had been unappealing, so was the room which greeted us on the first floor. The small bar which faced the entrance hardly seemed big enough to contain the woman enclosed within it. She was at least six feet in height and must have weighed in at over sixteen stones. This was the proprietor, Michaela, as Steinmann told me quietly.

The shelves behind her were crammed with assorted bottles and every other square inch of wall was occupied by drawings, prints, photographs, framed press cuttings, pieces of ornamental china and other memorabilia. Tables and chairs were scattered about in the confined space of the room and benches, the red upholstery faded and stained, ran along the walls.

It was early in the evening and there were only around a dozen or so customers, but the place seemed crowded. Steinmann waved a greeting to a group at one of the tables. One of them, a lady 'of a certain age' had long hair, dyed purple, and an array of piercings in her ears and nose, and one of the men had a Mohican haircut. The third member of the party had a swathe of blonde hair, thick make-up, and a bright green dress. I glanced at her hands, which were huge and guessed that she probably wasn't quite what she appeared to be.

Steinmann informed me that the woman with all the ironmongery was 'Stephanie, the performance artist.'

'Very interesting,' I muttered unconvincingly. 'What a fascinating place this is.'

'Yes, it has quite a history. It's a haven for all sorts of artists, a few are even successful, like Stephanie over there, but most are wannabes, poseurs, perverts of all sexes, drunks and con-artists.'

'Well, we'd better have a drink then.'

'I don't recommend the wine,' Steinmann warned me. 'Bottled beer or spirits for safety. Do you mind if I have a gin and tonic?'

I walked over to the bar and asked Michaela for two G and Ts.

'You're new here, aren't you, dearie?' she said in a surprisingly light, almost girlish, voice. 'How do you know Larry?'

'Oh, through work. I do a bit of writing.'

'Scribblers are always welcome here.'

I took the drinks over to a corner table and sat on a bench next to a haggard-looking man who was holding forth to his two companions about the Tate Modern and its duties towards aspiring British artists. I nodded at him and said to Steinmann, 'Perhaps we should ask him about Corbett.'

'Maybe, but the best bet will be Michaela herself. She knows everybody and, especially, who's doing what to whom.'

'Well, the sooner the better, Larry. This place isn't exactly my scene.'

'I don't blame you. I'm only a member for professional reasons. It's a great source of gossip.'

Steinmann then cleverly led me into a conversation about art fraud and we swapped some of the well-known stories about Elmyr de Hory, Wolfgang Beltracchi, Tom Keating and, of course, Derek Headlam. 'I gather that you're involved in a book about Headlam,' Steinmann said, his voice loud enough for our neighbours to hear.

'Yes, and I want to talk to one of his old friends who features a lot in the book. Charlie Corbett. Have you heard of him? Any idea where I might find him?'

The interest kindled in the man sitting close to me at the neighbouring table was tangible. 'Sorry to interrupt you,' he said, 'I'm Edmund and I couldn't help overhearing you. Charlie Corbett. Yes, he used to come here quite a bit, though I haven't seen him for some time. He's probably found himself another meal ticket. A rich one no doubt. That bitch has always had his eye on the main chance. Show me the money is his rule in life.'

'Do you know who the meal ticket might be?' Steinmann asked.

'No, but Michaela might. Michaela darling', he shouted, 'd'you remember that nasty piece of work, Charlie Corbett? Any idea where he might be found?'

'Well, Edmund, to quote the lovely Dylan Thomas "what do you want to find him for?" Anyway, who's after him? He used to drink down the road, you know.'

'Who did?' asked Edmund.

'Dylan Thomas.'

Steinmann strolled the few yards to the bar and explained that I was helping to prepare a book about Derek Headlam, that Corbett was an important part of the story and that I wanted to check some of the facts, and the allegations, that had been made about him in the book.

'Oddly enough,' Michaela said, 'I think he's shacked up with a lawyer, and maybe he'll need one by the sound of it.' She gave a high-pitched giggle.

'A lawyer who lives in Kensington. Oh dear, that's not much heip, is it.' She was silent for a moment or two. 'He isn't a member or I'd have his details. Maybe I've got his business card somewhere. I used to ask people for their cards if I didn't know them. Have another drink, dearie, while I have a look around.'

A few minutes later Michaela called Steinmann across to the bar and handed him a business card. 'Jot the details down, dear, will you, and bring it back, please. You never know, I might need a good lawyer one day.' She emitted another of her high-pitched giggles.

We both looked at the card. The lawyer's name was James Tallis of Storey and Tallis, Solicitors, and their office was in Chancery Lane.

'So, how do I find his home address?' I asked Steinmann. 'Somehow I don't think I'll get anywhere by calling his office and asking for it.'

'No, but don't worry, I can help you with that. I'll give you a call in the morning.'

CHAPTER 11

Steinmann was as good as his word and gave me James Tallis's address before 10 o'clock on the following morning. I knew the street, which was on the north side of Kensington High Street and was notable for its rows of compact Victorian houses.

I thought about the part that Charlie Corbett had played in Derek Headlam's story and tried to analyse what he might be able to tell me – if anything. According to the memoirs Headlam had been blackmailed into becoming a part, and a crucial one, of the plot to unload great numbers of fakes on the art market. But it was frustrating that he had not given the names of his co-conspirators. Presumably he had been too frightened to do so; and that had proved to be a precaution too far since, according to his nephew, Tim, he had been murdered anyway.

But would Corbett have any knowledge of the other members of the band of fakers? By that time in Headlam's life their relationship was over; in fact it had ended in acrimony with Headlam claiming that Corbett had stolen a car from him, 'something called a Spider' as he put it, and that he had later retaliated by refusing to stand bail for Corbett when he was arrested for possession of cocaine.

I wasn't sure how I could put any significant pressure on Corbett to help me, but decided to pay him a visit anyway. It was just after 10 o'clock and presumably Tallis would be out of the way by now and pursuing his legal calling, and the 'kept man' would be out of his silk dressing gown and ready to face the day.

The house was at the closed end of a cul de sac of Victorian houses, its side overlooking the graveyard of a small and charming church, so that precluded any problems with noisy neighbours. A compact paved area, where potted plants were scattered, led up to the front door. A window box alongside was bright with flowers.

I pressed the doorbell and heard it ring. I waited for a moment or two for a response and then tried again. I then became aware that someone was inspecting me from the safety of the front window. I lifted my hand in greeting and smiled.

I saw the figure move away from the window and then heard the noise of locks turning and bolts being drawn. Finally, the door opened and someone I assumed to be Charlie Corbett stood before me.

'Yes. What can I do for you?' The tone was bored, almost dismissive.

'Mister Corbett? Mister Charles Corbett?' I asked.

'Who's asking?'

'I'm Chris Ludlow and I was given your name by Derek Headlam's nephew, Tim.'

'I don't know him.'

'But you knew Derek, I believe, and I wondered if you can help me. It's in connection with Derek's memoirs. I'm helping Tim with their publication and there are some aspects of the story that we need to check.'

'Well, you'd better come in, though I've an appointment in half an hour, so I'm pushed for time.'

Corbett was dressed in well-cut dark trousers and a shirt which was a little too tight for a forty-ish man with the beginnings of a paunch. His cheeks also bore the marks of good living. He took me into a living-room just off the hallway. It was comfortably furnished, with one wall covered in bookshelves, while the other walls were covered with drawings and paintings.

I gestured at a group of four drawings above the fireplace. They showed four different aspects of the same youthful face and I guessed it was Corbett's. 'Headlam's work?'

Corbett nodded and waved me into a chair, but remained standing by the fireplace.

'What a brilliant man your friend Headlam was,' I said. 'All those fakes...'

'... copies,' Corbett interrupted.

'If you wish. But was he as prolific as he claimed?'

'I don't know. I wasn't involved in his work, his business.'

'But you knew enough to tell someone in the Home Office that your former friend had placed some of his so-called copies in some very important places. For instance, a Cossa drawing in the Pierpont Morgan Library in New York, a Breughel in the Metropolitan Museum and a Piranesi drawing in the Danish National Gallery. Not bad for starters. But I need to know who that Home Office bureaucrat is, because Headlam doesn't give any names. I assume he was scared of what might happen to him.'

Corbett looked hard at me, suspicion written large on his face. 'I don't remember her name. I only met her briefly and it was some time ago.'

'But you helped her, did you not, because you'd been caught in possession of a large quantity of cocaine and you were under threat of imprisonment?'

'It was planted on me.'

'And Headlam wouldn't help you, would he? Because a few years before you'd stolen a car from him and you weren't exactly in his good books any more.'

'What bloody nonsense. The car was a gift and Derek made up the story when our relationship ended.'

'But you gave this mysterious Home Office lady enough information about Derek to enable her to force him into churning out forgeries for her and her chums to sell on the open market.'

'That sounds ridiculously far-fetched to me. Derek was just a talented copyist, he wasn't in the big time. When I was with him, he just wanted to make enough money to enjoy *la dolce vita*. Not that the *vita* ever became very *dolce*, I'm sorry to say.' He moved towards the door to signal the end of the conversation.

'Well, if you do remember any names. . . ' I gave him my card and he put it on a table without looking at it.

'You must excuse me,' Corbett said, 'I've things to do.' He ushered me towards the front door.

'What about the gentleman from the CIA who was involved in this art scam? Do you have any idea who he is?'

Corbett laughed. 'Now that's a real Derek fantasy. Typical of him.' He held the door open for me. 'Do remember, Mister Ludlow, if I feel I'm being harassed by you or anyone else, I'll ask my lawyer to deal with the matter.'

'Mister Tallis?'

'Yes, my good friend Jimmy Tallis. He is very professional.'

I decided to walk a part of the way home but, since Fairfax's office was nearby, called there first. I looked at some correspondence about the Cyprus project and was about to leave when Dan Fairfax came through the door.

'Ah Chris, a word please. My office.' His tone was peremptory. He'd obviously been watching too many drama series on television.

When we were both seated he said, 'I must give you credit, first, for introducing Roley Jenkins. He's almost on board for Cyprus. So that's good. But on the debit side I've heard that you've got on the wrong side of Jeremy Foote.'

'What makes you say that?'

'Because Lofty Lazenby told me. That you and that sodding journo, Greenslade, were winding him up at the Ritz a couple of days ago.'

'We tried to talk to him about the problem of drugs in golf.'

'And he told you that there isn't a problem. So, Chris, lay off.'

'I am not the one who's making inquiries into the matter.'

'No, it's Greenslade, but don't get involved because Foote is much too prominent a figure in golf to mess with. That's stating the bleedin' obvious, since he's the head honcho at the bloody European Golf Tour. We, and that means you and me and this agency, have got to have him on our side.'

'Sure, Dan, but I can't stop Toby writing about the subject.'

'Maybe not. But his editor probably can.' Fairfax picked up his telephone, nodded a dismissal and I took the hint and left.

A walk through London's streets is one of my great pleasures, since there is so much to enjoy: the superb buildings, the smart shops, and the people in all their guises and eccentricities. Kensington is a special favourite, but on this occasion nothing much penetrated my consciousness. The ramifications of the Headlam book occupied my mind almost entirely. I had to unveil the identities of Headlam's co-conspirators in order to make sense of his story.

When I reached home, I decided to look again at a passage in the memoirs when Headlam is sent to Berlin to authenticate, if that's the right word, some drawings and paintings being offered for sale to his partners in crime by an ex-Stasi thug. They were just a few of the hundreds of thousands of art-works plundered by the Nazis during the Second World War. In this passage Headlam is under the protection of the CIA man, whom he calls S.

> I'd seen some fleapits in my time, but couldn't remember a meaner or dingier one than this. I sat on the sagging bed and waited with S for the merchandise to arrive.
>
> Our German friends were late and I was becoming increasingly nervous. Eventually there was a double tap on the door and S opened it. The two men who entered were clad in cheap and

nasty clothing, and suited the room down to the filthy ground.

The older of the two men carried a suitcase and the other one stationed himself by the door. That didn't make me feel any better, I can tell you.

S asked the man with the case if he had the merchandise, and the German said, in a sing-song German/American accent, 'Yes, if you've got the money.'

Well, that was clear enough and I was told to check the goods. The kraut put the case on the bed and opened it. I took out a rolled-up canvas, unrolled it with great care and moved towards the window to take advantage of the light.

The kraut blocked the way and told me to steer clear of the window, and S told me to use the bathroom. Herr Beckenbauer, and I assumed his name was an alias, brought the case in for me.

The first canvas was genuine, a Monet, and worth a bloody fortune. But the rest were copies, good copies, but worth next to nothing.

I am now shit-scared of what might happen, because I don't like the cut of the other kraut's jib. He looks like a heavy from a Hollywood gangster movie, like Robert Mitchum, but bigger and nastier.

I went back into the bedroom and gave S the bad news. One genuine Monet and five bits of crap.

Then Beckenbauer freaks out and shouts 'Don't give me that shit' and of course he pulls a gun out of his jacket pocket. 'Hand over the money,' he snarls. Now I know I'm in a bad movie, except that I'm about to crap myself. I just stand by the window, frozen to the spot.

S seems calm, even icy, as he says, 'Derek, only one of the paintings is right, yes?' All I can do is nod my head. 'We'll buy the Monet, Beckenbauer, and you can shove the other rubbish.'

'You'll buy the lot,' says the kraut, 'for one hundred thousand dollars.'

I know that the Monet is worth a helluva lot more than a hundred grand, but say bugger all.

Suddenly S turns towards a door leading to another room and shouts, 'Okay, Greg, come on in.'

The door flies open and the cavalry in the form of Greg, tall and lean and holding a machine-pistol, has arrived. S grins and says, 'I think we've got the superior fire-power, Mister Beckenbauer, don't you. The kraut lowers his gun. 'Fifty grand for the Monet? Okay?'

Beckenbauer nods and S puts bundles of used notes on the bed. With Greg covering the two ex-Stasi bastards we leave with the Monet. S's parting words are, 'A pleasure doing business with you.'

Not in my book, it wasn't.

CHAPTER 12

I wondered if another story about Headlam's book could be planted in a newspaper in order to flush out any of the people involved in the scam. My one and only recourse on 'the street of shame' is Toby Greenslade and I called him at around five o'clock in the hope that I would find him at home as he recovered from his lunch and contemplated which hostelry he would favour with his custom that evening.

His voice was gruff and he sounded rather subdued. 'Is everything alright, Toby?'

'Up to a point. However, my articles about drugs in golf may be cancelled. That misbegotten shyster of an editor has told me that he's not sure that such speculations, yes, speculations he called my material, are appropriate. Therefore, they're not in the best interests of the game.'

'He's been wound up and I think we know by whom.'

'That stuffed shirt, Jeremy Foote. And, of course, Lofty Lazenby, who's very close to Foote, is undoubtedly involved.'

'In what way?'

Toby paused for a moment and then continued. 'Because he does quite a lot of business with *The News*. For instance, he wants Gary Peters to do some bits and pieces during the Open. The usual stuff, such as a hole by hole analysis of the course. And that former England cricket captain, who does a column, if you can call it that, is also one of Lazenby's clients.'

'But at least you can use the material in your book.'

'That's the plan.'

'Toby, would you help me with Headlam's book, please?'

'Of course, if I can.'

I explained that I was hoping to provoke a reaction from those persons unknown who had been involved with Headlam in the scam. 'Would you be able to plant a story in *The News* about the book? Along the lines that it has been bought by a major publisher and that the revelations about the extent of the fraud are even more extraordinary than at first thought. And that highly influential people, from both the British and American Establishment were involved.'

'It sounds fun. Is any of it true?'

'Yes, but since Headlam didn't name names. . .'

'Well, I'll do what I can. Maybe a piece in the gossip column. The semi-literates who compile it owe me a favour.'

As I was weighing up the competing attractions of a glass of crisp white wine or a gin and tonic, my telephone rang and it was Jane. I was uneasily aware that I had neglected her during the last few days. Her voice sounded a little tight as she told me she'd like to pop over for a drink and a chat.

As I awaited her arrival I wondered why she was so often a prey to problems, some of which seemed to me to be imaginary. But, when she arrived at my door, I forgot my reservations since she looked so lovely, and her fleeting smile as we kissed enhanced that innate appeal.

I opened a bottle of white Burgundy, settled Jane in a comfortable chair by one of the windows and waited. I thought it best to let her tell me of her problems and preoccupations first and then we could enjoy our evening together.

'I told you that husband Hugo has been watching me,' Jane began.

'So you say, but I'm still doubtful.'

'Well, I am not in any doubt.' I shrugged. 'And now I think he's gone further than that, I think he's been in my apartment, having a nose around.'

'What on earth makes you think that?' I said, the disbelief clear in my voice. 'Why would he bother? By the way, does he have a key?'

'Bound to, it's the kind of thing he'd have arranged, I can assure you. And he'd bother, as you put it, because he wants to make it clear to me that he's determined to remain a part of my life.'

'But how could you tell that he'd been at large in your place?'

'Oh, just small things. An ornament moved on the sideboard, and I'm sure that some books on a table were in a different order. But the noticeable thing was in one of the bedrooms.'

'Go on,' I said with a leer that I made as lascivious as possible, 'this is getting interesting.'

Jane scowled at me. 'Don't be juvenile, Chris, it doesn't suit you. Some of my clothes in the wardrobe weren't right, it was as if they'd been shuffled about, as if he'd been looking for something.'

I got up, re-filled Jane's glass and kissed her on the forehead. 'Well, don't worry. The first thing to do is change the locks.'

'Really, Chris, you're not taking this seriously, are you? I feel. . .well, almost violated. I'm worried what Hugo might do next.'

'Don't, it's not worth it. By the way, was any underwear missing?'

Jane frowned. 'A needlessly smutty remark, Chris.'

I laughed and gestured at the bedroom door. 'Talking of smutty. . .'

CHAPTER 13

Early on Friday morning I walked down the road towards the local newsagent's shop to buy a copy of *The News*. The sun shone brightly and nearly everyone seemed to be as cheerful as the cloudless heavens. I bought the newspaper and walked on a few hundred yards to a café, ordered a double espresso with some milk on the side and began to leaf through the paper.

Like all the tabloids it was mostly concerned with scandal about politicians and show-biz celebrities. There were several pages about women's fashion, and some detailed accounts of murder and violence from various corners of the country. I kept turning the pages in the hope that Toby had managed to place something about Headlam's book and finally found the gossip column, which went under the catchy title of 'Gemma's Jottings'.

The headline read: 'Uproar in the Art World' and the report went as follows: 'A memoir by Derek Headlam, a renowned faker of paintings and drawings by many of the greatest artists in history, is guaranteed to cause chaos and confusion within the cloistered world inhabited by the leading auction houses and among the owners of pictures reckoned to be worth millions of pounds. Headlam claims to have 'copied' works by a dazzling array of artists – from Michelangelo to Matisse.

'He died two years ago – some say he was murdered – and his memoirs are about to be sold to an international publisher by top literary agent, Chris Ludlow. In it Headlam gives a full account of his life as a faker: of how he fooled the now-disgraced spy and art expert, Anthony Blunt, by selling him a fake drawing by Poussin; and how he became a part of a huge conspiracy to dump hundreds of fakes on to the international art market.

'When the book is published, there will be many collectors of art who will be looking with fearful eyes at their stupendously expensive works; and many an auction house whose so-called experts will be wondering how these fakes escaped their notice. They can probably look forward to some litigation from their billionaire clients.

'Finally, one wonders how the Queen will react to such revelations. After all, Anthony Blunt was in her employ as Surveyor of the Queen's Pictures. Let us hope that he didn't slip any dodgy works into HM's renowned collection.'

Toby and his colleague had done me proud and I hastened back to my flat in order to give him my thanks. Nine o'clock in the morning was a little early for my journalist friend, but I risked his wrath anyway.

To my surprise he picked up his telephone at once and said, 'I guessed it was you, Chris.'

'Yes, and I'm immensely grateful. That's quite a spread *The News* has given the story.'

'Yes, Gemma liked the idea anyway, but nevertheless I am now much in her debt and she will undoubtedly extract her reward in full.'

'I'm sure you'll be equal to the task.'

Almost as soon as I put down the 'phone, it rang and Tim Headlam was the caller. 'Wonderful news, Chris. Who's the publisher?'

'Ah, I'm sorry to disappoint you, Tim, but there isn't one. We planted the story in the hope that we'd provoke a reaction which might lead us to those unnamed associates of your Uncle Derek.'

There was a pause as Tim digested the news and his disappointment was plain to hear as he thanked me briefly and asked me to keep in touch.

I managed to forget about the Headlam memoirs and all their ramifications for the next few hours as I compiled a report on the Cyprus project for Dan Fairfax. When I had finished the first draft, I slung on a track suit and went for a run across Wimbledon Common. It was a day to be out of doors, to free the mind by exercising the body.

Later that evening my brother Max would arrive and we were both looking forward to a round of golf on the following day.

Little did I know that our enjoyable day on the golf course would be followed by violence and confusion.

By six o'clock in the evening my idyllic day on the golf course with my brother had gone seriously awry as I confronted my two intruders.

My response to their demand that I destroy all copies of Derek Headlam's book and forget the project, 'that I would think about it', certainly hadn't hit the right note.

During our round of golf I once again recounted to Max all that had happened since he had introduced me to young Tim Headlam: the sale of the book to Grant Jezzard, his murder, and the subsequent withdrawal of the offer by the American publisher. Max's considered advice was to forget about the book and get on with my work for Dan Fairfax. This seemed to be very much the right thing to do when the smaller of the two intruders said, 'Maybe a bullet in your shoulder and another one in your knee will help you think about it.'

It was difficult to see how this scene would play itself out, except for my being seriously injured. I was, however, wondering what the hell Max was doing, though I was glad that he was staying out of trouble. On the other hand, he had got me into this mess. Perhaps he was trying to contact the police.

Suddenly the door to the second bedroom flew open. Startled, the gunman turned to his right and started to raise his gun. But Max grabbed his wrist, twisted it and forced the man's arm behind his back. The gun hit the floor with a clatter and then I heard a loud scream, just as I hurled myself at the other thug. The best I could do was to hit him amidships with my shoulder, but at least he went sprawling and I then managed to deliver a hefty kick to his ribs as well.

Meanwhile, Max had taken possession of the Glock and had stepped back, so that he could cover both villains with it. Not that the one Max had attacked was likely to offer any threat, since he was half-lying on the floor and moaning loudly. I guessed that Max had dislocated his shoulder.

My brother took command. 'Stay where you are,' he said to the man I had tackled. 'If you don't I promise I'll use this.' I'm not sure the other man believed him, but I certainly did. 'OK, Chris, tie the bastard up.'

I looked questioningly at my brother, since I don't keep supplies of rope around my home. 'Sticky tape', he said.

I went swiftly into my study, found some of that thick brown tape which is used to secure parcels and tore a couple of lengths off the roll. Then I went towards the man I had knocked over and told him to hold out his wrists. He backed away, shaking his head. Max then intervened and walked a few paces towards him, the gun at the ready.

'You haven't got the guts to shoot,' the man said.

Max held the gun a few feet from the man's left knee and said, 'You want to bet on that?' Before the man could move he slammed the gun into his neck. Down he went, out for more than the count of ten. 'Tie him up, Chris, and then keep your eye on him.'

While I did that, Max turned his attention to the other thug, who was still on the floor and moaning with pain. Somehow he dragged him over to a chair, sat him on it and told him that he'd put his shoulder back into its joint as soon as he told us who had sent him.

The man was stupid enough to tell Max to fuck off. He clearly didn't understand how dangerous my brother can be.

Max gave me the gun, with the warning that the safety catch was off, went into the kitchen and moments later re-appeared with a towel, a part of which he proceeded to stuff into the thug's mouth. I turned away as he forced the man's dislocated shoulder further away from the joint. Even through the towel I could hear the man's scream of agony. 'OK, let's try that again,' Max said.

There were more profanities from the injured man; I had to admit that he was either very brave or very stupid. Then he gasped out, 'If I tell you anything about the man who pays us, I'll be dead within days. The boss don't put up with any shit.'

I could see that the other man was stirring and I saw a familiar glint in Max's eyes. It didn't bode well for the injured thug since my brother had a ruthless side to his personality. It went with his somewhat shadowy past. For instance, he had spent more than a year in Northern Ireland working for what he called 'an economic intelligence unit' and no specific details were ever forthcoming. I didn't relish the thought of what he might do and said, 'Max, forget it. We're not going to get anywhere with him. He's more frightened of his boss than he is of you.'

'You're probably right. But I'm intrigued by his accent. Eastern European, of course. And who's got all the fast money these days?' He turned to the injured man. 'Where do you come from? Moscow? St Petersburg?'

'No, I'm from Smolensk, you prick.'

'Good,' Max said, 'now we know something about them and, maybe, their boss.'

'We'd better call the police,' I said.

'Much good that'll do us,' Max retorted. 'I don't want to press charges against these two idiots. Do you?'

I shrugged. 'No, but I want to find out who's so eager to bury Headlam's book.'

Max walked over to the thug in the chair, told him to keep still, grabbed his shoulder and heaved on it. The man yelped and Max grinned. 'Your shoulder will be alright in a few days, I've put it back in place.' The man glared at him and Max said playfully, 'Now, come on Sergei or Boris or Fred or whatever your name is, say thank you like a good boy.'

Understandably there was no response and Max followed up by saying, 'You two can piss off and thank your lucky stars that you're not going to prison for armed assault. We'll keep the gun and if you come anywhere near us again, we'll use it.' He walked across to the front door and opened it. The two thugs didn't hang around, except that the smaller one spat over his shoulder, 'You two'd better watch yourselves. Bastards.'

Max raised the Glock threateningly and the two men galloped towards the road. Max stood by the door for a few moments and then turned to me. 'I wonder who that was?'

'Who what was?'

'I swear I saw someone by the main gate, looking at us.'

I shrugged. 'Just a passer-by, I suppose. Probably wondering why our Russian friends were in such a hurry.'

When we were back inside my flat I told Max how relieved I'd been that he'd come to my rescue. 'I thought I was about to be beaten to a pulp. Mind you, you're the person who got me into this predicament in the first place with your introduction to young Tim.'

'True, and I'm sorry. But, as I said earlier, this is probably the time that you bow out. You seem to have stirred up some very serious enemies.'

'Maybe, but first let's have a drink. I think we need one and then we can discuss the problem.'

We went into the living room and piled into large glasses of a vintage Armagnac, which I kept for special occasions. And avoiding a beating, or worse, was worth celebrating.

CHAPTER 14

After savouring that lovely, curative drink, we reverted to our original plan and strolled down to a pub near the river. The Saturday crowd was there in force, but we found a corner table and downed a couple of refreshing pints of bitter from a local brewery. We avoided any discussion as to who might be our attackers or who might have sent them until we were sitting at our table in the restaurant and had ordered our food. We decided to share a plate of seafood, followed by steak and chips for Max and chicken Kiev for me.

'What we've got to establish, if we can, is who stands most to lose, either in terms of money or reputation, from what Headlam has revealed in his book,' Max began.

'Let's start with the art establishment itself,' I replied. 'All those auction houses, dealers, experts. If what Derek Headlam claims about the number of fakes he and his associates sold is true, then the credibility and the integrity of these people will be in ruins. And the market will go into free-fall.'

'What integrity? There are hundreds of thousands of fakes littering the market. And do those dealers and auctioneers give a damn? Of course not, just as long as they can continue unloading them on to a gullible public. To quote Seneca, "He who reaps the profits has committed the crime".'

'Quite. But on second thoughts I'm not sure that the amorphous entity called the art establishment would be capable of organising itself to do battle against Headlam and his book.'

'Agreed, nor do I really think that its members would condone murder. And one must assume that the murder of Grant Jezzard is part and parcel of the same plot.'

I supped some of my wine, a rich and fruity white from Sicily. 'What about Headlam's partners in crime? They wouldn't want anyone to know their identities, would they? Maybe they arranged for Headlam's death in Rome and thought that was the end of the matter.'

'Until something that they could not have anticipated made its appearance. The book.'

Having made short work of our starter, we then began to make inroads into our main courses. Max said contemplatively, 'Of course, the presence of two Russian thugs suggests that a crooked Russian plutocrat is behind all this. One of those oligarchs who made billions out of oil and other natural resources when Boris Yeltsin was President of the country.'

'You mean someone who's got houses all over the world and has filled them with what he thinks is great art.'

'Exactly, and now has grave doubts about the authenticity of many of his pictures.'

'And the value of his investments, because that's what the pictures mean to him. So he decides to deal with the problem in the traditional way.'

'There are rather a lot of Russian oligarchs to choose from,' Max said reflectively. 'Up to a hundred thousand of them have flooded into London, and a good proportion of them are multi-billionaires.'

'Yes, and they've got their villainous hands on some of the best property in our city, in Belgravia, Chelsea, Kensington, Hampstead. And most of them bought with laundered money hidden away in tax havens around the world.'

Max laughed. 'Well, not so much Hampstead. Apparently, such houses must be within ten minutes' walk of Harrods. And if you've bought millions of barrels of oil for a dollar apiece and sell them on for thirty dollars, you can certainly afford these grand mansions. However, you sound bitter, Chris.'

'Not really, I don't aspire to live in such exclusive neighbourhoods, but these mega-rich Russkies spoil things for other people. A while ago, I was chatting to a very successful English stockbroker who has a lovely home in a Knightsbridge square. Then a Russian moved in next door and the nights are now filled with blaring music and the slamming of car doors as the tarts come and go in their droves.'

'So, he'll end up selling it to another Russian. That's life. But I take your point.' Max paused. 'But to get back to our discussion, we're not exactly narrowing the field for our investigation, are we? Let's see, the art establishment would have a strong motive for silencing Mister Headlam. Then there is an unknown number of Russian oligarchs who want to conserve the integrity of their art collections and of their investments therein. Let's say at least two or three hundred of them.'

'And then there are Headlam's former associates, about whom we know next to nothing. According to his book, one of them was employed in the Home Office and another was a CIA operative.'

'So, they each present their own intrinsic difficulties,' Max said. 'The innate secrecy of government agencies. Anyway, I'll take a good look at the memoirs before I leave tomorrow. Maybe there's something in there that will give us a clue.'

On the following morning Max was up early. While I made some coffee at just after seven o'clock, he brandished the Headlam manuscript at me and said, 'What a fascinating book. And a remarkable man, if only half of what he claims is true.'

'Any clues which might lead us to his partners in forgery?'

'Well, forget the CIA man, we'd never get anywhere trying to unmask him. But I was wondering about D, the civil servant. Headlam mentions that she's a Home Office wallah, and it's interesting that she seemed to know a lot about Anthony Blunt. There's a sequence in the book in which she taunts Headlam about his friendship with him. She says what a pity it is that he's not still around because he could've helped them by giving favourable attributions to some of their forgeries.'

'In the same way that Bernard Berenson assisted, if one can put it that way, the dealer Joseph Duveen, perhaps?'

'Yes, another dodgy pair of art experts. Anyway, D says to Headlam, "what a pity the old bugger Blunt isn't still around to assist our little group, Derek. And you'd have the added fun of doing a bit of cottaging with him. He favoured that loo near Marble Arch, didn't he?" Headlam gives her a very frosty reply, but the point is that D's remark suggests an unusual familiarity with Blunt's activities. I just wonder, and this is a long shot, whether D was in one of those Secret Service agencies that monitored Blunt. If she were, we might have a better chance of finding a way to unmask her.'

'Even though these agencies are supposed to keep their secrets secret?'

Max grinned and I assumed that he might know somebody who knew somebody. 'And I am fascinated,' he continued, 'by the way they changed their approach to the scam after that fright in Berlin with the ex-Stasi boys.'

'You mean how they decided not to bother acquiring genuine works to be sold alongside the forgeries?'

'Exactly. It was too much bother, too risky. And I really liked the cover story about the reclusive Jewish family. How they hid their treasures away during the war, recovered them eventually after the war and then decided to sell them. Very much a feel-good story, clever and plausible.'

'And it was also clever how they set up Headlam with that arrest at Heathrow for possession of cocaine.'

'A bit of entrapment that's typical of the so-called Secret Service,' Max said with a grimace.

'Do you think you'll be able to shine any light on the elusive D?'

'Maybe. There are still people in Cambridge who know plenty about the intricacies of Blunt's life. Someone might have come across her.'

When Max had left, I turned to the passage in the book in which Headlam describes how he was blackmailed into joining D's art scam.

First he was stopped and searched at Heathrow and a significant quantity of cocaine was found in his luggage. I tended to believe his protestations of innocence and assumed that D had used her Home Office or Secret Service connections in order to entrap Headlam.

He describes how he ends up on that very same evening at D's house, though unfortunately he gives no details of its location.

I told the bitch how humiliating the whole business at Heathrow had been. The body search. Disgusting. And she tells me that I'd been caught with enough coke to make me a dealer and ensure a lengthy prison sentence, and that I'd only been released because of her influence. Oddly enough I thought that there was something familiar about the so-called customs officer who dealt with me. Was he a cop maybe? From that half-arsed art squad they've got at New Scotland Yard? I said as much to her and she told me not to be ridiculous.

She then got to the nitty-gritty, that she wanted my services as a forger and I told her to fuck off. So she threatened me. 'Do you want to be strip-searched at every airport in Europe?' she said in that prissy public school voice. 'Do you want to be on the black list of every art dealer in London?'

Then the cow compared me to Tom bloody Keating, that dauber, and that really hacked me off. I pointed out that I was a true artist and I'd never tried to deceive the so-called experts. 'I show them a drawing and let them decide what I'm selling to them and what it's worth.'

'That's a precarious moral balancing act, isn't it?' the bitch replied, all superior.

As I then pointed out to her, Michelangelo used to do fakes. He carved a 'Sleeping Cupid', aged it artificially and sold it as a classical statue. A fake, but by a genius, so how do you value it?

That stopped her for a moment or two and then she looked at me with her hard eyes and said, 'Do you want to make lots of money, Derek, and enjoy my protection or would you prefer a prison sentence and lots of harassment in the future?'

Not much of a choice, was it? And then she told me I'd be off to Berlin on the following day to case some art works. If they were authentic her associate would buy them and they'd eventually be sold along with some of my copies. So, it seemed like a clever idea and I had to go along with it.

She happened to mention Blunt during our little chat and out of interest I asked her how she got to know him. 'Let's just say that the Queen introduced us,' she said, with that supercilious smile on her face.

I smiled to myself at the woman's final remark about how she met Blunt. She sounded not just hard-nosed, but masterful, one of those powerful women who can be very appealing. I was ruminating on how I would like to meet her or, rather, how important it was that I did meet her in order to resolve some of the mysteries surrounding Derek Headlam's final years, when the telephone rang and jerked me out of my reverie. It was Toby.

CHAPTER 15

Without the usual civilities, Toby launched himself into an undoubtedly one-sided account of his editor's latest misdemeanours. 'Do you know what that misbegotten son of Satan has done now?' he began.

'Do you mean that highly-regarded man of letters, the sports editor of *The Daily News*?' I replied lightly.

'The very same dribble of slime from the gutters of Fleet Street.' When aroused Toby has a colourful range of invective.

'He's made you the paper's fashion correspondent?'

'He might just as well have done. No, Chris, but he's confirmed that he's axing my articles on drug usage in golf. All the other writers will do their bits – football, rugby, tennis, cycling and athletics of course, but nothing on golf.'

I heard a snort of indignation, or perhaps of sorrow, from Toby and asked, 'And the reason?'

'I expect you can guess. It's the usual codswallop. It's not in the interests of the game. Golf has never been afflicted in any serious way with drugs, it's not like other sports and there is no point in wasting time and newsprint on a non-story.'

'So, he's been got at.'

'Of course. By that supercilious bastard Jeremy Foote.'

'Or by Lofty Lazenby,' I suggested.

'Both, I imagine. They're as thick as thieves, aren't they?'

'So, what are you going to do?'

'Have a bloody good drink.'

'And then another good drink?'

'Yes, Chris, that's my immediate plan. Why don't you join me?'

'I would, but I'm going to the theatre.'

'To see?'

'A fringe production of "For Whom the Bell Tolls, the Musical".'

There was a silence and then I heard Toby's booming laugh. 'A musical version of Hemingway's blockbuster action novel. I wish you luck. To quote a couple of lines from a satirical poem I read years ago, "Sing Goddess, if you must, but be polite, We mourn for Slugger Hemingway tonight". Are you going with Jane?'

'Yes.'

'Oh well, that's some consolation.'

It was indeed some consolation, since although Jane was casually dressed in jeans and a pale pink cashmere sweater she looked lovely. A mini-cab took us to the outskirts of Clapham and, as we got out of the car in a dreary street, that's when my heart, and my expectations, began to sink. The street had a selection of small concrete blocks of flats, various fast food restaurants, and a supermarket which was open for 24 hours a day every day; amongst this dross was our venue for the evening. The fringe theatre was housed in what must once have been a small factory. Two tiny windows flanked the entrance and the whole edifice was topped with a sloping corrugated iron roof.

The interior was just as unprepossessing with its dim lighting and a décor of discoloured plaster walls with a few faded playbills posted haphazardly thereon. I could just about identify a makeshift bar in one corner, but its customers were thronged several feet deep in their efforts to obtain a drink before their theatrical experience began.

'I wonder if they can rustle up a couple of champagne cocktails at that lovely bar,' I said light-heartedly to Jane.

'Chris, don't be so snooty. This theatre has done some fine work in its time. For instance, it's unearthed some promising playwrights. It may seem a bit rough and ready, but keep an open mind, please.'

'Of course. Let's forget about a drink and find our seats.'

There were no reserved seats, since the policy was one of 'first come, first served', as I was told by one of the theatre's staff as we walked into the cavernous interior. The girl's shaven head, sleeveless T-shirt and ripped jeans were presumably designed to mark her out as an artistic person. I led Jane to two canvas chairs on the end of a row near the back of the theatre. I thought it prudent to have an easy escape route.

Despite the crowded bar at least half the seats were empty as the curtain rose on what seemed to be an ill-lit cave. As a cacophony of whistles, drums, gunfire, screams and, inevitably, a tolling bell opened this musical entertainment I glanced longingly at my escape route. At once Jane admonished me with a sharp instruction 'not to fidget'. More than fidget, I wanted to make a run for the nearest pub, if there was a half-decent one in this unpromising part of London.

I couldn't properly comprehend what was happening on-stage, though one of the songs, as far as I could make out, was about 'the fight for freedom'. But much of the action was concentrated on a sleeping bag in which our hero Robert Jordan cavorted vigorously with his new love, Maria.

And so it went on, in the semi-darkness. At one point the noise was so overwhelming that I put my fingers in my ears; why hadn't I had the foresight to bring a pair of earplugs? I received a smack on the wrist from Jane for, I supposed, my lack of artistic sensitivity.

Finally, the curtain came down for the end of the first act and I turned to Jane and said, 'What do you think of it so far?'

'Moving. Very brave. Symbolic of hopes and loves lost and regained.'

I looked blankly at her as we stood up to stretch our legs. 'Er, well,' I began and then stopped as I saw her put a hand to her mouth, as she stifled a scream.

'Christ, he's here,' Jane said.

'Who is?'

'Hugo. Over there. Look.' She pointed at the other side of the theatre and all I could see was a crowd heading for the exit to the bar. 'The one in the dark shirt and jeans, it's him, I swear it.' Jane put her hand over her eyes and began to cry.

I took her in my arms and tried to quieten her. Several people were looking at us and I said, 'Come on, let's get out of here. Let's see if we can spot him outside.'

'No, no, Chris, you don't understand. He'll be gone by now. He just does these things to upset me.'

'And he succeeds,' I said testily. I took her hand. 'Let's go outside for some fresh air anyway.' When we arrived on the pavement, we stood aside from a band of desperate and dedicated cigarette smokers and I asked Jane again how she could be so certain that it was Hugo whom she'd seen.

'Because I know the way he holds himself, the position of his head, the way he walks. I know I'm not mistaken.'

'So, is it a coincidence that's he's here tonight, d'you think?'

'Of course not.'

'But how did he know that you'd be here?'

'He must have followed us.'

I didn't see much point in pursuing this line of enquiry. Either Jane's disengaged and possibly deranged husband was mounting a determined campaign of surveillance and harassment, or Jane herself was on the brink of a nervous breakdown. I was at a loss, so took the obvious way out and said, 'Let's try and forget about this. Let's make our way into the centre of Clapham, with its many and varied attractions.' I smiled at Jane. 'We'll have a drink and a meal. Let's try and enjoy the rest of our evening.'

That was difficult, since Jane kept looking anxiously behind her at the other people in the street; and her twitchy behaviour continued when we had settled ourselves into an agreeable French restaurant just off the High Street in Clapham.

In the taxi on the way back to my flat, I suggested to Jane that I should turn the tables on her husband by mounting some surveillance on him. 'Or I can knock on his door, ask a few pointed questions about his activities in relation to you, and maybe he'll get the message and leave you alone.'

'No, he won't. In fact, that will only encourage him. He'll see that I'm worried and re-double his efforts to upset me.'

'What if I warn him off?'

'No, he can be very violent. I don't want you to get hurt.'

I looked at her in the gloom of the taxi. 'Has he ever attacked you?'

'No, but he has threatened me.'

I changed the subject. I knew where Hugo lived and where he worked, and despite Jane's warning decided that I would don my trench-coat and trilby hat and do a bit of nosing around in the near future.

On the following morning, Jane left quite early. She wanted to walk home in the sunshine that was already the harbinger of a sparkling summer day.

I made myself another strong cup of coffee and listened to my telephone messages, only one of which was of immediate interest. Tim Headlam had called on the previous evening to ask if I was making any progress with 'Uncle Derek's book'. He sounded a little querulous as, towards the end of his call, he asked if the project had a future or should he assume that it was not of interest to the publishing world.

I didn't blame him and decided to return his call and try to re-assure him. He answered on the second ring and I told him that I was still trying to approach the story from a different angle. 'It's an interesting story, Tim, but it needs more substance. I want to try to establish who these shadowy, unnamed people are who master-minded this conspiracy with Derek. That would make a great story even better. And one of those people might well have murdered your uncle.'

'But what are your chances of doing that? There's a woman from the Home Office – maybe – and a bloke who worked for the CIA. Shadowy, you said. That's putting it mildly.'

'I agree, but there's also another interesting line of inquiry. Maybe some mega-rich individual, possibly a Russian oligarch, had Derek killed to preserve the integrity of his art collection. You're in the art business, Tim, so do you know how we might establish who have been the big buyers of very expensive art in the last ten years?'

'Unfortunately, the big auction houses don't reveal the names of the buyers, many of whom use agents anyway. So there are usually at least two layers of confidentiality to penetrate.'

I paused for thought and then said, 'We can narrow things down a bit, can't we? Derek and his fellow-conspirators really got going in the mid-eighties, didn't they? And they ran the scam for, what, three or four years?'

'Yes, and he began to put his memoirs together in the early nineties. And he was killed a couple of years ago.'

'As I said, Tim, you are in the world of art, so could you look at the important sales of Old Masters from the mid-eighties until the end of the decade?'

There was a silence on the telephone and then Tim said, 'Heavens above, Chris, have you any idea how many sales of Old Master drawings and paintings there are in one year alone? And just in London, let alone Paris and Rome and New York?'

'No, not really.'

'Hundreds.'

'But can we not assume that the works from this dodgy syndicate would be offered for sale in London and through the big auction houses?'

'Well, okay, let's limit the research to Heathcote's.'

'And that other bunch.'

'You mean the illustrious house of Westerby's.'

'Er, yes. With your expertise you might see some sale which fits the profile, if I can put it that way, of our fraudsters.'

'That's a very long shot,' Tim protested, 'because Derek copied such a wide variety of artists. You name one and he'd probably have imitated him.'

'But surely he had some favourites?'

'Yes, of course. Don't you remember, there's a sequence in the book when he's with that Home Office woman, he calls her D, and they're discussing the works Derek might create, interleaved with genuine paintings and drawings. Hang on a minute.' Chris heard some shuffling of paper and then Tim continued. 'He gives D an outline of the people he'd imitate. This is what he says in the book: that Durer is a must, and Rembrandt of course. But he warns that caution is needed with the latter because it would look bloody suspicious if a load of unknown Rembrandt drawings suddenly came to light. And he's absolutely right there.'

There was a pause and then Tim said: 'then D re-assures him that they'd be sold over a long period of time and the old boy really gets the bit between his teeth, as he bangs on about works by followers of Rembrandt . . . Ferdinand Bol, Flink, Lambert Doomer, and so on. And, as Uncle Derek says, if some of them were attributed to the master himself, there wouldn't be any argument. He recommends slipping in a few Corots maybe, Ingres, Goya, van Dyck, his old friends Castiglione and Tiepolo. As he rightly states, the possibilities are endless. And he agrees to mix some of his own drawings in with some of the genuine ones.'

'And what about paintings?' I asked.

'Poussin of course, he loved his work. And Utrillo, but he's one of the most copied of all painters. "Because of the deceptive simplicity of his painting" as some pseud put it. Along with Picasso and that charlatan, Dali, and Hockney, too. Of course, many of the abstract artists like Rothko and Mondrian were child's play to Derek.'

'So, he had an extensive portfolio, to put it mildly. How the hell did he perfect all those different styles?'

'As you know, it's in his memoirs. He had to kid himself that he was assuming the identity of the other artist. He'd become Utrillo for a few hours. And there must be no hesitation, the work had to be done without fear. Then the chances were pretty good that it would appear to be the real thing. Another very important point, which was much emphasized by Derek, was never to copy an existing work by an artist. To get it spot-on the copy had to be a brand-new work in the style of the man he was imitating.'

I had to get Tim back to the point and said, 'But you will have a look, won't you? You've got much the best chance of spotting something, a sort of pattern, that might relate to Uncle Derek and his work.'

'And then what? Do I ring up Heathcote's and ask them for the names of the buyers? They'd tell me to get stuffed, but not as politely as that.'

'First things first. Can you at least make a list of any sales that catch your eye? After all, Derek had his favourites, as he tells us in his memoirs, so if several of them turn up at the same sale, we might be on to something. We can then try to cross-reference them to any coverage in the newspapers about new and important acquisitions by art collectors. And there might be comments in the gossip columns, for instance, that might help us.'

'That's quite a daunting project, isn't it. I suppose I can use the university library for some of the research.'

'And of course there was that story that Derek's associates created about the reclusive Jewish family who hid their collection of art from the Nazis, re-discovered it several decades after the war and were selling it all as one lot. That surely must have made it into the papers or the trade press.'

'Okay,' Tim said, 'I'll have a bash at it.'

'By the way,' I said quickly, 'why did Derek pull out of the scam after two or three years? Surely the money was good. And it can't have been an attack of conscience.'

'No. I suppose he was getting older, into his 'sixties, and he was becoming unreliable. Mainly because he hit the bottle harder and harder, like his old chum Anthony Blunt. Above all, he was devastated by the death of one of his boyfriends, young Jason. Again, it's covered in the book.'

After putting down the telephone, I flicked through the pages of the book and found a reference to Headlam's boyfriend, Jason. The process served to remind me that he had encouraged Headlam to write his memoirs.

> I owe a lot to young Jason. He brought some fun, some levity I suppose, into my life when I was on the wane in every way.

One evening I was very down in the dumps, staring out of one of the apartment windows and thinking of what little lay ahead for me, after a life that once had held so much promise, was so full of light and fanciful imaginings. Though I suppose that most people, unless they're completely dull and indifferent, have such thoughts. Then lovely, lithe, pretty Jason came over and put his arms around me. I could feel the affection that was pulsing out of him. I nearly burst into tears. And then he said, 'Come on, Derek, love, snap out of it. You know what you should do, don't you? You should have a go at your memoirs. Christ . . . the life you've led . . . the scams you've pulled off . . . the people you've known.'

I told Jason that I wouldn't like to let anyone down and he laughed and said that we were in the 'nineties now and the newspapers would pay a bloody fortune for my story. As he said, 'All those toffee-nosed wankers in the art world, how you took the piss out of them.'

I cheered up for a while until Jason told me that he wouldn't be with me in Rome for Christmas. He had to go home to Blighty to see his mum. Oh well, it was understandable, I suppose.

I read a few more pages, though I knew that Headlam was about to be shoved to the brink of despair when Jason's mother turns up at the apartment.

I was more than a little puzzled when I got back to my apartment. Expecting only Jason to be there, I found him with a middle-aged woman. She was decently turned out, I suppose, in jeans and a sweater, Marks and Sparks no doubt, but I didn't catch on straight away as to what she was doing there.

I always try to be polite so I did my best, told her my name and held out my hand to shake hers. The ill-mannered cow ignored it and said, 'I'm Alice Scott, Jason's mum, and he's coming home with me.'

I tried to stay calm, though I could feel my hands trembling with tension, and I asked her to sit down and discuss any problems.

She ignored me again and simply told Jason to get his things together. The dear boy protested that he was old enough to make his own choices, but she told him, as cold as ice, that if she had to leave without him, she'd go straight to the British Embassy and ask one of their officials to take her to the Italian police. 'I don't suppose they like drug-pushers, Mister Headlam.'

I told the bitch that I didn't do drugs, but she ignored me and poor Jason had to do what he was told.

Ten minutes later they left. Because of her, Jason didn't even give me a farewell kiss, and I never saw him again.

But Headlam did see Alice Scott again, less than a year later, when she re-visited his apartment.

It was quite a shock, and a bloody unpleasant one, when I opened the front door and there was Alice Scott again. I asked her how Jason was and, without any preamble, she said, 'Jason is dead and I'm here to collect the rest of his things.'

I staggered into the living room and collapsed into a chair. I didn't know what to say and muttered, 'Oh God, Jason. What happened?'

She snarled at me that it was drugs that killed him and that I bore the blame. What could I say except to protest, again, that drugs weren't my thing. I really had tried to stop him taking them.

She then meandered on about how she'd never wanted Jason to do his hitch-hiking around Europe, he was too young but he didn't have a job and he said he could look after himself. And his father wasn't around to lay down the law.

I asked her where his father was and she told me he was dead, 'murdered by some IRA bastards'. So, he'd been a soldier; but I couldn't remember Jason telling me that, or even talking about his dad.

She then asked again for Jason's things and I took the opportunity to go into the bedroom, away from her. When I came back she was looking at some drawings and I had a sudden thought. 'I did some drawings of Jason,' I said. 'Would you like some?' And I didn't mean any of the nude studies I'd done. I didn't think she'd appreciate those.

She nodded bleakly. I handed over a suitcase with the few bits and pieces that he'd left behind, and then rummaged in a drawer. I found two lovely head and shoulders drawings of the dear boy and handed them over.

'They're very nice,' she said through gritted teeth and gave me what I assumed was a curt nod of thanks as she put the drawings into her bag. I told her how sorry I was about her son.

I opened the front door and she walked past me into the corridor and then paused. 'So you should be,' she said, her eyes glittering with venom. 'May God forgive you. If my husband was alive, he'd kill you.' I wanted to scream back at the bitch that I loved Jason. But no words would come.

I just stared silently after her and then, head down in misery, went back inside my apartment. I grabbed a bottle of brandy and sank two large glasses, one after the other. Poor, dear Jason.

Then I grabbed a pad of paper and a pen and sat down by a window. At the top of the first page I wrote: The Memoirs of an Artist. By Derek Headlam.

CHAPTER 16

It was around six o'clock and I needed a drink and some contemplation, since so much was happening in my life, much of it difficult to put into those pigeon-holes that normal people use to keep control of their day-to-day existence. Jane was a worry; Mrs Bradshaw and her grasping and possibly unscrupulous relatives was a slight concern; and the whole business of Headlam and his book was a challenge.

I had just taken a fulsome draught from my glass of white Burgundy when the telephone rang. One of Fleet Street's finest was the caller and he came to the point without any ambiguity. 'Chris, I need your help.'

'Er, yes,' I replied, unused to such a direct approach from my old friend.

'Yes, with this book of mine. "Caddie Confidential". I need your professional help.'

'You mean I'll be paid?'

There was a distinct pause on the line and then Toby replied, 'Well, in due course. Some money and a share of royalties. Yes, I think I can manage that. And you'll get a credit in the book, of course.'

'My goodness, such generosity,' I said nastily. 'Have you sent the outline to a publisher yet?'

'Er, not yet, but you will no doubt help me with that, after all the hard work I've put into promoting your art fraud book.'

It was a flimsy claim, but had a small element of validity and I asked him what he wanted me to do.

'You know all the caddies, so would you talk to some of them. Just tell them it's a light-hearted look at the lives of caddies, those Jeeves of the fairways.'

'Not many of them will know what that means.'

'Perhaps not, but you were after all one of them, so there's a chance that they'll let their hair down for you. But one of the main points of the exercise is to find out who has used or does use illegal drugs of the performance-enhancing kind.'

'If they know anything, I am betting that they won't tell.'

'They're more likely to tell you, Chris, than me. Try the obvious ones, Scotch Billy, Burlington Basil, Jigger Davies, Cowboy Ken, you know the ones.'

'I think it's a waste of time, but since it's you, Toby.'

'Good, so why don't you start on Wednesday? At the pro-am before the Starlight Insurance Open. They'll all be there.'

On the Wednesday morning I dutifully set off for the south Midlands at well before seven o'clock in the vain hope of avoiding the worst of the rush-hour traffic. The event was being staged at a course built about twenty years before, during one of golf's growth periods when new clubs were springing up in the unlikeliest of places; and the Halgrave Golf and Country Club was certainly one of those. The designer, an American with a grossly inflated reputation as a golf architect (whose fees matched his reputation, as Toby never failed to point out) had admittedly faced an almost insoluble problem since the terrain marked out for the course was unrelievedly flat.

Water, water, everywhere was his solution and the resulting lay-out might have passed muster in Florida, but looked markedly out-of-place in rural England. Virtually every shot held the dismal promise of a watery grave and the course seemed to me to be better suited to the staging of a regatta than a golf tournament.

The press pass which Toby had provided was useful, since I was able to by-pass lengthy queues of vehicles which were heading for the public car parks.

I began to wonder whether I would manage to isolate any of the caddies for long enough to extract any useful information from them. As I knew from my days working for Jack Mason, a caddie's day could be protracted. Jack is a serious and very talented professional golfer, but not perhaps as assiduous as some of the others. Nevertheless, even his golfing day during a tournament would typically span around nine hours when the pre-round warm-up, the round itself and a couple of hours of practice afterwards were taken into account. Mercifully, however, the need for a few pints of strong ale sometimes took precedence over the practice session.

Above all, a caddie's first and only duty is to his golfer, who expects his trusted helper to be attentive and fully aware of all his needs. I knew that I wouldn't get a word in edgeways while a caddie was actually at work with his employer; I would have to try to nab him well before the round began or when it had been completed.

I wandered into the press tent, poured myself a cup of coffee and studied the order of play. I saw that Jamie Winter was due to start at just after one o'clock. There was a chance that his caddie, Scotch Billy, would be in the caddies' tent; he liked to prepare for his day with several cups of strong tea and a large whisky. 'Just to keep the flies at bay' was his excuse for the latter.

The caddies' quarters were at the back of the clubhouse and I glanced inside to check who was there. Even though his back was turned to me, there was no mistaking the squat figure of Scotch Billy, with his long grey hair swept back over his ears and secured in a pony-tail. While wandering over to his table I noticed that Burlington Basil was also nearby and tucking into a bacon roll.

'How goes it, Billy?' I said as I stopped by his table.

'Great heavens. It's the upper crust caddie. How are you, young Chris?' A few years back, the press had attached that ridiculous description to me and it had stuck. As always I had to make a serious effort to tune in to Billy's deep Scottish accent. It always caused me problems, but I thought it unwise to ask him to use sub-titles.

'Very well,' I replied. 'May I join you? Have you had your good luck whisky yet? Scotch Billy shook his head and I told him I'd set it up for him.

His rheumy eyes studied me suspiciously and when I returned with a large Chivas Regal, he said, 'So what are you after, Chris?'

'Just a bit of information. Background stuff. I'm helping a friend with a book. About being a caddie on the European Tour. The highs, the lows, the problems, the fun, the good guys and the bad.'

'Why doesn't Toby do his own interviews?'

I grinned at Billy. 'He thinks I'll get more and better stories because I used to do the job myself.'

'And you had a bloody good bag, too, in Jack Mason.' He looked at his watch. 'I've got half an hour or so. Fire away.'

I led Scotch Billy through the obvious questions. How had he got into the business? For whom had he worked? Who was the best of his employers? What had been his biggest pay-day? The biggest thrill of his career?

Then It was time to ask the fifty-thousand-dollar question. 'There's a lot of talk about drugs on the Tour, Billy. Do you know any golfers who are users?'

Billy finished his whisky and then looked contemplatively at the dregs in the bottom of his glass. His voice became lower, even more of a growl. 'Come on, Chris, there're always a few of the lads who smoke a bit of pot, take uppers or downers. So what? It's a part of growing up, d'ye know.'

'I don't mean the recreational stuff, I mean the drugs that are really frowned upon. Anabolic steroids, growth hormones.'

'Well, my man Jamie's not on 'em.' Scotch Billy laughed. 'I've just got time for one more belt, Chris, if you're buying.'

I returned swiftly with another double whisky and Billy said, 'That's what you're really after, eh, the drugs business?' I nodded. 'I've heard a few rumours.' He leaned forward and the reek of whisky hit my nostrils. 'Gary Peters's been mentioned. But you already know that, I expect.'

Scotch Billy downed his whisky in one long swallow, rose to his feet and thanked me for the 'drams'. 'There are worse things going on in pro golf than a bit of steroid abuse, I can tell you that.'

Before I could question him further, he had given me a wave and strode off. I wondered what on earth his cryptic comment signified. Maybe Toby would be able to throw some light on it.

I glanced around the tent and saw that Burlington Basil was still present. No one on the golf tour could remember how he got his nickname, but he had come late to the profession, if one could call it that, of caddying and it was clear that he had done a more genteel job in his former life. But he resolutely refused to discuss his past; some claimed that he had worked in the City, others that he had been a schoolteacher. As I approached his table, I saw that he was reading *The Financial Times*, rather than the caddie's usual stand-by of *The Sporting Life*.

I noted again Basil's neatly brushed white hair and quiet demeanour; rather than being a part of the rough-and-tumble world of caddying, he could have been a kindly local doctor or solicitor. He greeted me with his usual genial smile and in his well-modulated voice asked me politely how the world was treating me. 'You certainly look in the pink, dear boy.'

I assured him that I was in good order and then we exchanged the standard platitudes about the weather and the state of professional golf. 'How's your man playing?' I asked him. He carried the bag of Edgar Smith, a young player who had won the British Amateur Championship two years before and was now languishing in the lower reaches of the Order of Merit.

Basil sniffed. 'Edgar has real talent, but he's confusing himself with different theories about the game. It's a simple game, as you know, Chris, but only if your head keeps it thus.' I nodded. 'And he keeps banging on about needing more power. I keep telling him, that'll come, as his body matures.'

'Is he fit? Does he do his stuff in the gym?'

'Oh yes, he's trying hard to build up his physique.'

I saw my opportunity and said, very quietly, 'Well, Basil, there are things that could help him. There are players around who are not averse to some of those pills that work wonders.'

'Is that what you were discussing with Scotch Billy?

'Amongst other things.'

'Yes, well he might know things that have passed me by. And one must be realistic, dear boy. If steroids and so on are used in other sports, they've undoubtedly made their way into golf. More's the pity.'

'But you can't name names?'

'Afraid not. But what's your interest?'

'I'm helping someone with a book about caddies.'

Basil smiled knowingly. 'If I hear of anything of interest, I'll let you know, off the record of course. You're helping that old devil, Toby, I suppose.' I nodded. 'Yes, I heard Lofty Lazenby slagging him off the other day. He said that Jeremy Foote had warned him off the topic of drugs in golf. Is that right?'

'As if that would make any difference to Toby.'

'Quite. A pretty pair, those two.' Basil sniffed in disgust. 'Lazenby wanted to represent Edgar a while back, when he turned pro. Luckily the lad turned him down. His sister looks after things for him. A bright girl, and of course Edgar is intelligent, too.'

'Maybe he would help me and Toby.'

Basil pursed his lips. 'Maybe. But, first things first, I must get to work with him on the course.'

'Play well,' I said and shook Basil's hand. 'By the way,' I concluded, 'Scotch Billy made a rather odd remark to me about there being worse things going on in golf than a bit of steroid abuse. Does this mean anything to you?'

Basil paused. 'Not really, but quite a bit of gambling goes on. Perhaps he was referring to that.' He smiled amiably and left to pursue his unlikely calling.

I realized that I had achieved very little for Toby, but, nevertheless, decided to take a look at what was happening on the course. Pro-am days at professional tournaments are surprisingly popular, since the ordinary golf fan is joined by many spectators who are there to goggle at the celebrities, among whom are invariably many household names from the glitzy world of showbiz. To give them their due, they are ever ready to chat to their fans, sign autographs and pose for photographs. The stars are fortunate in that they have an adoring audience who are eager to enjoy their every remark, however banal or derivative. A casual aside about the weather will provoke such merriment that you might begin to wonder whether Oscar Wilde has re-appeared on earth with a new panoply of witticisms.

My old boss, Jack Mason, used to detest pro-ams and did his considerable best to avoid them. He felt uneasy in the casual and jokey atmosphere, not that he was short of humour. If forced into the pro-am ranks his usual mode of defence centred on several bottles of strong ale, whose consumption would smooth his way happily through the round. I noticed, however, that Jack had managed to avoid playing in this particular event.

I strode over to the 17th hole, which seemed to me to personify the peculiar eccentricities of the golf course. A short hole of just over two hundred yards, its island green was imprisoned in the centre of a lake. I wondered how many balls plummeted into its waters every week. How the members must love it.

A golfer called Nick Goddard, whom I knew from my days as a caddie, was standing on the tee. I gave him a wave and he grinned back at me; considering that he was three over par and his team, even with the best ball from among his three partners counting towards their overall score, was only standing at level par, he did very well to raise a smile.

Goddard strolled over and shook my hand. 'Going well, Nick?' I asked mischievously.

'It's bloody purgatory. We've been out here for nearly five hours already. That bloke over there is Ernie Fellowes, you've probably heard of him. Star of that comedy show on the telly. Well, he obviously thinks that he's the world's funniest human being, God's gift to the rest of us talentless bastards. And his golf . . .' Goddard shook his head in disgust. 'He shouldn't be allowed on a golf course. If he could even hit it sideways that'd be an improvement. The other one is the boss of an electronics company and wants to talk incomprehensible technicalities to the rest of us. And the other bloke, he's that ex-rugby player, Lester Freeman, well, he can play but he keeps trying to show me how good he is. You know the scene, Chris, he asks me what club I've hit into the green and then says it's probably one less for him. I grinned in sympathy and he moved back to the tee.

Goddard hit a soaring iron shot behind the flag and it spun back to within about eight feet of the hole. He deserved the loud applause he received from the spectators. Then his amateur partners hit their shots from a tee which was about thirty yards nearer the green. The first two shots were best forgotten, but Lester Freeman, who had an excellent free-flowing swing, put his ball on to the front edge of the green. As Goddard walked past me, he said quietly, 'These bloody amateurs, they're always short of the pin.'

It is a hoary old jibe, but accurate, and it always amuses me.

I looked at the order of play and saw that a caddie called Jigger Davies was about to leave the 18th tee with his charge and I thought that it was worth trying to chat to him for a few minutes when he finished the round.

Jigger Davies was as different from Burlington Basil as one could imagine and fitted the traditional raffish image of the caddie perfectly. As a youth he had been in all sorts of trouble and a life of petty crime seemed to be his destiny. After spells in reform school he ended up in prison for a series of misdemeanours. But a prison visitor had discerned some of the undoubted good in him and secured him a job as a caddie at a busy club on the outskirts of London. Eventually, Jigger had seized an opportunity to carry the bag of a professional golfer on the European Tour.

I watched Nick Goddard and his new bosom pals finish the hole, and enjoyed watching him hole out for a birdie. I walked along the 18th hole, skirting many acres of water as I did so and caught up with Davies as he waited outside the scorer's hut while his golfer checked his card before signing it.

I strolled up to him and asked how the round went. Davies shrugged. 'Oh, not bad, Chris. The boss was two or three under par, not that he gives a damn. The pro-am's just another practice round to him. Anyway, what are you up to? You're not doing any caddying these days, are you?'

I shook my head. 'I'm nosing around, Jigger, especially into the question of drugs on the tour.'

'I've given 'em up, mate. Too pricey these days and anyway the boss is as straight as they come. He's a born-again Christian. I'd be out on my ear if he thought I was on the stuff.'

'No, I didn't mean that. Anabolic steroids, growth enhancers, those drugs.'

'Oh, I see. What the cyclists and the runners use.' I nodded and Davies looked studiously at the bag of clubs he was guarding and then towards the scorer's hut. 'I've heard rumours, nothing definite. You know how it is from your days in the game. Gossip, a nod and a wink, but all I can say, Chris, is that I've seen no evidence of that kind of thing and I don't want to, neither.'

'Why do you say that?'

Davies looked around, as if afraid of being overheard. 'I've gathered that it's not healthy to get involved in all that, that's all I'm saying. But don't quote me, eh?' He looked up, shouldered the heavy bag and said, 'Must go. There's the boss and he wants to get some more practice in. See you, Chris, look after yourself.'

He strode off and I pondered what he meant. One thing seemed clear, that it was another warning.

I decided that it was time to return to London. As I threaded my way through the spectators, many of whom were taking their lunches on the move and were clutching sandwiches, bottles of beer and the inevitable burgers, I pondered what I had achieved during my visit to the Starlight Insurance tournament. Very little, I decided, except for some vague hints of possible impropriety on the tour. Nothing new, in other words. And those insinuations were not going to propel Toby's book on to the best-seller lists.

I entered the VIP car park and, as I strolled along, became aware of someone on the far side of a line of cars. I recognized the tall figure of Lofty Lazenby, who was pursuing a parallel course to mine. Since I didn't know him especially well and had heard little good of him, I did not acknowledge his presence.

Eventually I found my car, with Lazenby standing next to it.

'Chris Ludlow,' he said stiffly.

'Lofty Lazenby,' I replied.

'I hear that you're back where you belong, Ludlow. Among the caddies.'

News travels fast, I thought, as he walked around my rather tired-looking Porsche and stood in front of me, and rather closer than was necessary.

His obvious intention was to intimidate me and it worked, since Lazenby was not only well over six feet in height, but also broad-shouldered; and he looked in good physical order. 'I enjoyed my days as a caddie,' I said with a smile. 'Especially when I worked for Jack Mason.'

'And now you work for Dan Fairfax.'

'On a casual basis, yes.'

'He's a good friend of mine. We do business together. So why are you helping that third-rate journo, Greenslade, to stir up nonsense about drug abuse in the game?'

'Because it isn't nonsense, and it will be an important strand in Toby's book about caddies.'

'His editor has already told him to lay off the subject in *The News*.'

'At your instigation?'

'Let's say that some interested parties had a word with the people who matter at the paper.'

'Jeremy Foote, in other words.'

Lazenby shrugged and moved even closer to me. 'And my word to you, Ludlow, and your scribbling friend, is the same. Lay off the subject.'

'Why are you so concerned, I wonder? Is it because your most important client, Gary Peters, is under suspicion?'

I'd had enough of the conversation, moved away from Lazenby and felt in my trouser pocket for my car keys. It was definitely time to go. To my alarm, Lazenby grabbed me by the right arm and slammed me hard against the side of my car. 'I mean it, Ludlow,' he said, his face beginning to redden with anger. 'You and Greenslade had better keep your prying eyes out of my business. Or else.'

He still had a strong grip on my right arm and his other arm was against my chest. I could feel the adrenalin surging through my system, but I was aware how much bigger and stronger he was than me. I had to await my chance, catch him unawares. Like most bullies, he probably did not anticipate any resistance.

'Okay, okay,' I said placatingly. 'You've made your point. Now let me go, please.'

Lazenby gave my arm a final and painful squeeze and then pushed me contemptuously in the face with the heel of his hand. Then he half-turned away from me in order to walk back towards the exit. This was my chance and I didn't hesitate. With my right fore-arm I hit him as hard as I could on the lower jaw. He didn't fall over, but sprawled against the rear of my car. I hooked my leg behind him and used all my strength to throw him to the ground. Groaning, he massaged his damaged jaw. My final act of farewell was to give him a solid kick in the ribs. 'That's from Toby,' I said. I am not a vindictive person; I'd merely given Lazenby what any bully deserves.

I looked around quickly and it was fortunate that there were no witnesses. I jumped into my car and set off towards the exit. I looked back in my rear-view mirror and saw that Lazenby was already levering himself to his feet.

As soon as I was on the main road back to London, I scrabbled amongst my collection of CDs and found the Miles Davis version of 'Porgy and Bess'. The mellifluous tones of the great man's trumpet calmed me down and eased my journey. But I wondered when Lazenby would attempt his retribution and what form it would take.

CHAPTER 17

On the following morning I was determined to clear my head and try to sort out the various options that faced me both in my personal and my business life. Some people discuss such opportunities or problems with their close friends; others sit down and write a list, followed by an analysis of it in an attempt to plot a new course. My favourite method is to go for a long walk and let my thoughts take me where they will. It's a random walk through my own subconscious mind.

As I strolled along the edges of Wimbledon Common, I came to several conclusions. It was increasingly obvious that the misuse of performance-enhancing drugs was a serious problem in golf. The muted reactions of the caddies to whom I had spoken, added to the crassly bullying attitudes of Lofty Lazenby and of Jeremy Foote, the man at the helm of the European Tour, confirmed it in my eyes. But there was also the hint of another scandal in the game; unfortunately the veiled remarks of Scotch Billy, Burlington Basil and Jigger Davies had given me no leads and were meaningless without some concrete evidence.

As for the Headlam book, everything surrounding it was even more convoluted and I seemed to be at an impasse. Although I had not given him much time as yet, I needed Tim Headlam to come up with some leads following his research into major art sales in the latter half of the 1980s. If he could only provide a list of the buyers of highly-priced pictures and drawings this would give me a chance of identifying the plutocrats who had most to lose from Derek Headlam's revelations. It was unfortunate that what had once seemed to be a fascinating part of the Headlam story – the identities of his co-conspirators – had hit a dead end. Nevertheless, I resolved to contact my brother Max to see if he had anything to contribute.

When I returned to my apartment the light on my answering machine was blinking but I ignored it while I made myself a cup of coffee.

Having scanned the sports pages of *The Daily News* and seen that Toby had only contributed a short article about the main contenders in the Starlight Insurance Open, I listened to my messages. There was only one and it was from Dan Fairfax; in his usual peremptory style he summoned me to a meeting in his office on that morning at midday. I had planned to go to my golf club for some much-needed practice, but unfortunately business had to come first. I guessed that the main item on the agenda would be Lofty Lazenby, who was not the sort of man to wait too long for his revenge.

When I arrived at Fairfax's office at just after midday, Lindy was as usual perched on the edge of her desk, telephone in hand. I wondered fleetingly if she was Fairfax's 'bit of spare' as he would undoubtedly put it. She covered the mouthpiece of the telephone, pointed at Fairfax's office door and said, 'He's waiting for you.'

Fairfax was also engaged on a call and waved me to a chair in front of his desk. 'OK, old son,' he said, 'she'll do the jobs for you. Let's call it ten grand for the two appearances, yeah? Half of it in cash which'll go into that Gucci handbag of hers. OK? Good, all agreed. Must go, one of the lads is waiting to talk to me. Cheers.'

He looked at me steadily for a few moments. 'Easy money, Chris. Two grand in commission, some of it in readies, and no hassle. Better than pissing about with books on art, eh?' I shrugged and waited for the subject of the agent Lazenby to be broached. 'Anyway, we're getting somewhere with the Cyprus project. Some of your leads are still positive and I want you to follow them up and try to get their signatures on an agreement, OK? Especially that Roley Jenkins bloke, he's now dragging his feet a bit.'

We discussed the investors in question and then Fairfax continued. 'There's another bit of business I want you to look into, Chris. A clothing manufacturer has been in touch, golf stuff, from China. He needs a distributor over here in Britain, and Europe maybe at a later date. So, can you do some research for me? The state of the market, the competition, the pricing structures. You know the sort of thing.'

'It's a crowded market, Dan, to state the obvious. All the big golf equipment manufacturers are already in there, with their star professionals wearing their gear.'

'Sure, Chris, most markets are tough to enter, business is tough.' The impatience in Fairfax's voice was evident. 'But this firm has very modern factories with cutting-edge machinery, so the quality is top-notch. And their labour is cheap, to put it mildly, so the margins are bloody good. Anyway, have a go, Lindy's got all the info waiting for you.'

I was rising from my seat to go when Fairfax said, 'Did you hear what happened to Lofty yesterday?' I shook my head and tried to look concerned. 'The poor bugger was mugged. In the car park at the Halgrave Club. A couple of yobs set on him, they were after his wallet and credit cards of course.'

'At the golf club? Is nothing sacred? Didn't anyone help him?'

'There was nobody around apparently. Anyway, Lofty fought them off. He's a big sod, as you know, and he gave as good as he got. They buggered off pretty sharp-ish.'

'Good for Lofty,' I said with a show of approval. 'You have to be careful wherever you go these days. Even at golf tournaments.'

As I left Fairfax's office, I felt a fleeting admiration for the way in which Lazenby had re-worked his account of our melée. Rather than admitting that he'd been duffed up by someone who was well under his own fighting weight, and a former caddie to boot, he had portrayed himself in a semi-heroic light as a man who had sorted out a couple of ruffians.

I was greatly relieved that Lazenby's vanity had triumphed over his need for retribution. Otherwise, my job with Fairfax would have come to an end just as I was beginning to enjoy some aspects of it.

During the afternoon I settled down in my small office at home and did some basic research into the state of the golf clothing industry. Much of the gear was already imported and, as I had told Fairfax, the market was dominated by the powerful and well-entrenched manufacturers of golf clubs and balls and by some specialist companies, which concentrated on the more expensive end of the market; at the other extreme were the department stores and chains which sold relatively low-priced items, such as polo shirts, which were ideal for wear on the golf course.

My conclusion was that the new range that Fairfax was keen to promote would have to be exceptional in every way to stand a chance. The next step was to see the full range of clothing. Maybe I could persuade Lindy to model the women's range for me. It was a cheering thought, but I was then uneasily reminded that I was taking Jane out for a meal that evening.

After the debacle of our visit to the musical version of 'For Whom the Bell Tolls', I felt that I owed her a special treat and had encouraged her to choose a restaurant which she really fancied. She had read about a new place in Notting Hill, which had a young and trendy chef who was already becoming a media darling.

I arranged to meet her at the restaurant, since I had to meet Toby beforehand to report on my conversations with the three caddies on the previous day.

I had persuaded him to meet me in a pub in Notting Hill and, despite his protests about the location, he was comfortably ensconced in a booth, a bottle of champagne in its cooler in front of him, when I arrived.

'Well, it's not as bad a place as I anticipated,' he grumbled. 'And I passed George Orwell's old house up the road. I had to stop and bow my head respectfully. A great writer, even if his politics were dodgy.'

'Perhaps the power of his writing came from his political beliefs.'

Toby did his trademark harrumph, which means that he doesn't agree with you, but cannot be bothered to argue the point. 'Maybe. Anyway, have a drink. And to more mundane matters, did you uncover anything of interest yesterday?'

I gave Toby a concise account of my conversations with the caddies and apologised for their inconclusive nature.

'So, we have nothing new to look into?'

'Except those vague hints that something else of an unsavoury nature is going on.'

'So vague as to be meaningless,' Toby said severely. 'It could be anything. Sex orgies, gambling, cross-dressing, the mind boggles.'

'You've been working for *The News* too long. But, to be positive, I think you'll have to concentrate on the Gary Peters angle. That is obviously the most fruitful area. In particular, I would like to find the source of his drugs supply. That would be a good start. What about chatting up your colleague at the paper, the athletics correspondent? Surely he'll have some inside information. For instance, that runner, Ron Rigby, has been accused of misusing drugs and maybe your fellow-scribe could tell us who supplies him. It's a starting point anyway.'

'Yes, I agree. And of course Rigby's agent is Lazenby. It's remarkable how our lofty friend keeps cropping up, isn't it?' Toby supped some of his champagne reflectively. 'By the way, you've heard what happened to Lazenby, have you?'

'Fairfax mentioned something about a punch-up.'

'Yes, but the two ruffians made a big mistake in attacking Lazenby. Apparently, he duffed up the bastards.'

'Was he hurt?'

'A battered jaw and very sore ribs, that's all.'

'I wish I'd been there to help those two yobs out,' I said with a laugh.

'I'll drink to that,' Toby replied, as he filled up our glasses.

Toby had counselled that the restaurant chosen by Jane was the most over-priced in London. Its surroundings did not suggest such extravagance, since the décor was unpretentious to the point of plainness. However, as Jane and I sipped our glasses of wine and studied the menu, I realized that the prices were far from being unpretentious. I don't normally worry about such things, but I hoped that Jane would not opt for the 'tasting menu' which was offered at the very tasty price of £99.

The descriptions of the food were elaborate and I wondered what violet artichokes were, and how beetroot became 'candy' beetroot. In the end I chose the simplest-sounding of the dishes on offer and was relieved when Jane did the same. I managed to obliterate any thoughts of the cost of the meals from my mind; I would make a credit card payment and worry about the bill at a later date. I was there to enjoy the food and, even though it was fussily presented, I did.

The evening was an enjoyable one, since we both steered clear of any contentious topics, especially that of her unstable husband.

At my apartment we had a final glass of wine and listened to some music; then we orchestrated a thoroughly enjoyable finale to our evening.

I was awakened from a beatific and dreamless sleep by a change in the atmosphere. A rosy light was flickering through the bedroom curtains. It seemed a strange time to be lighting a bonfire and I eased myself out of bed, trying not to disturb Jane, who was sighing quietly in her slumber. I slid the curtains aside and peered out. Beyond a small square of lawn and a hedge was the car park and it was from there that the glow was coming. Suddenly, there was the boom of an explosion.

Jane shot up in bed and gasped, 'What on earth was that?'

I grabbed a pair of trousers from a chair, drew them on swiftly and put on some slippers. 'Stay here,' I said urgently. An awful premonition had me in its grip as I unlocked the door on to the garden and padded across the lawn. A small gate led to the car park and I saw that my lovely old Porsche was ablaze. There was nothing I could do to halt the inferno that engulfed it, and I was thankful that it was parked on one side of the parking area and well clear of the cars belonging to other residents.

Several of those residents had heard the explosion and had gathered in the car park. One of them, an accountant called Harry, who was interested in cars and had occasionally chatted to me about the merits of the older Porsche models, said, 'Do you think an electrical fault caused it?'

I shrugged and said I hadn't a clue, but must call the fire brigade. I left the growing gaggle of residents and did so. Before ten minutes had passed a fire tender arrived and the car was swiftly covered in some sort of foam, which put out the fire and confirmed the end of the car's useful life.

By this time Mrs Bradshaw had taken charge. She managed to disperse her fellow residents and make tea for the crew of the fire engine and for Jane and myself. The head fireman made some notes about the incident, also raised the question of an electrical fault, and instructed me to call the police. Jane had already done this and, when two of them arrived in the form of a male sergeant and a female constable, I went through a further recital of what had occurred.

Sergeant Wilkins, young and fit-looking, asked me if the car had been properly maintained. 'These old cars, sir, can be a problem, especially the electrics.' I confirmed that it was serviced regularly at a nearby garage. He nodded and took down the name and address. Hesitantly, he then asked me if the fire could have been started deliberately. 'Have you any enemies, have you upset anyone, someone of a questionable nature perhaps, who might have got his own back by torching the car? Sorry, sir, but we have to ask these questions.'

I assured him that I couldn't think of anyone who wished me harm; but the figure of Lofty Lazenby was looming large in my thoughts.

By the time that the two police officers had departed, dawn was inching up in the sky and we didn't bother to go back to bed. I was dreading all the form-filling that my insurance company would demand; and there was also the question of a replacement for my lovely old Porsche.

CHAPTER 18

Having spent the whole of Monday delving into the background to the golf clothing market in the UK, I was grateful to escape to Oxford on the following day. I had arranged to meet Tim Headlam to see if his researches had borne any fruit.

Since my car was now merely burned-out rubble, I travelled by train to the city of dreaming spires and met Tim at a brasserie just off Broad Street. Even at just after midday on a Tuesday it was already busy and I was lucky to grab a table for two people in a corner. The other customers were a mixed bunch of tourists, business types and 'ladies who lunch'. Not surprisingly there didn't seem to be any undergraduates amongst them.

Tim was only about ten minutes late for our lunch and ambled towards the table in what I assumed was his standard student kit of frayed jeans and T-shirt, with a back-pack on his shoulder, his long hair awry, and an apology on his lips.

Once he had settled down, I ordered some wine and then we both perused the extensive menu in silence for a few minutes. Tim grinned at me. 'If it's OK with you, Chris, I'd like the steak and chips. It's not normally what a research student can have.'

'Fine by me. I'll have a go at the fish and chips.'

The wine arrived and Tim proposed a toast to Uncle Derek. This prompted me to get straight down to business and I asked him whether he had managed to sniff out any traces of his fraudulent works at any of the auctions he had investigated.

'As we agreed, I looked at major sales of Old Masters at the two biggest auction houses. Heathcote's and Westerby's. There are at least a dozen sales which could have been infiltrated by Uncle Derek's copies.'

'Presumably you looked for sales in which Derek's favoured artists turned up?'

'Yes, of course. The usual suspects. Durer, Corot, Goya, Rembrandt, Castiglione, and so on. But they crop up frequently anyway, so it didn't really help us. And it did occur to me that Uncle Derek and his merry band of buccaneers might have inserted his copies in ones and twos and threes into various sales. That would be a safer and more sophisticated approach, perhaps?'

I nodded my agreement and then asked Tim about the Jewish family that the fraudsters had invented. 'Presumably the original plan was to unload a lot of the copies, mixed in with genuine works, in one fell swoop. They wanted to get rich quick, in other words.'

Tim drank some of his wine. 'I found a mention of the family in *The Courier*. A small item of news, without any details of the so-called treasures they were selling. This was in 1988 and there was no follow-up that I could find.'

'I just wonder if a private sale was arranged by Uncle Derek and his friends,' I mused. 'Perhaps they approached some well-known collector, and Derek would know most of them, told the sob-story about the Jewish family and did a deal.'

Our food arrived and Tim attacked his steak with gusto. 'That's a tantalising thought,' he said, through a mouthful of food. 'But anyone who made such an important purchase would want to keep a very low profile. For security reasons.'

'But the buyer would presumably employ an adviser, an agent. Perhaps someone from one of the auction houses?'

'Yes. I was just thinking that an approach to some of the people who work for Heathcote's or Westerby's might pay dividends. One of the archivists, most of whom happen to be women, so that would give you a chance, Chris, to use your charm on them.' Tim grinned mischievously at me. 'I will uncover some names and pass them on to you.'

'Talking of the gentle sex, how are you faring with the lovely Mandy?'

Tim had the good grace to look mildly embarrassed. 'She really was devastated by Grant Jezzard's death, but I've seen her a few times since then. She's got a job with another small London publisher and the good news is that one of their editors is looking at Uncle Derek's book and seems interested in publishing it.'

'Good news,' I replied. 'Keep in touch on that, because I'd still like to earn some commission as your agent.'

Tim looked blankly at me for a moment and then nodded. 'Yes, of course, I hadn't forgotten you.' He scanned the menu and ordered some treacle tart and ice-cream.

CHAPTER 19

On the following day I received an email from Tim in which he thanked me for an enjoyable lunch and, as promised, gave me the name of an archivist at Westbury's and another at Heathcote's.

I wondered how best to approach them and decided to obtain some advice from Larry Steinmann, who had such a wide range of contacts in the art world.

He answered his telephone on the second ring and greeted me warmly. 'Chris, nice to hear from you. How did you fare with that nauseating little creep Corbett?'

I explained that my conversation with him had been far from fruitful and then asked him if he knew either of the women recommended by Tim Headlam.

'Abigail Carey at Westerby's and Joanna Aston at Heathcote's? Well, I know the names, but I don't know the ladies themselves. However, there's someone else at Westerby's, she's their public relations guru. She's knocked around the art and media scene for years. She's quite formidable, very bright, attractive, fifty-ish. Araminta Brooks is the name. A bit old for you, Chris, but she might suit old Toby.' He laughed at the thought. 'Give her a call, tell her you know me and see what you can get out of her.'

I now had a proper introduction to someone at one of the main auction houses, rather than cold-calling one of those suggested by Tim. Steinmann's remark about

Toby also gave me a tantalising idea. I dialled Toby's number.

'Greenslade', he grunted down the line.

'Is that Toby Greenslade, notable journalist and author?' I asked brightly.

'Ah, flattery can move mountains. So, what do you want from me, Chris?'

'Some help with a lady in the art business,' I replied.

'Why me?'

'Because Larry Steinmann says that the woman in question, Araminta Brooks, is bright and attractive and of a certain age.'

'And you need her help? Some information?'

'Yes. I want to ask her if she knows about any noteworthy sales of valuable paintings and drawings to private and therefore very rich individuals in the last few years. And secondly whether she has heard any rumours of a reclusive Jewish family unloading their treasures to a private collector.'

'And why should she share this information with you?'

'Not me, Toby. With you. Because you are researching a book about the world of art, how the business works, who are the really important movers and shakers, and so on. And I am helping you with the research.'

There was a pause in our conversation as Toby mulled over my remarks and then he said, 'So you need me to use my considerable and mature charms on the no doubt lovely Araminta Brooks?'

'I couldn't have put it better myself.'

Araminta Brooks confessed that she had never heard of Toby, but was more than happy to talk about the business In which she worked, especially if some 'good publicity was generated for Westerby's'. She was very busy during the day and we agreed to meet on the following evening in a wine bar in Kensington.

Toby and I were already installed at a corner table in the busy bar when Araminta arrived. Dressed in a dark-grey suit and carrying a leather brief-case she was every inch the business executive, and Larry Steinmann had not exaggerated her attractions. I could sense Toby's interest quicken as she approached our table.

After the introductions were made, Toby explained that, although he was a golf writer, he had always been fascinated by the art world and was delighted to be researching a book about it.

Earlier in the day he had talked at length to Tim Headlam about the questions he should put to someone like Araminta, and he now covered all the obvious lines of enquiry: the estimated size of the various markets for paintings and drawings; the most coveted artists; the names of the leading auction houses; who were regarded as the most influential and informative of the art critics. Toby led the conversation well and scribbled the replies in short-hand into his notebook.

Araminta was relaxed and charming, and I noticed that she sipped only occasionally and sparingly at her glass of champagne.

Eventually, Toby reached the critical part of the meeting. 'What about the private collectors?' he asked. 'We hear so much about the Russian oligarchs and their obsessive collecting of important works. Is this really true? And, if so, who are they?'

'There is a lot of truth in that,' Araminta agreed, 'and firms like Westerby's benefit greatly from the money they spend, and from the money from the oil-rich magnates in the Middle East. And there are plenty of mega-rich collectors in other corners of the world, of course.' She reeled off a string of names and obligingly spelt out several of the more obscure ones.

As Toby paused for a moment and took a draught of champagne, I said, with feigned hesitation, 'I think I read, a couple of years back, about a Jewish family which had a hoard of Old Master drawings and paintings. They managed to conceal them from the Nazis and then reclaim them after the war. The story was that they were selling the whole collection. I wondered if you know how they sold their treasures, whether they came to Westerby's for instance. I'd love to know who bought them. It would make wonderful story for Toby's book. Full of human interest, as they say in media circles.' I smiled broadly at Araminta.

She didn't smile back but merely said, 'Unfortunately, Chris, I can't help you.' She looked down at her glass, which was still half-full and then turned her head to study the occupants of a nearby table.

'Do you have any idea who might have bought the works?' I persisted.

'I'm afraid not. I vaguely remember the story, but fear that it was just a bit of journalistic kite-flying.' She grinned at Toby. 'My apologies, Toby, but there is a lot of make-believe in the Press, as I'm sure you'll agree.' He nodded eagerly and it was obvious that he was smitten by the fair Araminta.

'So, perhaps it was a private deal,' I continued.

'Possibly. If there was any substance to the story.'

'But you can't throw any light on it?'

'No. Private sales are happening all the time, and in all corners of the world market. We can't possibly keep track of them, unless those involved in such deals make it known.'

I glanced at Toby, who was looking questioningly at his empty glass. 'It intrigues me,' I said, 'because the rumour is that many of the works in that collection were fakes, that it was a scam on a grand scale. Therefore, I thought that it might have caused some ripples of concern among the art professionals.'

Araminta pushed her half-full glass away, looked down to locate her brief-case and said, 'Not really. The art market is bombarded with tales of fakes and forgeries. Some of those stories may well be true, but most of them are nonsense.'

As she reached down for her brief-case, I said, 'Before you go, do you know anyone at the Art and Antiques Squad at Scotland Yard? One of them put a faker called Derek Headlam through the wringer at Heathrow a few years ago and we'd like to find him.'

'Ah yes, the notorious Headlam, a man with a fevered imagination. But I don't know anyone at the Art and Antiques Squad. Those people come and go because the police hierarchy doesn't take that department seriously. As a result, it's badly under-funded. For instance, a few years back it was disbanded for a while, despite all the appalling thefts that occur every year. Just imagine how vulnerable some of those stately homes are with all their treasures. They're sitting ducks for professional thieves.'

Araminta picked up her case, rose quickly to her feet and said, 'Toby, Chris, it's been great fun to meet you both and if you need any more help or information do give me a call.' She blew kisses in our direction and swayed elegantly towards the door.

Toby nodded at a passing waitress and another bottle of champagne was swiftly placed on our table. 'What did you make of all that?' he asked.

'She's a charming woman, but helpful only up to a certain point.'

'That well-defined point when you asked about forged works of art and that mythical Jewish family.'

'When the delectable Araminta became defensive, to put it mildly.'

'Yes, and I was hoping that she'd have dinner with me,' Toby said mournfully. 'Or even perhaps a dirty weekend could have been negotiated.'

I laughed and said, 'A dirty weekend. That's a rather dated term, isn't it? And it would have to be in Brighton, I assume? Anyway, she's a bit young for you, isn't she?'

Toby glowered at me and I asked him if any of the names Araminta had rattled off meant anything to him.

'I don't read the gossip columns, Chris, so they didn't ring any bells.' He glanced at the list he had made. 'Let's see. How about Ivan Smirnov? That sounds promising if you like a tot of vodka. Roman Kozlov, Ilya Orlov, Fedor Popov and so on. I was hoping for an Eisenstein or a Dostoevsky.'

'Maybe your newspaper's files will turn up something interesting about them,' I suggested.

'Maybe. I'll ask one of our trainees to look back through the files.' Toby paused. 'There are a few American names and some of Asian origin, oh, and here's an intriguing one. George Gawalas, I wonder where he springs from?'

'Greece, perhaps.'

'Yes, and he probably owns a fleet of oil tankers. We'll take a look at him, too.'

As Toby poured some more champagne into our glasses, I asked him if he was making any progress with his investigation into the use of drugs in professional golf.

'Not a lot, but our athletics correspondent at *The News*, Jack Marshall, told me what we already know. That there are numerous suppliers of illicit drugs to sportsmen. But he did give me the name of a doctor who is well-known for prescribing treatments and drugs to athletes which are supposedly on the right side of the regulations. Supposedly, but I have my doubts about that, Chris. What do you think?'

'I think we'll have to try him out.'

CHAPTER 20

I thought it might be helpful to talk to Jack Mason about the ramifications of drug abuse in the golfing world. He was guaranteed to have some interesting, and no doubt trenchant opinions on the matter. I knew that he usually visited a golf club near his home in Surrey on the days when he was not playing in a tournament. His usual programme was to practise for an hour or two, often help any young players who were present and then have some refreshment in the club bar.

The best time to catch him was around midday and I set off at just after 11 o'clock in my rented car. Every time that I got into it I experienced a brief but sharp pang of longing for my lovely old Porsche. I hoped that one day I would have sufficient proof of Lofty Lazenby's part in its destruction; then I would wreak a suitable revenge on him.

Traffic was relatively light and I arrived at the Micklesham Golf Club, a charming and unpretentious parkland course, at well before midday. As I made my way towards the clubhouse I could see Jack's imposing figure on the practice putting green. He was chatting to a teenage boy, who then addressed the ball and stroked it firmly into a hole about ten feet away.

'Well done,' I heard Jack say. 'Now your grip on the putter is much improved and so is your posture.'

What a lucky lad, I thought, to have the benefit of Jack Mason's knowledge and enthusiasm.

Jack saw me and waved a greeting. Then he gave the young golfer a few more words of instruction and strolled towards me. 'Good to see you, Chris. I hope you're not after a caddying job because young Marlon is doing fine so far.'

I smiled and shook my head. 'No, Jack, I'm after information and thought you might be able to help.'

'I'll do my best. Let's have some coffee on the terrace.'

When it arrived we covered some perennial golfing topics, such as the approaching tournaments, and which golfers stood a chance of doing well in the Open. Then we had a good laugh about the rumours which had been circulating in the American golfing press about a leading professional who had been 'outed' as a cross-dresser.

'I suppose the silly sod wants to play off the women's tees', Jack said.

We joked a bit more about the stories and then I asked him for his thoughts on the prevalence of illegal drugs in golf.

'Nothing like as bad as in athletics, of course. But worrying, nonetheless. You look at some of these guys and it's bloody obvious that they haven't acquired those bulging muscles in the gym.' Jack paused, sipped some of the watery coffee and continued. 'When you add in the advantages these high-tech modern clubs and balls bring, I can see the day coming when many of these pros won't be far short of three hundred yards with their drives.' I looked at Jack in disbelief. 'Chris, I'm serious. They'll make a mockery of many of our lovely courses. And then the only solution will be to make the courses longer and longer. And quite frankly, Chris, I don't want to have to compete on these monstrously long tracks. It's not golf as I know it. It's boring.'

Jack looked rather gloomily at me. I nodded in sympathy and said, 'Golf isn't supposed to be all about power, is it? Anyway, the reason I'm here is that I'm helping Toby, as you probably know, with his book...'

'... About caddies?'

'Yes. It's called "Caddie Confidential".'

'Well, tell him not to dish the dirt on me,' Jack said with mock-severity.

'None to dish, Jack. No, we want to identify the pros who are actually using these prohibited drugs, and who is supplying them. Any ideas?'

'I know that Toby's in touch with Gary Peters's caddie, Andy Massey, and I assume that you've talked to some of your old caddie mates.'

'Yes, and they're as tight-lipped as one would expect.'

'Of course they are, they don't want to lose their jobs. Or worse.'

'What do you mean?'

'I mean that there are people in the golf business who don't necessarily play by the rules.'

'Like Lofty Lazenby?' Jack nodded and I told him about my *contretemps* with him and my suspicion that he'd arranged for my car to be trashed.

Jack stared at me, his face showing both surprise and puzzlement. 'Your car was torched? Bloody hell. I know that Lazenby is an unscrupulous bastard, despite his airs and graces, but would he go to such lengths to get back at you? Are you sure you haven't upset someone else?'

'Possibly,' I replied and told Jack about the two Russian thugs who had nearly spoiled my evening with Max recently.

'Well there you are. Look no further for the culprits.'

'But that was an unrelated matter,' I insisted. 'They wanted to stop the publication of a book by a con-artist.' I grinned at Jack, who raised his eyebrows at the pun. 'And their warning was serious,' I continued. 'It was at the point of a gun. So why bother with what seems like a rather petty and spiteful bit of revenge?'

'You've got a point, Chris, and I was about to advise you to stick with golf.' He laughed. 'But now I'm not so sure because you're ruffling some feathers in that world, too.'

I shrugged. 'And I mean to do even more of it. So, how can we find out more about the drugs problem? For instance, could we use someone to let it be known that he needs steroids and other substances, and where can he get them.'

'A sort of stalking horse,' Jack said thoughtfully. He laughed. 'I wouldn't be much good in that role, would I? At my height and weight I don't need any building up. The other pros would soon guess that I was up to something, especially since Toby is a good friend of mine.'

'What about someone like Edgar Smith,' I suggested. 'He's young and ambitious and he could do with a bit of extra muscle.'

'But why should he get involved? It might be dangerous and the real culprits might turn the tables on him and shop him to the European Tour people.'

'You might be able to persuade him. That he's doing something to keep the game of golf clean.'

'He'd probably laugh at me. The game has moved on since the days of Bobby Jones and Walter Hagen. More's the pity. There's so much money at stake now and the pros are remarkably single-minded, even cynical, in their pursuit of it.'

We both paused and looked away to the golf course which lay before our eyes. The well-defined fairway of the first hole meandered to the right and then curved playfully back to give the golfer a view of the two-tiered green. It looked a deceptively simple hole, until you noticed the trees on both sides of the fairway; they represented severe obstacles for a wayward shot.

'That hole isn't as simple as it looks,' Jack said, as if reading my thoughts. 'Lovely trees. "There is a pleasure in the pathless woods", as the poet wrote.'

I looked at him with surprise. 'Is that Lord Byron?' Jack nodded. 'I didn't know that you liked poetry.'

'Some poetry. I find that it relaxes me and those wonderful phrases must be good for the soul.' I nodded in agreement and Jack continued. 'Just another thought about how we infiltrate the drug culture in golf. I wonder if your brother Max could help us?'

'I'm sure he would, but how?'

'He looks every inch a sportsman, so perhaps he could pose as an aspiring golfer. The story is that he's just joined the Challenge Tour and needs to bulk up a bit, acquire more power. It might work better than using Edgar Smith.'

CHAPTER 21

When I arrived home I decided to talk to Max about Jack Mason's idea. I was also anxious to know if any of his many and varied contacts among the academic luminaries of Cambridge University had thrown any light on the identity of 'D'.

However, before I called him at his office I looked again at the sequence in Headlam's memoirs in which he describes a meeting with D's American accomplice, S.

> I wasn't really sure why S had asked me to a flash Mayfair restaurant for 'a bite to eat', as he put it. A bloody expensive bite, that's for sure, and I'd rather have met him in a pub, to be honest.
>
> Not that I'm very keen on Yanks anyway. They gave us stick for not joining them in Vietnam but, as I always say, they were Johnny-Come-Latelys when we had to take on the krauts. Mind you, without the Yanks. . .
>
> Anyway, S does his best to be friendly and I certainly didn't forget how he'd stuck it right up those Stasi bastards in Berlin. To my everlasting relief.
>
> I'd often wondered how he'd come to know D. He wasn't a bad-looking bloke in some ways, in that rugged All-American style that some of them

affect and, as a really nice bottle of red plonk relaxed the both of us, I asked him about her.

He looked a bit startled and I imagine that you're not supposed to ask leading questions like that when you're with secretive bastards like him and D.

'Oh, we met here and there on bits of official business. You know, committees and conferences, that kinda thing.'

'And you got on well?'

'Sure. She's a really nice lady.'

I gave him the benefit of my best leer. 'And you had an affair, I suppose.'

'I couldn't possibly comment,' said S, with a smile. So, that was a given then, I thought.

I didn't pursue that line of chat, but I had long been intrigued by how D had become involved in an art scam. 'D has a good job, in the Home Office she told me, so why should she risk her career, her reputation, Christ, her rock-solid pension, for a get-rich-quick scheme like this?'

S chewed on his steak for a while, swallowed some of it and then some of his wine and said, 'Because D is a disappointed woman. She's damned good at her job and should, if there was any justice, be the head of a Government department by now. She told me once that she was fed up with missing out on promotion.' S grinned at me. 'I'll try to remember her precise words. They went something like this: she was being brushed aside so that some mentally-retarded misfit, whose only attribute was his Old Etonian tie, could be moved even further beyond the level of his competence.'

I laughed loudly at those words because I'd met plenty of those tossers in my line of business. 'So, she was bitter and twisted,' I said.

'To put it mildly. And our project is her way out. Make plenty of fast money and then she'll take early retirement and enjoy herself.'

I couldn't fault her for that and I raised my glass and said, 'Let's both drink to that.'

When Max answered his 'phone, I came straight to the point and said, 'How would you like to masquerade as an aspiring golfer who needs some extra help, in the form of drugs, steroids and so on, so that you can bulk up?'

'As long as nobody tries to check out my golf swing.' Max laughed. 'What's the plot?'

'We want to try to expose the doctors who are providing these illegal drugs to sportsmen and in particular to golfers.'

'So you want me to go along to some dodgy medic, who will no doubt be installed in great comfort in the environs of Harley Street, and ask for some of these illegal drugs.'

'That's it.'

'Why should he have anything to do with me. If he's got any sense he'll guess that I'm a fake, an *agent provocateur*.'

'No, because you'll tell him that he's been recommended by Ron Rigby and Gary Peters.'

'Let me think about it, Chris. I suppose this is going to help Toby with his book?'

'Yes, and talking of books have you found anyone in the Groves of Academe who can help us to identify the elusive D?'

'I've spoken to one or two of the older dons, who would have known the people who were keeping an eye on Blunt on behalf of our Government. But, as they all said, it was all so long ago.'

'Prime Minister Thatcher shopped Blunt in 1979, didn't she? So that's not so long ago, surely?'

'Correct. But Blunt was exposed as a Communist spy in 1964, partly because the Americans, in the person of the Attorney General, Robert Kennedy, made a fuss about the old bugger's activities.'

'And that's when Blunt confessed all?'

'Yes, in return for immunity from prosecution. Of course, he kept his knighthood, and his position as Surveyor of the Queen's Pictures and so on.'

'It's remarkable how the British Establishment closes ranks around one of their own,' I said lightly.

'Quite. And Blunt would have had some surveillance after that from the Secret Service people and maybe the Home Office. But it would have been moderated over the years, and the people watching Blunt could have been any one of hundreds of bureaucrats.'

'So, it's a dead end?'

'Not entirely. One of the people I spoke to told me that the Art and Antiques Squad were at one stage involved in shadowing Blunt. He didn't know why. Perhaps he was doing one of his chums a favour and trying to slide some paintings of dubious value or provenance into HM's collection. I wouldn't put it past the old devil.'

I thought back to the sequence in Headlam's book when he was searched at Heathrow Airport. He'd written that the so-called customs officer who'd stopped him seemed familiar, perhaps a member of the Art and Antiques Squad.

I mentioned this to Max and said, 'Could we try to identify him? He was probably a part of the conspiracy with D, so he might lead us to her.'

'Good idea. We ought to look at the newspapers for any stories about the Art Squad. They might possibly give the names of the officers involved. After all, the cops love to get some positive publicity.'

'I'll ask young Tim if he can help us on that one. I also wonder if there was anything in the press about D's retirement. She was seen as a high-flier after all.'

'Except that she was never allowed to take wing.' Max said with a laugh.

'Nevertheless, she probably had a reasonably distinct profile within the ranks of the Home Office. Intelligent, attractive, just the sort of person who would stand out among all those stodgy bureaucrats.'

'Those slaves of mediocrity, as someone once said. But I doubt there was any comment. Government departments take great pains to avoid negative publicity. But if we assume that D had been involved in keeping track of Blunt, then her retirement may well have been noted by those who retained an interest in the Anthony Blunt saga.'

There was a pause as Max spoke briefly to someone in his office. 'Sorry, Chris, I've got to attend a meeting shortly. Meetings, meetings and yet more meetings.' He sighed. 'By the way, have you made any progress in finding out who bought Headlam's forgeries?'

'Not really,' I replied and told him about Araminta Brooks and the mega-rich collectors she had named.

'Why not try to talk to some of them, see if they've ever been in contact with Headlam, if they bought a collection of pictures from a secretive Jewish family and so on.'

'These plutocrats don't exactly advertise their whereabouts, do they. We know how they protect themselves, Max, as you will recall from our encounter with their hired guns.'

'Perhaps we need to stir things up again, provoke this rich thug to come out of the woodwork to protect his investments.'

'First things first,' I replied. 'Let's line up an appointment with the dodgy doctor. I'll get his name from Toby and we'll take it from there.'

CHAPTER 22

Toby experienced no difficulties in naming several doctors who specialised in treating people with 'muscular disorders' and the caddie, Andy Massey, had also pointed his accusing finger specifically at the man who had prescribed various illicit medicines to Gary Peters and the athlete Ron Rigby.

My journalist friend had been very enthusiastic about our plan, since he said that our medical researches, as he put it, would become a salient part of an article he was preparing on the subject for a relatively new publication called *Golf Plus*. 'Since I'm prohibited from writing about the matter, and a highly important one, by that conniving scrote of an editor, I had to take it elsewhere,' he said with venom. 'By the way, Chris, tell Max that I'll pay any fees he incurs.'

It wasn't difficult for Max to secure an appointment with Doctor Cockburn and a few days later we were ushered into his presence on the second floor of a grand Edwardian building in Marylebone, a stone's throw from Harley Street.

A relatively short man, with a rounded face and a good head of crinkly grey hair, Cockburn was wearing a well-cut and expensive-looking suit and a tie which looked familiar. No doubt it signified his membership of an exclusive club and later Max told me that it was the Garrick Club.

First, the good doctor talked Max through his medical history. Any illnesses? Any psychological problems? Max had little to tell him; an occasional cold and a few minor muscle strains were the only afflictions he had experienced.

'So, how can I help you?' Cockburn asked, with an avuncular smile.

Max told him the story that we had agreed, that he aspired to gain entry to golf's Challenge Tour and realized that he needed more power in order to compete with the other players.

'Well, you need to spend lots of time in the gym,' Cockburn advised.

'I do that already,' Max replied. 'But I need some extra help. I would value your advice on which steroids or other medication to take to enable me to spend even more time building myself up and to greater effect. Can you help?'

Cockburn frowned. 'I hope you're not requesting drugs which might be seen as illegal by the people who run golf?'

'Not at all, but you were highly recommended by a leading golfer and a top athlete.' Max smiled conspiratorially.

'And they are?'

'Gary Peters and Ron Rigby.'

Cockburn studied his desk for a few moments. 'They both have physical problems for which I am able to prescribe treatments. They are classed as medical exemptions and are legitimate and completely above board.'

'Perhaps you can help me in the same way,' Max said brightly.

The doctor studied him briefly. 'Fine. I will prescribe a course of a particular type of steroid. You take such drugs at your own risk. Let's see how you fare with them.' He scribbled rapidly on a thick pad of paper and handed the result to Max. 'Come and see me again in about two months.'

I decided to take a part in the meeting and asked Cockburn if the drugs could be classified as illegal.

'I appreciate your concern for your brother,' he said, with a rather cynical grimace. 'They are not illegal if I say they're not. They fall into the category of a therapeutic use exemption, and TUEs are widely accepted in all sports. And, to be practical, the drug testing in golf is minimal. No blood tests, just the occasional urine test, which doesn't tell anyone very much beyond traces, perhaps, of recreational drugs.'

Cockburn stood up, shook hands with both of us and asked Max to settle the bill on his way out.

Max and I had an early evening drink with Toby at one of his many favourite watering holes in Chelsea and talked him through our meeting with Doctor Cockburn; we showed him the prescription Max had been given and the fee he had been charged.

Toby frowned when he examined the latter. 'They don't mess about, do they, these Harley Street medics?' He then confirmed that he would use the material as part of his article for *Golf Plus*. 'It's a comment piece and I aim to make it controversial. My objective is to stir things up, jolt these arrogant bastards like Jeremy

Foote out of their complacency and see what happens. I will of course send you both an advance copy.'

He then asked how we were faring with our researches into the Headlam conspiracy. We had to admit that progress was slow. 'In fact, that's putting far too positive a slant on it,' I said. 'We're grinding to a halt. Though Tim Headlam told me that Mandy, who used to be Grant Jezzard's assistant, is now working for a small publisher who is interested in taking on the book.'

'So do what I'm doing,' Toby said forcefully. 'Make it known that Headlam's book is in production and that his activities as one of the art world's most prolific and skilful fakers will shortly be revealed to the general public.'

Max laughed. 'And how do we accomplish that, Toby?'

'Larry Steinmann might be able to help. Have you heard him doing his arty bits for BBC Radio?' We shook our heads in unison. 'He does a piece on that awful Saturday morning show on Radio Four. All about forthcoming events. New plays, concerts, art exhibitions, books. He has a wide brief and he does it all very well. You know him, Chris, so give him a call and give him all the details. The publisher, the rough date of publication and so on.'

On the following day I contacted James Trimby at Purple Patch Publications. He was initially reserved when I told him that I was Tim's agent, but he grew more co-operative when I mentioned my plan to promote the book on BBC Radio. We agreed a tentative date for the book's launch, with the proviso that we would discuss the basic terms of the contract in the near future.

I then spoke at some length to Steinmann and he was as helpful as in the past; he promised to try to include the news about Derek Headlam's forthcoming revelations if he had enough time in the programme.

'It's the sort of item I really love,' he said enthusiastically. 'Speculative of course, controversial and likely to cause chaos and confusion among the fat cats in the art establishment. Great fun, so I'll do my best, Chris.'

CHAPTER 23

In the diminishing afternoon, as I was looking through various golf magazines as a part of my research for Dan Fairax into the golf clothing market, I took a call from Max.

'I've been thinking about Toby's remarks, that we should try to force the pace a bit, rattle some cages, as his newspaper would no doubt phrase it in their usual populist manner.'

'Larry Steinmann has promised to do a piece on the radio about Headlam, so that might help us.'

'Agreed,' Max replied, 'but I was thinking about that bastard who shook Headlam down at Heathrow Airport. I'm sure that we are right in thinking that he was not a Customs official, but was more likely to have been working for the Art and Antiques Squad. Would you agree?'

I was silent for a moment or two and then said, 'Yes. Since the elusive D had been associated in a professional capacity with Anthony Blunt, it's highly likely that she had good connections with the Art Squad.'

'And I did some digging. First I contacted the Art and Antiques Squad at New Scotland Yard and told them the truth, that I was doing some research for a book on art fraud, that one of their officers is mentioned but not named and I wanted to try and find him and verify some of the claims made.

'A woman gave the usual rigmarole about confidentiality, so I suggested to her that I looked back at some of the better-known cases which had involved the Squad. Robberies from stately homes, heists from art galleries, art fraud, of which there is a vast array, as we well know. She was friendly enough, but non-committal, so I had to trawl the newspaper archives and the Internet to see what I could find.

'Fortunately, the members of the A and A Squad are far from shy about publicity and, in a way, I don't blame them, because they're saying to these villains that, however clever and devious you think you are, we are even more clever and we'll catch you.'

'So, some of these guardians of our artistic treasures have quite a high profile?'

'Yes, and I singled out three or four of them for investigation. One of them, a bloke called John Ramsey now runs a bar in Spain and another, Rick Norman, seems to have ended up in Australia. It was all a bit hit and miss, but I settled on a bloke called Mark Preston, because he'd been with the Squad for over ten years. Therefore, he would have been around when D was still shadowing Blunt.' Max laughed and continued. 'This may sound fanciful, Chris, but Preston fits the bill very well. A likely lad, one might say. Good looks, one of those assured, intelligent faces, the sort of man someone like D would have taken a fancy to, perhaps.'

'And he would help her out for the money,' I said thoughtfully, 'or was it for love?'

'Probably a bit of both. Anyway, I've tracked him down. He left Her Majesty's employment a few years ago and owns an antiques shop in the Cotswolds.'

'Perhaps his ill-gotten gains from the Headlam conspiracy enabled him to retire and then set it up?'

'No doubt. And I thought that you, Chris, would be the right man to have a chat to him and try to find out where the no doubt lovely D is enjoying her considerable wealth.'

'You don't really think that Preston is going to spill the beans?'

'No, but we've got to try. By the way, Chris, have you still got that Glock pistol we took from those Russian thugs?'

'Yes, it's locked away in a cupboard. Why?'

'Well, Preston might get nasty and, like most ex-coppers, he's probably as hard as nails.' My brother laughed and put down the telephone.

I remembered that Headlam had given a brief description of Preston in his memoir and I read it again.

The bastard was a shade over six feet tall and nicely-dressed, which is unusual for a copper. He even sounded well-educated, which is even more bloody unusual, since most of them sound as if they've been dragged up in the East End of London.

He had dark-brown hair and blue eyes, and there was a small scar under the right one. A handsome bastard, that was for sure. If he hadn't been so obviously straight, I'd have tried to give him one.

Jane was on my mind and it occurred to me that she might be interested in a day out in the Cotswolds; and from a selfish point of view I thought that the presence of an attractive woman might make my conversation with Preston more equable; that is, if he even agreed to talk to me.

Jane agreed with enthusiasm and on the following morning, as we drove towards the Cotswolds, I felt that it was an opportune moment to question her about her husband Hugo's behaviour.

'I receive an email or a letter every day,' she told me. 'And several 'phone calls.'

'What does he say?

'That he loves me, that he will never accept our being apart and that he has seriously contemplated suicide on several occasions.'

'Moral blackmail, then. And of the worst kind.'

'You're very hard, Chris, aren't you? But you must understand that I've hurt him terribly, disrupted his safe and conventional life, destroyed his self-esteem. Knowing him, I doubt that he's even told any of his colleagues at work what has happened to us.'

I had to take evasive action as a lunatic in a red BMW came out of a slip-road and cut in front of me in order to overtake a large lorry. 'What an idiot,' I muttered. 'I didn't mean Hugo. No, I understand what he's going through and sympathise. But you've both got to get on with your lives now, haven't you?'

Jane sighed and, with mutual and unspoken consent, we both talked of other things until we reached our destination.

We found Mark Preston Antiques in a prominent position on the main street of an attractive, almost archetypal, Cotswolds town, the sort of place where celebrities, rich businessmen and well-placed politicians cluster at weekends. It was one of many up-market shops in the row: a men's outfitters with everything a proper country gentleman might need in its window; its counterpart for women was a couple of doors away; a kitchen equipment emporium; and a wine merchant with an enticing array of bottles from around the world in the window. A Methodist chapel, about fifty yards away on the opposite side of the road, struck an incongruous note.

I paused to look at the wines, while Jane walked a few yards to inspect the display of women's clothing. I walked over to her side and asked her if anything appealed to her.

'It's all a bit County, isn't it? But I like some of the cashmere sweaters.'

I looked at the prices and winced. 'Have you got your credit card with you?'

'Chris, darling, my card is always ready for action.'

'Fine. But let's have a word with Mister Preston first, shall we?'

We looked in the window of his shop. Small pieces of furniture, china and glass ornaments, several clocks, and a few paintings and drawings were neatly displayed. I didn't recognise any of the latter and wished that Tim Headlam was at my side.

'What a lovely display,' said Jane. 'Not too cluttered. Understated.'

I nodded, held the door open for her and took a swift look at the interior, which was much more spacious than the window suggested. There were larger items of furniture; some grandfather clocks which always appealed to me since my parents owned a lovely example; rows of bookshelves filled to capacity; and a number of prints, including a series by David Hockney.

My eye was also caught by a bundle of hickory-shafted golf clubs in a corner and, nearby, a painting of a golfing scene by Francis Hopkins and another by Muirhead Bone.

A few customers were inspecting the goods on offer and a smartly-dressed man, who I assumed to be Mark Preston, was seated at a beautiful antique desk on one side of the shop. As we approached the desk he rose nimbly to his feet. He was a shade over six feet in height, with a square jaw under an open countenance that hinted at good humour. I put his age in the late-forties and he looked to be in good physical shape. I noted that his eyes were as described by Derek Headlam, blue, and there was a small scar evident under the right one.

Preston wished us 'good morning' and asked how he could help us.

'If you have a moment or two,' I replied carefully, 'I'd like to talk to you about a man called Derek Headlam.'

Preston shot an appraising look at Jane and smiled briefly. 'The name rings a distant bell. Was he an artist of some kind?'

'Of an interesting kind,' I replied. 'Headlam was a forger, or copier as he put it, of high quality works of art. And he claims that you shook him down, so to speak, at Heathrow Airport a few years back.'

Preston looked hard at me and frowned. 'I never worked for the Customs people at Heathrow, or for anybody else there.'

'Well, no, Mister Preston, you worked for the Art and Antiques Squad and liaised closely with Special Branch and you were at Heathrow specifically to intercept Headlam. In his book, he tells how you questioned his possession of some Old Master drawings, including one by Piranese, and that you found a quantity of cocaine in his luggage. Headlam claims that the drugs were planted on him.'

'They always do, don't they.' Preston said with a smile.

'Headlam describes you very well, by the way. Your height, the blue eyes, with the small scar under the right one, and so on. I won't tell you all he wrote about you, since it might embarrass you.'

Preston frowned and looked quickly around his shop, in which only an elderly couple now remained. 'That's quite a fairy tale, Mister Ludlow. Perhaps you would allow me to look after my customers and then we can continue the conversation around the corner. Holly's Café is quite decent. I'll close the shop early and see you both there in half an hour.' Once again he smiled, but only in Jane's direction.

I deliberately paused in the doorway as we prepared to leave the shop and saw that Preston, telephone in hand, was already preparing to make a call. Perhaps to one of his former colleagues in Special Branch, or perhaps to the elusive D who had been the prime mover in the Headlam art scam. Or perhaps I was being fanciful and it was merely a routine business call.

Jane smiled at me. 'Well, Mister Preston is rather dishy, isn't he? And once in the Special Branch, so he has an interesting past.'

'Possibly more interesting than you would wish to examine,' I said nastily.

'Yes, what was all that about Derek Headlam being set up? I'm surprised that Preston agreed to speak to you about it.'

'He wants to talk to me to find out how much I know, or think I know. It seems obvious that Preston was involved in some way in the conspiracy, since he definitely set up Headlam with that nonsense at Heathrow Airport. That paved the way for D to force Headlam to join in the fun. The question is whether Preston took a full part in the ensuing scam or not. And what was his relationship with D? Had they worked together in the past? Were they lovers?'

By this time we had reached Holly's Café, whose tables were well-populated by a variety of mostly middle-aged and elderly people. We secured a table in a corner and studied a menu which offered the usual array of sandwiches, cream teas, tea cakes and crumpets, and all manner of cakes and pastries.

Jane licked her lips theatrically and ordered a cream tea, while I opted for some anchovy toast.

When he entered the tearoom about forty minutes later, Preston was greeted warmly by the waitresses, one of whom smiled broadly and said, 'Your usual, Mister Preston?'

He nodded and smiled back and, as he joined us, he continued the smile in Jane's direction and said, 'China tea. Nice and refreshing.'

To appear to be courteous I asked him how his business was faring and he grimaced and said it was steady but unspectacular.

'Do you live in town?' I asked.

'Yes. Just down the road and I have a little flat in London, too.'

Then it was his turn, as he asked me what was my interest in Derek Headlam. I told him about the book and how I wanted to cast some light on the other conspirators.

Preston sipped his tea and looked at me carefully. 'And you think that the mysterious D is one of them? Am I supposed to know her?'

'Since you liaised with her during the 'eighties, when she was one of the team shadowing the traitor Blunt, yes, I think you know her.'

Preston laughed and said to Jane, 'Your boyfriend has a fevered imagination. But, even if I knew D, and I deny that absolutely, I wouldn't be able to reveal anything about her.'

'The Official Secrets Act and all that?'

'Exactly.'

'All right,' I said quietly, 'but can you tell me whether the Art and Antiques Squad was aware of a bumper sale of fraudulent works of art towards the end of the 'eighties or early in the 'nineties? Perhaps there was a package deal negotiated with a major collector in London, one of the Russian oligarchs, for instance.'

'That would have been a dangerous thing to do. Those mega-rich people don't take their retribution in the law courts. They take it with a knife or a gun, or by means of an untraceable poison.' He smiled again at Jane. 'You've no doubt read those dreadful stories in the newspapers.'

'And maybe they took their traditional mafia-style revenge on Derek Headlam,' I said.

'I don't think so,' Preston replied, 'it was a hit-and-run accident in Rome.'

'I thought you said earlier that you had little or no knowledge of Headlam. But you know how he died.'

'Oh, I remember reading about the accident, or heard something on the radio.' Preston looked steadily at me. 'Now, I must get back to the shop and do some admin.' He rose quickly to his feet. 'A pleasure to meet you, Jane. I'll settle the bill on the way out. Goodbye, Mister Ludlow.'

As we drove home to London, I asked Jane what she thought of Preston. 'The soul of discretion, to put it mildly. He obviously knows a lot more about Headlam and this woman D than he cares to admit. And who can blame him?'

'Quite. He was certainly on the defensive, wasn't he. I wonder where his flat is. If I can find out, we might arrange a bit of surveillance. Maybe he'll lead us to D.'

'I wouldn't want to get on the wrong side of Preston. He looks as if he could be dangerous. Which adds to his considerable charms,' Jane concluded brightly.

I glanced quickly at her. 'And he is obviously charmed by you. Perhaps you would be willing to pop back to the Cotswolds and try to wheedle some information out of him. A little bit of pillow talk can work wonders, you know.'

Jane turned in her seat and glared at me. 'You are a foul-minded and salacious person, Chris Ludlow, and I sometimes wonder why I have anything to do with you.'

CHAPTER 24

On the following morning Jane and I awoke in my apartment to a Saturday morning of solemn and overcast skies. We sipped our way through several cups of tea and half-listened to the Today programme. Politicians ranted and pontificated and were in their turn interrupted by hectoring presenters, and correspondents gave detailed reports of disasters from around the world.

It was a relief when the weather forecast indicated the end of the programme. After a quick shower, I went into the living room to give my full attention to the next hour of radio. I was hoping that Larry Steinmann would have time to mention Headlam's book during his 'arts round-up'.

The presenter of this hour-long magazine programme was, mercifully, a calming presence amid the laughter and giggles of the contributors as they trawled through fashion tips, show-biz gossip, cookery fads and travel advice. It was all such jolly fun, wasn't it.

At last, just as a fully-dressed Jane joined me in the living room, Larry Steinmann's contribution to the programme was announced. He began with a series of trailers: a new play at the National Theatre, a tour by an American pop singer, an exhibition of Modigliani's paintings at the Tate (and I wondered how many of them were forgeries), and a new novel by one of Britain's finest writers.

The final item was what I had been waiting for and this is how Larry reported it.

'Finally, the latest news about the book by Derek Headlam, renowned as one of the most prolific and accomplished forgers of Old Masters works. The manuscript of his "Memoirs of an Artist", coffee-stained and scribbled upon, was found in a dusty drawer at his brother's house several months ago. Headlam himself perished in suspicious circumstances a couple of years back and the first publisher who agreed to take on the book, Grant Jezzard of Galbraith Publications, was brutally murdered.

'However, an enterprising publisher will have the memoirs ready for this year's Christmas market. He does not wish to be named yet, and in view of what befell Grant Jezzard, who can blame him?

'Headlam's revelations will cause a furore throughout the art world. He claims that he forged thousands of works by Old Masters and that, near the end of his life, he, along with certain highly-placed but unnamed officials of the British Government and of its United States counterpart, sold a substantial collection of these fakes to one of the many billionaires who have a presence in London.

'As a result, chaos, recrimination and disputation will certainly blight the art market, especially in London. No doubt the writs will fly like confetti. There will be lots of happy lawyers, but many more disenchanted art collectors.

'Truth is, as ever, stranger than fiction and the film and television producers will no doubt be slavering as they open their cheque books and prepare to bid for the rights to Derek Headlam's extraordinary revelations.'

Steinmann had barely finished his broadcast when the telephone shrilled and Tim Headlam was the caller. 'What a wonderful piece by Steinmann. I'm so glad you told me to listen, because I'm usually tuned in to the jazz on a Saturday morning.'

'I'm glad you approve, Tim, and it should give the book some momentum when it comes out.'

'Yes, full speed ahead now.'

'Well, yes,' I replied hesitantly, 'but I still want to throw some light on his accomplices, if possible.'

'I realize that, Chris, but James Trimby wants to get on with the final edit.'

'Fair enough, just give me a little more time.'

'Fine,' Tim said, 'and I'm really grateful for what you've done.'

'So far.'

Tim laughed. 'Point taken.'

Jane grinned at me and congratulated me on my 'little broadcasting coup' and then Toby called and told me how lucky I was to have such influential friends. 'On another subject,' he continued, '*Golf Plus* will be published on Thursday and my piece about drug abuse in the game will be therein.'

'Written in your usual trenchant style, Toby?'

'In my usual considered style, I trust, young Chris. I'll get an advance copy over to you early next week.'

James Trimby was next on the line to thank me for my efforts and I felt fully appreciated on all sides. It made me even more determined to unearth the identities of Headlam's associates.

I hadn't yet heard from Max and decided to contact him and give him an account of my meeting with Preston. His telephone rang several times and I was on the point of giving up when Max replied. I could hear some music in the background and above it a female voice suddenly shouted. 'Milk and sugar, darling?'

I laughed and Max said, 'Sorry, Chris. Just an old friend of mine.'

'A close friend, I take it. But one who doesn't know how you like your tea.'

'Well, er, I'll tell you more when I see you next.'

I gave him a brief summary of my encounter with Preston and mentioned that he had a flat in London.

'It's a long shot,' I said, 'but if we had his address we could follow him when he's in town and he might just lead us to D. His shop is only open until three o'clock on Sunday and closed on Monday, so presumably that's when he's in London.'

'OK, we can find his address easily enough and I might be able to persuade someone I know to track him. But it is, as you say, a very long shot. Surely, if he wanted to warn D about something, he would simply pick up the 'phone.'

'Of course, but let's give it a try.'

Jane was in the kitchen, making some toast and brewing some coffee, when my doorbell rang. It was proving to be a busy morning. I heard Mrs Bradshaw call out, since she knew that I was cautious about opening the door after my encounter with the Russian thugs. 'It's only me, Chris,' she cried.

As she entered I enquired about her health and was told that the plaster on her arm would be removed in about ten days' time. She refused Jane's offer of some toast and coffee and I settled her in an armchair. 'What a wonderful plug for your book,' she said. 'This

Headlam saga is becoming more and more interesting. Mister Steinmann must be a good friend of yours.'

'Of Toby's really,' I replied and, since Mrs Bradshaw rarely visited me without a good reason, I guessed that she had some news for me and asked her what she had been up to.

'Battling against the wiles of my duplicitous nephew and his ghastly wife,' she said. I looked startled and she continued. 'They've obviously been in touch with social services and one of their band visited me yesterday. Without warning, I should add. Now, I have a high regard for the people who work for these arms of the state because they receive little thanks and even less praise for doing a difficult job. However...'

Mrs Bradshaw paused and Jane again offered her a coffee or tea and she opted for a cup of tea.

'So what happened?' I prompted her.

'As you well know, Chris, I don't want the social services to mess up my private life. I can cope quite happily on my own.' I nodded my agreement. 'Anyway, this child walks into my home, rather tubby, and with bits of metal stuck here and there in her face. Heaven knows what she's got stuck in other parts of her poor body. She started her preamble, that her department had sent her to see what sort of care I needed and so on and so forth. I didn't want to be nasty to the poor girl, so I made her a nice cup of tea, told her that I had no need of her services, and sent her on her way.'

'And that's that, I hope.'

'So do I, Chris, so do I.'

Mrs Bradshaw sipped some of her tea and I said, 'Going back to the book, you once told me that your husband, when he worked at the Home Office, had some contact with Anthony Blunt. Can you recall if he mentioned any of the people who were in close contact with Blunt?'

'You mean the people who were trying to ensure that he didn't betray any more of our secrets to the Russians?'

'Yes. Members of the Secret Service and Special Branch had him under surveillance, but some Home Office people had a role to play also, I'm told.' I explained how the woman, known only as D, fitted into the Headlam story.

'Well, Henry was never up close and personal with Blunt, thank heavens. One wonders how our dear Queen could bear to deal with such a scoundrel, by the way. I'm staggered that he was able to cling on to his job at the Palace. Surveyor of the Queen's Pictures indeed.' Mrs Bradshaw snorted with disbelief.

'The Government agreed to give him immunity from prosecution in return for his revealing everything about his past activities.'

'I know what I'd have given him,' Mrs Bradshaw said and Jane nodded vigorously in agreement. 'Anyway, something odd did occur within the circle of people who were helping to shadow Blunt. I remember that Henry mentioned some sort of scandal. It must have been twenty-odd years ago, in the early-'seventies, I suppose.'

Mrs Bradshaw frowned as she tried to recall what her husband had told her. 'There was a very bright woman in the group shadowing Blunt, a high flyer, tipped for the very top in the Home Office. But she became pregnant.'

'She was single presumably?' Jane asked.

'Yes. That was the problem and she insisted on having the baby. Apparently it was adopted as soon as it was born. The poor woman hardly saw her child, I imagine. Then she returned to work, but was never again considered for high office.'

'That sounds like the woman we're looking for. Do you have a name, by any chance?'

'I'm afraid not, Chris. It happened so long ago. If only Henry were here, he'd remember. But, I'm still in touch with some of the old crowd, so I'll make some inquiries. Someone may come up with a name.'

CHAPTER 25

After a relaxing weekend, which included a dinner party with some golfing friends, I was fed a goodly dose of reality on Monday, when I was summoned to a series of 'meets', as Dan Fairfax put it, with him and his 'main man', Simon. We covered the projects in which I was involved, including the agency's possible entry into the golf clothing market, and the progress of the fund-raising for the golf resort in Cyprus.

I came out of it with my credibility more or less intact, but to say that I was unscathed was debateable. The remorseless questions that Fairfax posed in his usual aggressive way, and his 'wise guy' patter, was hard to take. I wondered how Simon, a mild-mannered man in his 'thirties, had managed to survive such treatment for so many years.

It was a relief to head for home in the late-afternoon, with Fairfax's admonitions and well-used aphorisms gnawing at my brain. Exercise was essential and I donned a track-suit and covered a few miles around Wimbledon Common. When I returned, a package containing *Golf Plus* was lying inside my door. I put it on the living room table and looked forward to reading it later.

After a refreshing shower and some stretches on the bedroom floor, I was ready for a glass of wine and a good look at the magazine. I flicked through the pages, which were an amalgam of golf news, instruction, book reviews, travel tips, and reminiscences from golfers and writers, until I came upon Toby's article, which was entitled 'Opinion Piece'. This is what my friend had written.

'Anyone with even a passing interest in sport will be aware of the wide-spread use of performance-enhancing drugs. Athletics and cycling, for example, are both sports which are no longer about how well a man or a woman can perform these disciplines, but much more about how a participant can obtain the most effective drugs and remain undetected.

'In their perverted pursuit of some kind of national glory, the Russians sponsor such drug abuse; and, at the international level, the people who run athletics and other sports routinely destroy the results of drug tests in order to protect their so-called sportsmen. Above all, these officials are determined to protect their privileged way of life and the regular flow of bribes which secure their continued co-operation with dishonest athletes and their corrupt medical advisers.

'It is an Augean Stable and its stench is now, unfortunately, all too evident in the world of golf. In their pursuit of more muscle and, therefore, more power, many professional golfers are now using banned substances such as anabolic steroids and growth hormone drugs.

'It is sad to report that the people who run professional golf have no conception of how far this drug abuse has spread in the game. For example, at a recent meeting with the Chief Executive of the European Tour, Mr Jeremy Foote, I was told firmly that drugs were 'not an issue' in the game. Perhaps the real problem, Mr

Foote, is that no real effort has been made to discover how widespread is the use of banned drugs. On rare occasions, urine tests are carried out and they do not reveal much. Blood tests, which do, are not yet imposed on professional golfers.

'The game of golf has a long and glorious history at the top level. But its precious traditions are now in grave danger of erosion, owing to the incompetence and hypocrisy of its administrators.

'A young man of my acquaintance recently showed how easy it is to obtain these illegal drugs. He simply made an appointment with a Harley Street doctor, told him that he was an aspiring professional golfer and asked for his recommendations of drugs such as steroids. He walked away with a prescription for various substances which are deemed illegal in the professional game.

'Your correspondent has the name of a prominent British golfer who is known to ingest performance-enhancing drugs and is high up the world rankings. I would be prepared to reveal his identity to the authorities, since it would be a great shame if they remain indifferent to the sleaze lapping at the edges of the game. Unless firm action is taken it will soon engulf it.'

As soon as I finished reading Toby's article, I called him with my congratulations. 'I like the quality of your indignation,' I said.

'That wasn't difficult to summon up. This kind of cheating sickens me and I was delighted to put the boot into that pompous ass, Foote.'

'And I imagine you'll provoke a strong reaction from him.'

'No doubt. He'll undoubtedly make his feelings known very quickly, so why don't you come over to my place on Friday for a drink. Then we can have a meal together. A new brasserie has just opened around the corner. We'll go there.'

'Fine. Max is in town again, so may he join us?'

'Even better. See you at seven o'clock.'

Max and I arrived at Toby's modest end-of-terrace house in Fulham at just after the agreed time and, as expected, our host had opened a bottle of champagne. 'Don't fret,' he said, as he greeted us warmly, 'there's another bottle in the 'fridge.'

'As if we would have doubted you,' Max replied with a smile. 'I enjoyed your *Golf Plus* article immensely, Toby. Long may the vitriol flow from your pen.'

'Thank you,' Toby replied, as he filled our glasses and replenished his own. 'There has already been some favourable comment in the nationals, including *The Times*, and apparently the odious Foote has demanded what he terms a "right of reply" in the magazine.'

'And the editor will agree?' I asked.

'Of course. All grist to the mill of controversy. Anyway, Max, what are you up to in your ivory tower in Cambridge?'

'Oh, trying to think the unthinkable, hunting the snark, trying to locate the ghost in the machine.'

Toby grinned. 'It sounds as if you're helping Stephen Hawking out.'

'No thanks. I've never been at home with his theories about time. I think that Auden understood it far better. "O let not Time deceive you, you cannot conquer Time". And he put it more succinctly, too.'

'Max is actually trying to work out how to hit a one-iron,' I said.

'That would be really useful,' Max agreed. He sipped some of the champagne. 'I have actually been pondering the question of drugs in golf. Should we condemn a pro golfer for taking a drug to help him muscle up a bit, so that he can hit the ball further? In essence, is it any different from obtaining the most technologically advanced driver, for instance, so that he gains another twenty yards or more off the tee? Or if he hires a coach who improves his putting to the tune of a couple of strokes a round? It's simply the idea of marginal gains applied to golf. Or, to put it more crudely, he's just stealing a march over his competitors.'

As usual, Max was playing devil's advocate with practised ease. 'Drugs are, in essence, artificial aids,' I replied, 'and that's why they're deemed illegal. Whereas, a new and advanced driver is completely above board and can be made available to any golfer who wants it.'

'Let's continue this interesting discussion in the restaurant,' Toby suggested drily, and we strolled a few hundred yards to a brasserie whose interior would not have looked out of place in the Latin Quarter of Paris. The walls were adorned with colourful prints of Parisian scenes, the tablecloths bore their traditional red and white checks, and the maitre d's French accent was strong, even if it wavered into shades of Essex occasionally.

Despite all the French connotations the food we devoured was excellent; my cassoulet, with all the anticipated ingredients, was rich; and Toby and Max shared a seafood extravaganza. After some cheese, Toby urged us to return to his home for 'a drop of my best Armagnac'. Why not, replied Max and I in unison.

We settled ourselves into some creaking armchairs in the living room and sipped our glasses of Armagnac. 'That maitre d' puts on a good show,' said Max, 'but he reminded me more than a little of René from 'Allo 'Allo.'

We were all laughing when we heard a loud thump from the front door. 'Another wine delivery?' asked Max lightly.

Toby levered himself out of his armchair. 'I'm not expecting any parcels,' he replied, as he strolled out of the room.

We heard the door open, followed by a loud and urgent cry from our host. 'Chris, Max, quickly. I need help.'

We got in each other's way as we raced down the short hallway and saw Toby trying to cradle the body of a man whose mouth was gagged and his hands and feet bound. I recognised the long hair and skinny body of the caddie, Andy Massie, at the same time as Toby.

Max took hold of Massey's feet. 'Get his arms and shoulders, Chris. Let's get him inside. Very gently, he's in a bad way.'

Massey's eyes were flickering as we laid him, with the utmost care, on to a long sofa which sat in front of the living room windows. I closed the lower shutters, as Max removed a filthy black rag from the victim's mouth. There was a deep sob as Massey breathed in some air.

'Get a sharp knife' I said to Toby. 'Let's get these bloody ropes off him.' When he returned with a lethal-looking carving knife, Massey whispered, 'Careful, Chris, the bastards broke some of my fingers.'

I looked down and saw that the first two fingers of each hand were hanging limply down. Very gently, I sawed through the cord and we all looked in horror at his distorted fingers. Toby had turned away from the harrowing scene and I asked him if he had some bandages and some tape. 'I'll try to bind the fingers together,' I told Max, 'while you call an ambulance.' He grabbed Toby's telephone and dialled 999.

'What the hell happened, Andy?' Toby asked urgently. 'What bastards did this to you and why?'

Massey groaned. 'I wish I knew, but there were two of them and they grabbed me as I left the golf club. Being an artisan member I had to use the back door and they got me as I walked out.'

'Did you see their faces?'

'No chance. They had hoods on and scarves around their faces.'

'What about their voices? South London, middle-European accents, for instance?'

'No, they hardly said a word. Just stuck that stinking gag in my mouth, dragged me across the car park and used the ball cleaner near the first tee to break my sodding fingers.'

'What?' I gasped, appalled.

Tears were coursing down Massey's face, and I finished the makeshift splints on his hands as quickly as I could. 'Yeah, they shoved my fingers, one by one, into the hole where the golf ball goes and then rammed the lever downwards. Bingo. And agony.'

'Then what?'

'Luckily, they heard someone coming before they broke all my fingers, and they threw me in the back of a van, tied me up and drove me here.'

'Why here?' Toby asked.

'Because there's a note for you in my back-pocket. For that bastard Greenslade, one of them grunted at me.'

Max and I gently lifted Massey to his feet and found the scrap of paper in the back pocket of his jeans. I managed to read out the almost illegible scrawl to the others. 'Lay off the drugs thing, Greenslade, or what happened to Massey will be nothing to what you'll get.'

Toby grimaced and went in search of some painkillers, while we did our best to make Massey comfortable. Toby re-appeared with the pills and a glass of whisky to wash them down.

After some time we heard the noise of a siren, and a rap on the door announced the arrival of the medical men. While Toby opened the door, I said to Massey, 'Who's got most to lose from a drugs scandal?'

'Peters's agent, of course. Lazenby.'

'But I don't see him as a criminal. For heaven's sake, he's got a good business.'

'Yeah,' Massey replied, as we reached the open door, 'but if you're a compulsive gambler, you need all the extra help you can get.'

The paramedic told me that they would take the victim to the Chelsea and Westminster Hospital. I asked Massey if he wanted to report the attack to the police and he shook his head. 'No point, Chris, no bloody point at all.'

We watched the ambulance speed down the narrow street, with its siren screeching. Predictably Toby stated that he was in dire need of a drink and Max and I joined him. 'I get it, but I don't get it,' Toby said plaintively. 'What does the perverted bastard who's behind this hope to achieve?'

'He wants to put the frighteners on you,' I replied.

'Well, yes, and he's certainly succeeded. But such an extreme and crassly violent reaction only serves to show that there's an even more serious drug problem in golf than I thought.'

'And where do we go from here?' asked Max. 'Apart from stationing some ex-SAS men outside your door.'

'One of the things I can try to do,' Toby replied, 'is to put as much pressure as possible on the accursed Foote to introduce random blood tests for European golfers.'

'Some chance,' I said.

'Agreed. But my *Golf Plus* article will be the first salvo in a serious campaign against the plague that could ruin our game, in the same way that it's ruined athletics and cycling and many other sports.'

'Maybe you should challenge Gary Peters to take a blood test,' I suggested. 'And if he agrees,' Max interjected, 'then he's in the clear. If he declines, we can all draw our own conclusions.'

'Except that Lazenby is bound to wriggle his way of of any trouble and any damage to his valued client's reputation,' Toby replied. 'With the help of course of his great friend, Jeremy Foote.'

Max and I were still in a state of shock when we got back to my apartment and continued our speculations about the people behind the vile attack on Andy Massey.

Max summed it up. 'The villain of the piece must be Lazenby. It became obvious who was leaking information to Toby. Massey. And Lazenby went for him.'

'Agreed. But does he really think that violence and threats directed at Toby will work?'

Max shrugged. 'Clearly he does, because he's not the most subtle of men, is he?'

I poured two more cups of coffee for us and said, 'I was intrigued by what Massey had to say about Lazenby's gambling. He suggested that he was up to his ears in debt.'

'So, he would need successful clients, from whom he could derive lots of lovely commission. However that success was earned.'

'And this gambling business ties in with hints dropped by both Scotch Billy and Burlington Basil when I talked to them at the Starlight event. It was nothing specific but Scotch Billy muttered something about worse things going on in pro golf than steroid abuse. It didn't register strongly because it's the sort of thing that grumpy old buggers like Billy are prone to say.'

'And Burlington Basil reinforced it, did he?'

'In a way. He was straight-forward, he said that a lot of gambling goes on.'

'Which brings us back to Lazenby,' Max stated. 'Performance-enhancing drugs and gambling. A lethal combination.'

'So, we need someone on the inside to tell us what's going on,' I mused.

'That someone might be tricky to find, after what's happened to Massey,' Max said.

'I wonder if Jack Mason would help. He could put it about that he needs money and doesn't much care how he gets it.'

'And Jack's not the kind of man who is easily intimidated.'

'Far from it,' I agreed. 'But his story will have to be convincing, because Lazenby is well aware of my past connection with Jack, who'll be contaminated, so to speak, in Lazenby's eyes.'

'Jack can put it about that he was taken for a ride by one of those crooked investment companies.'

'There are plenty of those,' I replied.

'And you should know, Chris, since you worked in the City long enough,' Max said nastily.

'True. The story will be that Jack was the victim of one of those ghastly Ponzi schemes and lost most of his hard-earned money, and now needs to recoup his losses.'

'Exactly. And he doesn't have to be too specific about who took him for a ride.'

'No, and anyway it's too painful to talk about it.' Max nodded his agreement. 'Fine. I'll talk to Jack. And, on another subject, Max, have any of your well-connected chums in Cambridge thrown any light on the possible identity of the elusive D?'

'As you might imagine, the real insiders are reluctant to say much. The repercussions of the Blunt affair have never dispersed, and probably never will. But I am seeing a man who works at the Home Office tomorrow. We're having a drink at his club. A history professor from St John's arranged the introduction. I'll let you know what he tells me. If anything.'

I told Max about Mrs Bradshaw's vague recollection of a scandal involving a woman at the Home Office over twenty years ago. 'Mrs B's husband worked there at the time. The woman in question was a high-flier, tipped for the very top, but she became pregnant and never got back on track. Since it was a long time ago we'll be lucky to find out anything interesting.'

'Maybe Mrs B's husband was the father.'

I laughed. 'I doubt that very much. You'd have to be a very brave man to cross that lady.'

'I don't want to be pessimistic,' Max concluded, 'but even if we find D, why should she admit anything about the art fraud conspiracy, much less tell us who bought the forgeries?'

'You're right, but we must follow up every lead. I'll talk to Mrs Bradshaw tomorrow and see if she has gleaned any information from her old pals.'

CHAPTER 26

Saturday dawned with menacing black clouds lurching across the sky. Before Max and I had finished our first cups of coffee the rain hurtled down and the strong winds dashed it noisily against the windows of my apartment.

We decided to forego our plans for a round of golf and instead to pay a courtesy call on Andy Massey.

On the way to the hospital Max asked me what I knew about the injured caddie. 'Practically nothing,' I replied. 'The environment in which caddies work and live has never seemed to encourage chat about personal matters. It's all about golf, golf, golf. How the boss played today, how he might play tomorrow – if he listens to his caddie, that is.'

'Such an enclosed world,' Max muttered. 'So, you obviously don't know whether Andy is married, where he was born and so on.'

'No idea. Let's ask him when we see him.'

We found Massey in a ward at the back of the hospital. With the help of a rather motherly nurse in her middle years he was finishing a breakfast of fruit and cereals.

'Great to see you both,' he said with a smile as we approached his bed. He bit into a banana. 'And many thanks for helping me out last night. When those bastards shoved me into the back of that van, I thought it was going to be curtains for me.' His grimace at the memory changed into a smile. 'But where are the bunches of grapes and a copy of *The Sporting Life*?'

Max began to get up from his seat, saying, 'I'll pop out and...'

'Only kidding, mate,' Massey replied. 'You've both done more than enough already.'

We went through the usual enquiries about Massey's health and the extent of his injuries, though they were obvious enough. The nurse cleared away the debris of Massey's breakfast and warned us not to tire out the patient too much. 'The poor lad's had a rough time,' she said in a soft Irish accent as she left.

'You can say that again,' Massey agreed, with a tired smile.

'When will they discharge you?' asked Max.

'Probably tomorrow. They need the beds.'

'Have you got someone to look after you, Andy?' I asked. 'Wife, girlfriend, mother?'

'No. I'm divorced and the old mother died a couple of years ago. I'm in a bed-sit in Wandsworth. Well, the estate agent calls it a studio flat. That's why I like caddying. When I'm at a tournament, the digs can be really decent, eh, Chris?'

I nodded. 'But what's going to happen now? You won't be carrying a bag for Peters again, will you?'

'No, and I was making good money, too. Maybe I'll get another bag, but I expect Lazenby has spread the poison about me. And you know what the pro game's like, Chris.'

'Perhaps it's time to spread some poison about our lofty friend, Lazenby,' Max said.

'As you see, that can be dangerous,' Massey said ruefully. 'But there's a lot more to his business activities than people realize.' He looked around the ward as if afraid of being overheard, even though many of the patients were dozing after their breakfasts. 'I've heard talk that Lazenby is way behind with his payments to his clients. Peters is owed hundreds of thousands of quid for his endorsements, apparently.'

'Surely there's a code of conduct for agents,' Max said.

'Some chance,' Massey replied with a sneer. 'I'm told that there are some honest agents in sport, but that bastard Lazenby isn't one of them. Far from it.'

'In effect, Peters and Lazenby are tightly bound together,' I said. 'If Peters shops Lazenby for fraud, or even if he sacks him as his agent, Lofty could dish the dirt on him for using illegal drugs.'

'But tell us more about Lazenby's gambling,' Max asked. 'If it's the usual stuff, horses, casinos, and so on, well, he's just stupid. But is there more to it?'

'Much more,' Massey said quietly, 'but I don't really know any details. But it involves betting on golf, that I do know, and in a big way.'

The Irish nurse bustled up and told us that we must let her patient rest, and we left Massey with assurances that he must tell us if he needed any help. He was a little tearful as he thanked us, and we headed for the exit.

It was mid-morning when we arrived back at my apartment and the wind and the rain seemed to be increasing in violence.

'At what time are you seeing your Home Office contact?' I asked Max.

'Not until five o'clock this evening.'

'OK, so let's ask Mrs Bradshaw in for coffee and see if she has any information about D.'

She arrived at my front door holding a plate, on which a large slab of cake reposed. I was glad to see that her arm was now in a small sling around her wrist.

'Lemon drizzle cake,' she said cheerfully. 'It will go nicely with our coffee.'

I settled her into a comfortable armchair, brought in some plates for the cake and served up the coffee. Mrs Bradshaw was right, the lemon drizzle cake was delicious.

After a few minutes Mrs Bradshaw told us that she realized that we wanted to know if she had uncovered anything of interest about the mysterious D. 'I reckoned that Daisy Newman was the most likely source of information, since her husband Patrick was quite high up in the Home Office. The poor fellow died about a year ago.'

Mrs Bradshaw sipped at her coffee. 'Daisy did indeed remember some sort of scandal. At the turn of the 'seventies. She said that it was all rumour and nothing was ever proved or made public, but the woman concerned and she was, as I told you before, a rising star at the Home Office, suddenly disappeared.'

'Disappeared?' Max said quizzically.

'Yes. The story was that she was having a sabbatical and that she was assisting some department of the Secret Service with a special project.'

'And how long was she away from the Home Office?' I asked.

'About a year and the baby was never mentioned when she returned. But it was a brief return because she moved on to another department and changed her identity.'

'That's very odd,' Max said. 'And presumably the baby was adopted and she gave up her rights ever to see it again.'

'It seems strange that such a clever woman, and one with apparent strength of character should behave like that,' I mused.

Mrs Bradshaw nodded her agreement and Max said, 'Could it have been the identity of the father which caused all the trouble? After all, D moved in high circles, including helping to watch over Anthony Blunt.'

'Well, he wouldn't have been the father, would he?' giggled Mrs Bradshaw.

Max smiled back at her and continued. 'I wonder whether her liaison was with someone who was considered to be a security risk?'

'Could the father have been S, who was her partner in the art fraud project?' I suggested.

'But he was with the CIA,' Max replied. 'Would he have been seen as a security risk?'

'Certainly,' Mrs Bradshaw said emphatically. 'There was no love lost between our spooks and the American spooks in the 'seventies. The respective heads of government were Ted Heath and the odious Richard Nixon and they were far from being bosom pals, and they set the tone.'

'Perhaps this Home Office wallah you're meeting later will throw some light on the matter,' I said to Max.

'Here's hoping.'

Shortly afterwards Mrs Bradshaw left us and Max headed off to the British Library 'to do a bit of research', as he put it.

'What's she like?' I asked playfully.

My brother did not bother to respond to my rather childish remark and told me that he would be back in the early evening after his meeting.

Minutes later my telephone shrilled and, aware that I had been neglecting my girlfriend, Jane, I braced myself for her annoyance. But it was the jovial tones of Jack Mason which greeted me. He told me first how much he had enjoyed Toby's article in *Golf Plus*. 'When he's in the mood old Toby can put the boot in with great accuracy, can't he?' I agreed and then Jack continued. 'But what on earth happened to Andy Massey? Do you know who did him over?'

'I wish I did. But how did you hear about it?'

'Toby again, of course. Haven't you seen his piece in *The News*?'

'Not yet.'

'Hang on, I'll read it to you.' I heard the shuffling of paper over the telephone and then Jack's voice. 'The headline reads "Top Caddie Assaulted" and then Toby goes on as follows: "Andy Massey, caddie to Gary Peters, one of the world's leading professional golfers, was yesterday brutally attacked. He was taken to hospital with four of his fingers broken in a vile act of torture. It is unclear what was the motive for the assault. However, he was dumped, late at night, on your correspondent's doorstep. Perhaps the villains who carried out the attack think he is associated in some way with my enquiries into the misuse of performance-enhancing drugs in golf. This assumption is incorrect, but for my part I will not halt my pursuit of the truth about this grave problem". Uncompromising stuff, eh, Chris?'

I then told Jack of our belief that Lofty Lazenby was behind the attack in order to protect his client, Gary Peters; and Jack agreed that the way in which Peters had gained strength and bulk in a relatively short time was highly suspicious.

It was a good opportunity to tell him about the rather indeterminate rumours we had heard about Lazenby's involvement in gambling in golf, and to ask for his help.

There was a pause and then Jack said, 'Lots of people suspect that Lazenby's a wrong 'un, but I didn't know to what extent. You say he's holding on to his clients' money. That's bloody despicable. But I don't get the drift of the golf gambling thing.'

'Neither do we, but you are better placed than us to find out. Would your caddie, Marlon, know anything?'

Jack laughed. 'Apart from golf, Marlon has only one interest in life and that's his motor-bike. He's a dedicated petrol-head.'

I told him about our half-formed idea that Jack himself might pose as the victim of a Ponzi scheme, and that as a result he needed money, and quickly.

This time the pause on the line was lengthy and finally Jack said, 'Since it's you, Chris, but above all because the good name of golf is in danger, I'll put the story about. Mind you, I've just bought myself a lovely new Mercedes.' He laughed. 'I'll have to use the missus's car instead, won't I? Otherwise the tale of financial woes won't stand up to much scrutiny, will it?'

CHAPTER 27

Since the weather was so unpleasant, the idea of playing even a few holes of golf still did not appeal to me. Briefly I considered donning a track suit and going for a run on the Common, but discretion prevailed and I made myself another cup of coffee instead. I pondered what I might have for lunch. A modest sandwich perhaps and then a look at some of the sport on the television.

For once I did not have any commitments. I sampled my coffee and then picked a CD at random from my collection of jazz. It was a compilation of Duke Ellington numbers and I sank into an armchair, closed my eyes and tried to empty my mind of all the conundrums that were threatening to overwhelm me.

Within a few minutes my reverie was rudely shattered by the ringing of my telephone. It was Jane and, as I heard her voice, I was again conscious that I had neglected her recently.

'How are you, Chris? I'm so glad I've found you.' Her voice, normally so agreeable, was brittle with sarcasm.

Even as I made my excuses, I knew how feeble they must appear to her. 'You are too busy for your girlfriend, are you? That's rather sad to hear, because I thought we had an important relationship. Well, it's important to me, I don't really know how you feel.'

I tried to re-assure her that my feelings for her ran as deeply as ever. 'I'm sorry, Jane, that I've been so elusive, but all that business of the art scam, Derek Headlam and his band of fraudsters, has taken up more and more of my time.'

Jane did not respond and I continued. 'Let's get together tomorrow and I'll tell you all about it. The weather is supposed to be fine apparently, so let's take a walk along the river. We can have lunch at that lovely pub in Kew. I'll pick you up at midday.'

'That's fine. I suppose I'll still recognise you.' Jane put down her telephone.

For a time I was concerned about her. She was clearly upset, despite her sarcasm, and I began to wonder what she wanted from me. A commitment, of course, but to what extent? Just to see her regularly, or was it more than that? I certainly didn't want to set up house with her. I decided to broach the subject tomorrow – for good or bad.

Max arrived at just before seven o'clock and was carrying a bottle of Pol Roger champagne. 'It's chilled,' he said brightly, 'so let's open it.'

When we had settled down in the living room, I asked him about his meeting.

'An interesting bloke. Richard Mather, he's called and he helped the Professor I know with some research, years ago, into the history of MI5. Very much the career bureaucrat, measured in his opinions, and so on. He plays golf.'

'Where does he play?'

'You could probably guess. He's a member at Rye, Sunningdale and Hunstanton.'

I grinned. 'And he pronounces the latter as "Hunston" no doubt.'

'Of course. Anyway, I asked him about D and whether her disappearance was simply to cover up an unwanted pregnancy and he confirmed that this was true.'

'So, what's her name?'

'He doesn't know, because, as Mrs Bradshaw told us, she changed her name and went to work for another, highly confidential, arm of the Secret Service. She was well-versed in under-cover work, as we have been told, since she had been a part of the team shadowing Blunt.'

I grimaced. 'Mather wasn't much help to us, then. And there are no clues as to who adopted the child.'

'No. Except that Mather told me that D, owing to her involvement with Blunt, had discovered that someone very important in the Home Office was leaking information to the Russians. As a result, she was able to blackmail him and ensure that the child was never registered in her name, but registered in the name of the adoptive parents.'

'I wonder if Blunt was involved in all this?' I asked tentatively.

'Why should he be? Not really his scene, was it?'

'No. Just a thought.'

CHAPTER 28

As soon as I awoke from a deep sleep on Sunday morning, I eased aside the bedroom curtains and checked the weather. The forecasters had been accurate, since the skies were clear, except for a few wispy clouds.

Max had already left for Cambridge and, after a cup of coffee and a shower, I ambled down the street to the nearby newsagent and bought a couple of newspapers, including *The Daily News*. Toby had followed up his trenchant piece about the assault on Andy Massey with more comments about the rising tide of corruption in the game of golf.

On glancing at the arts pages of one of the broadsheet papers I had bought I found an article written by Larry Steinmann. I knew that he was one of their guest columnists and was heartened to see that he had once again managed to plug the Derek Headlam book. It was only a short piece, but named a date in mid-November when 'Memoirs of an Artist' would be published. I made a mental note to contact the publisher, James Trimby, to discuss the terms of the contract. I hoped that Tim Headlam was not trying to exclude me from the deal.

It was an unworthy thought, since Tim telephoned me about an hour later and told me that Trimby would like to discuss a deal with me.

'I'll call him tomorrow,' I said, 'but I don't suppose he'll offer much of an advance. He runs quite a small outfit, after all.'

'I don't mind, Chris. As you know, I just want to see the book in print. Mandy told me that James will probably offer five grand as an advance payment.'

'She's a useful contact to have. How is she?'

'She's in fine form. Would you like to speak to her? She's right here.'

I laughed. 'That's OK, Tim. Please say hello to her.'

I arrived at Jane's apartment just before midday and we headed west along the bank of the Thames in the warm sunshine. To our right the scene changed every few hundred yards: there were parks and playing fields, outcrops of apartment blocks, scatterings of houses with enviable views of the river, and industrial buildings to be seen in the distance. But the real pleasure was to look through the trailing branches of the many trees and bushes at the river itself. 'Liquid history', as someone called it. It was busy, too, with rowers of all types enjoying the day; there were single and double scullers, several fours and many eights to be seen.

Jane and I relaxed in each other's company and I decided that there were too many pitfalls involved in starting a discussion about our relationship. The only irritations were caused when we had occasionally to take evasive action to avoid the lycra-clad loonies who were using the pathway as a cycle track. Some of them were obviously enjoying a fantasy of riding in the Tour de France.

After an hour or more of steady walking we reached the pub. It was crowded, especially the long terrace overlooking the river, and I was glad that I had taken the precaution of booking a table. I felt that the only wine which would properly mark the mood and the occasion would be champagne. Jane warmly welcomed my suggestion.

'You're getting as bad as your friend Toby,' she said with a wide smile. Despite all the problems which seemed to attach themselves to Jane, I realized once again why I liked her so much. If it wasn't love, it was an emotion fairly close to it.

The food was excellent, the atmosphere lively and the other customers exuded good humour. We ended our meal with some coffee and Armagnac and decided to take a minicab back to Jane's apartment.

We were deposited outside the building and left the bright sunlight for the comparative gloom of the entrance hall. As Jane fumbled in her handbag for the key to the main building itself I just about registered the dark shape of a man moving quickly towards me. My instincts made me duck away from him as he screamed, 'You bastard'. Then I heard the resounding crash of some sort of blunt instrument he was carrying as it hit a wooden cupboard where letters were deposited for the tenants.

I heard Jane scream. 'No, Hugo, no, please.' He was off-balance after his wild blow and I closed on him and kicked him as hard as I could in the side of his right knee. Hugo staggered and I kicked him again and then smashed my forearm into his face. He fell to the floor and lost his hold on the weapon he had tried to use on me. I grabbed it. It was an old-fashioned policeman's truncheon and it would certainly have made a nasty dent in my head.

I stood over him and tapped the truncheon thoughtfully against my other hand. 'I'm going to teach you a lesson, Hugo,' I said quietly. 'I'm going to smash both your kneecaps. How do you feel about that?'

Through her tears, Jane said, 'No, Chris, no more violence, I can't stand it.'

'I don't like violence, either, but your husband deserves all he gets.' I raised the truncheon and saw the look of terror on Hugo's face. I pretended to bring the weapon down, but stopped halfway. 'I suggest you piss off, Hugo, before I change my mind.'

As he raised himself slowly to his feet, I added, 'I'm going to make sure that Jane obtains a restraining order against you, you idiot, but in the meantime don't come anywhere near her.'

Hugo had limped over to the exit to the street and looked at me with a half-smile on his face. 'A pity about your Porsche, Ludlow, wasn't it?' he sneered. 'The next accident will involve you, not just your car.' Quickly he left and I now wished I had smashed his knees.

I looked at Jane. 'So, it wasn't Lazenby who torched my lovely Porsche. It was your ghastly husband.'

Jane was still weeping, silently but copiously, as we entered her apartment. 'I'm sorry, Chris, so sorry. But at least he didn't hurt you.'

She sat down on the sofa, her head in her hands. I went off to the kitchen and made some tea; I know what we Brits do in a crisis. We sat together on the sofa, mainly in silence. After some time Jane told me that she was alright and would like to be left alone to think things over.

I told her that I thought Hugo was deranged and that she must start the process of obtaining a restraining order against him.

'Maybe divorce proceedings as well,' she muttered. 'Are you going to report him to the police, Chris?'

'No point. I'm unharmed.'

'What about the car? Will you report that? To the insurers?'

'Again, not much point. He would deny it and there's no proof that he was the culprit.'

Jane nodded and told me again that she was so tired and upset that she must rest quietly for a while. I took the hint and set out to walk back to Putney. I kept a wary eye out for Hugo, but judged that the punishment I had meted out to him would deter him from trying to attack me again. Anyway, I had the truncheon tucked into my trouser pocket, just in case.

CHAPTER 29

I made my way into the offices of Gold Medal Management quite early on Monday morning. A series of 'meets', as Dan Fairfax put it, had been organised over the next few days and I was involved in several of them. The Cyprus project, which seemed to be at a standstill, was one of the important topics and so was the range of golf clothing. The distribution of this had been farmed out to a specialist company and the orders had reached an encouraging level.

After two days of Dan Fairfax's company, of listening to his homilies about business and how it should be conducted, I was in desperate need of a change of environment. But there was one more meeting on Wednesday morning.

This was to signal a new departure for the agency since a script-writer had sent in an idea for a comedy series. His big idea was that Mitzi Moorcock should be the star.

The writer was the main focus of interest when we all gathered in Fairfax's office in the late morning. Fairfax introduced Simon, Lindy and me to Eric Ogilvy, who seemed to have a very lined face for someone claiming to be in his early thirties. His fair hair was scanty and his narrow shoulders were covered by a dark-green T-shirt. His jeans strained against the beginnings of a pot belly and Ogilvy was clutching a

Tesco carrier bag, from which he produced a sheaf of papers.

'This is the script of the first episode of "From the Ground Up",' he said in a rather deep and gravelly voice.

'And it's going to be a smash hit for Eric, for Mitzi and for us,' Fairfax interrupted. 'The series will focus on an allotment in a reasonably affluent part of London, with all its goings-on. The rivalry to produce the best veggies for the annual show...'

'The biggest marrow,' Simon said with a laugh.

'The in-fighting over who gets the best plot in the allotment, how the busy-bodies on the committee behave and so on, the affairs that blossom. Oh, sorry about that,' Fairfax guffawed loudly, 'and the fierce rivalries.'

'But it is a sit-com,' Ogilvy stated. 'So, the emphasis will be firmly on the humorous aspects of the various situations which arise.'

'And where does our client, Mitzi Moorcock, fit into the series?' I asked.

'Well, that's the really clever bit,' Fairfax replied. 'Tell 'em, Eric, old son.'

'Mitzi will be the outsider,' Ogilvy said. 'She's not really from the same class as the other allotment holders, who are a mixed bunch of men and women from the professional classes, I suppose one would say. Bankers, medics, lawyers, company directors and their spouses. You know the type.'

Ogilvy paused and flicked the pages of his script. 'Annie Spencer's a bit common, let's say she's from Essex.'

'I'm from Essex,' interrupted Lindy, 'and lots of it is lovely, and so are the people.'

'OK, Lindy, I'm sure you're right. Nevertheless, just for fun, we'll say she's from Basildon. And she's married to a professional footballer. So, she doesn't fit in, except that most of the blokes on the allotment fancy her.'

'As you can see, there's plenty of scope for both comedy and a bit of drama,' Fairfax said forcefully.

'And for social comment, I suppose,' Simon added.

'What about Mitzi's acting?' I asked. 'Can she act? Has she ever acted?'

'You should see her do her after-dinner turns,' Fairfax replied. 'She can act, believe you me. No problems there.'

'We will of course have a cast of top-rated comedy actors,' Ogilvy stated, 'and they'll carry her along.'

I glanced at Lindy, who surreptitiously raised her eyes to the ceiling; she was as sceptical about the idea as I was. I asked the obvious question. 'Eric, have you sold the idea to one of the networks?'

'Not yet, but the Beeb love my work. They've used me on a lot of series in the last ten years.'

'But have you ever done your own series for them?'

'Well, no, not really, but I've worked as a writer on other people's sit-coms.'

'Like?'

'Oh, er, "High Life and Laughter", and "Fun and Frills". You know the kind of thing.'

I didn't and remained silent. Fairfax looked at me grimly. 'What's with all the pessimism, Chris? You've got to be positive in this life, my son, or you get nowhere. Look, we've got a top writer in Eric here and a top celeb in Mitzi. The Beeb and ITV are crying out for new comedy. All they do is repeat stuff from years back like "Dad's Army" and "Only Fools and Horses".

So let's get on with it. Simon, it's your project. You and I will decide who to approach and take it from there. Eric, you must have some good contacts.'

Ogilvy nodded eagerly and Lindy suggested that some of the bigger independent production houses should be approached.

'Or you could form your own production house,' I said playfully.

Fairfax ignored me and pursued his own path. 'And don't forget all the repeat fees and the spin-offs. A book of the series, maybe a cookery book based on freshly-grown veggies. And then there's the licensing deals – gardening tools, special plants, the prospects are endless.'

On this note of febrile optimism the meeting broke up and Fairfax took Simon and Ogilvy off to lunch at a nearby restaurant. On my way out, I asked Lindy what she thought of the project. She shrugged and said, 'I'm not sure, but I didn't like the way that Eric bloke kept staring at my tits.'

I laughed, resisted the temptation to tell her how delightful they were and left the office.

Jane and I had agreed to go to an early showing of a film at a cinema in Chelsea and we thoroughly enjoyed a comedy of errors, directed by a little-known Frenchman. The scenes shot in Paris were beguiling and, as we left the cinema, Jane told me how she would love to spend a few days in the French capital with me.

'I'll bet you know a lovely hotel in the Latin Quarter,' I said teasingly, 'with the traditional paper-thin walls, creaking floorboards and so on.'

'Creaking beds, too, my darling,' she said and squeezed my hand. 'No, I have a friend who will let us borrow her apartment. It's lovely. Near the Opera, and Harry's Bar is just down the road.'

'Wonderful. Let's do it, as soon as we can.'

After that conversation it had to be a meal at a French restaurant and if the food was merely passable, it was a thoroughly enjoyable evening.

I knew that Jack Mason was playing in a golf tournament on the Lancashire coast and on the following day decided to contact him.

There was some coverage on television and I saw that he had started his round early and returned a creditable score of two under par. I dialled his mobile 'phone in the late afternoon when I was fairly sure that he would have finished his practice session and would possibly be ensconced in a bar, with a pint of the strongest ale he could find within easy reach. He answered on the second ring and I congratulated him on his round.

'Not bad for an 'owd 'un, Chris,' he replied. 'But it's a fine course. Traditional in the best sense, well-bunkered and the bunkers are in the right places and not the monstrous carbuncles that those misguided American designers disfigure their courses with. Nor are there acres of sodding water everywhere. Just a few small streams, and they're natural to the terrain.' I heard a hearty slurp as Jack took a mouthful of his beer. 'The greens are superb and the spectators know their stuff. It's fun.'

Jack held strong opinions about how golf courses should be laid out, as his remarks had just demonstrated and, if he was enjoying himself, he was likely to do well in the tournament.

'I know you've only been on the scene for a couple of days, Jack, but have you managed to drop any hints about betting?'

'I'm being as subtle as I can. Otherwise, the villains might smell a rat. But I've dropped a few hints here and there. Lazenby's the key, isn't he, so I collared Gary Peters's new caddie, Geoff Curtis. He's been around and used to gamble more than a bit.'

'What about the Andy Massey incident? What are the reactions?'

'Amazement. Disgust. But a rumour has started that Massey was heavily in debt to a betting syndicate and that's why he was duffed up.'

'That's rubbish, as you'd guess. Anyway, good luck tomorrow, Jack. Play well.'

Hard work doesn't come easily to me, as many of my friends would attest with relish. However, I devoted most of Friday to the Cyprus project. I contacted around a dozen people with the financial resources to invest in such an enterprise; some of these calls were made to people who had expressed interest and then gone cold on the idea, and others were to new prospects. It was hardly rewarding work and I grew accustomed to the withdrawn tones of people who did not wish to offer me much encouragement, but didn't want to be too dismissive.

It was dispiriting work and I gave in at around four o'clock, put on my tracksuit and went for a run along the towpath as far as Twickenham Bridge. On the way back I looked across the river at Jane's apartment building. Perhaps she had spotted me; it was an unlikely thought.

I was exhausted, did a few cursory stretches and then gave myself the luxury of lying in a hot bath. To add to my enjoyment I read some more of one of George MacDonald Fraser's wonderful Flashman stories.

A walk down to one of the pubs near the river was an appealing idea, but I rejected it in favour of a gin and tonic at home. Gin is not one of my regular tipples, but rather an occasional indulgence. I let my mind wander and hoped that the various matters which had been demanding my attention over the last few weeks would resolve themselves: the Headlam book and the Mister Big who was intent on preventing its publication; the drugs and betting problems in golf; and my fluctuating relationship with Jane.

That was enough to be going on with, I thought, and was debating whether to pour myself another gin and tonic, when my telephone rang.

I stated my name and a woman's voice replied, 'Mister Ludlow, this is Maria Headlam, Tim's mother.' The voice was clipped and assured. I waited and she continued. 'I thought I should call you since you're involved with Tim in this accursed book by Derek.'

'I wouldn't quite use that term, Mrs Headlam.' I didn't bother to hide my exasperation.

'Wait until you hear what's happened to Tim,' she said severely. 'He is in hospital. Last night some thugs intercepted him as he entered his rooms, forced him inside and knocked him about very badly.'

'I'm very sorry to hear it,' I replied inadequately. 'How badly?'

'His nose is broken and he's lost a tooth, he has cracked ribs and his body is badly bruised. And these hooligans threatened to kill him.'

'These thugs, does he have any clues to their identity?'

'Not really. They were large, and wearing hoods and had foreign accents.'

'Russian, perhaps?'

'Tim couldn't say, but the point is that they warned him not even to think about publishing Derek's book. That's why I called it accursed. My poor boy. It's simply not worth it.' I heard a distinct catch in her voice.

'I'm terribly sorry, Mrs Headlam, I'd like to see him. Which hospital is he in?'

'The John Radcliffe in Oxford, but leave it, will you please. Tim should be back home in a day or two, so let's meet here. I want to talk to you both. I will call you, Mister Ludlow.'

CHAPTER 30

I was dismayed by what had happened to Tim, but consoled myself with the thought that he had perhaps been let off lightly, given that Grant Jezzard had been killed.

I decided that one way to disconcert the person behind the attack on Tim was to make it public. Although I knew that Toby would not see the story as grist to the mill of The *Daily News* I called his mobile number.

I heard a scuffling sound as my call was answered and several irritable grunts. My journalist friend disliked his mobile intensely and regarded it as an 'intrusion on his privacy'. However, he had to use it because his editor insisted upon it.

I could hear a lot of background noise, and it was apparent that Toby was on licensed premises. 'A nice pub, Toby?' I asked.

'Very, because it's free, I'm in the sponsor's tent.'

'Of course. Did you see any of Jack's round yesterday or this morning?'

'Not really. He was one of the early starters yesterday and I was busy this morning. I see that he's doing well, he's two under par again.'

I told him about the attack on Tim Headlam and then said, 'I want to retaliate in some way, try to make these bastards break cover. Do you have any bright ideas?'

'As you can guess, my paper wouldn't be interested in the story, but why don't you try Larry Steinmann. He might use it in his column or when he does his arts piece on the radio.'

Within minutes I was talking to Steinmann and he promised to do his best to run the story on the following morning and to place it in the broadsheet newspaper for which he wrote occasionally.

On Saturday morning I listened intently to Radio 4's magazine programme and in due course Steinmann's resumé of the week in the arts world began. He covered the openings of various art exhibitions and the premiére of an all-female version of "Othello". Then he continued: 'The saga of the much-heralded book by the famed forger, Derek Headlam, continues and becomes murkier. His "Memoirs of an Artist" is due to be published in a few months' time and his nephew, Tim, who found the manuscript and is master-minding the project is in hospital with serious injuries. It transpires that he was attacked late on Thursday night by two thugs who told him that Headlam's book must not be published. If it was, worse things would happen to him.

'Listeners will recall that the original publisher of the book, Grant Jezzard of Galbraith Books, was murdered several weeks ago. Clearly some deranged person is determined that the Headlam book will never see the light of day. It is probable that he is a billionaire art collector who has too much to lose if Headlam's tales of art forgery on such a grand scale are heard.'

It was a trenchant piece of broadcasting and I hoped that it would have the desired effect – to force the villains of the piece either to abandon their murderous plans or to break cover. I felt sure that the thugs who attacked Tim were the ones who had threatened me.

On the following day, alerted by Steinmann, I bought a copy of the *Sunday Post* and found an abbreviated version of his radio broadcast in their arts section. Steinmann was a very useful ally to have, as Toby emphasised when he telephoned me later on Sunday afternoon to tell me that Jack Mason had finished the tournament in a tie for sixth place.

On Monday morning it was fortunate that I had not been summoned by Dan Fairfax to a 'meet', since I received two interesting telephone calls. The first was from Jack Mason and I congratulated him on his sixth place on the previous day.

'Nice to win some prize money,' he said. 'If only I could putt. . .' I sympathised with him, although Jack was one of the steadiest putters on the European Tour.

'I think I've had a tickle,' he continued.

'Lucky you,' I replied. 'What's she like?'

'Don't be vulgar, Chris.' A quick laugh spoiled his rebuke. 'To be serious, a tickle regarding betting. It happened last night, as I was loading up the car after the final round of the tournament. As you know, I like to get home if it's at all possible.'

I heard him refuse a cup of coffee and he continued. 'This bloke came up to me and said that he'd heard that I needed money and plenty of it. I asked him who'd told him and he muttered something about the grapevine.'

'But he didn't give a name? What did he look like?'

'No name of course. A nondescript kind of fellow, in his forties maybe, decently dressed, not really any distinguishing features, as they say on the cop shows. So I asked him what I had to do. And he gave me a telephone number, scribbled on a bit of paper. He told me to call it this week and a meeting would be arranged.'

'It sounds very secretive, doesn't it.'

'Not surprisingly, if it's some sort of illegal betting scam.'

'And you'll do the meeting?'

'Of course.'

My second call of the morning was from Tim Headlam's mother and, as soon as I heard her patrician voice, I became full of forebodings. She wished me 'good morning' and I asked her how her son was faring.

'He will be coming home tomorrow, thank heavens, and everything is in place to take proper care of him.'

'I'm delighted to hear that. And when will I be able to see him?'

'Tomorrow, mid-morning. I hope that will suit you because someone else will be present. A woman called me yesterday and said that she was very concerned to hear about the assault on Tim and that she had some important and highly relevant information about this business of the book. She sounded very serious and is clearly a well-educated woman. One of us, Mister Ludlow, if I may put it that way.'

I cringed. Thank goodness she didn't know that I had been a professional caddie. 'Did she give you any details?'

'No, but I thought it sensible to hear what she has to say. She sounded very concerned about Tim and the last thing I want is any more violence. I hope that she will help us to avoid that.'

I had a sudden and wild premonition and said, 'What's her name? I suppose it begins with a D.'

'Oh, the D about whom Derek writes. As a matter of fact her name is Diana Wheeler, so I suppose it could be her.'

On Tuesday morning I drove westwards along the motorway and without difficulty found the place where Mrs Headlam lived. It was an archetypal English village and her house was one of several which overlooked the spacious village green, which, it was heartening to see, had a cricket pitch with a modest wooden pavilion. Just to the rear of it a pub sprawled alongside the road; low-slung, with a long terrace and a wide garden sprinkled with tables, it suited the village perfectly. Fifty yards away there was a small and ancient church and I remembered one of Toby's dictums – parsons and pints are invariably well-aligned in the English shires.

Mrs Headlam's house was a compact Victorian cottage with a small garden at the front. I parked my car on the road, strolled up the garden path and used the brass knocker to tap on the door. Almost immediately it was opened by a diminutive woman who was clad in a floral dress; her hair was cropped short and her eyes were bright behind her glasses.

'Mister Ludlow,' she greeted me with a brief smile. 'Come on in and see what those thugs did to poor Tim.'

They certainly had done some damage, as I could see when Tim rose painfully to his feet to greet me. His broken nose was taped up and both his eyes were blackened from the blows he had taken.

I told him how sorry I was and asked him if he could throw any light on the identities of his attackers. 'Not really. I hardly had a chance to look at them. I was on the floor trying to protect my vital parts, so to speak.

But they were big sods and sounded foreign. Middle-European, I suppose, not that it helps us.'

'Any tattoos?'

Tim sighed. 'Oh yes, even more than the average professional footballer. On their hands and arms and necks and heaven knows where else.'

'They sound like the men who attacked me and Max.'

Tim nodded and Mrs Headlam said, 'I cannot think why you two are continuing with Derek's book. It's madness. Tim has been badly hurt and you, Mister Ludlow, were threatened with death. For heaven's sake, just abandon the idea. However much money is at stake, it's not worth it.'

'Mother, it has nothing to do with money, as I've said before.' The exasperation was plain in Tim's voice and so was his determination. 'Uncle Derek's book is a very important one. It's a great story in its own right about how he took the mickey out of the art establishment, but it also adds a very interesting dimension to the history of art in the last thirty years or so.'

Mrs Headlam sighed theatrically and said, 'That may be so, even if I think you're exaggerating. We'll resume the discussion later. I think our guest, Diana Wheeler, has arrived.'

As she was ushered into the living room, Diana Wheeler had the assured air of a successful businesswoman. Elegantly dressed in a dark blue suit with an off-white blouse, she was quite tall and carried herself with grace. Her figure was slim and well-defined and her chiselled features were marked by widely-spaced blue eyes.

When Mrs Headlam had served some coffee, we all settled down in easy chairs around a rectangular table, in the centre of which sat a chess set.

Diana Wheeler took the lead. Her voice had a low and studied timbre. 'I hope we can dispense with formalities,' she said. 'I'm Diana, I know about Tim and I believe you are Chris.' She smiled at me. 'But Mrs Headlam, may I use your first name?'

'Of course, I'm Maria.'

'Excellent. As you know, I read about the vile attack on Tim and decided I had to intervene. I hope that somehow I can help to identify who is behind this violence.'

'How on earth. . .' Mrs Headlam began.

'It's a long story,' Diana Wheeler said quickly, 'and goes back to my days in the Home Office.'

'When you were a member of the team shadowing Anthony Blunt,' I said.

'You knew Blunt?' Tim said, surprise and excitement in his voice.

'Yes. But, Chris, how did you learn about that?'

'Because I know you played a very important role, albeit a very brief one, in Derek Headlam's life.'

Tim was staring fixedly at Wheeler and it was clear that he had already realized who D was and her part in his Uncle Derek's life.

'As Tim has already guessed,' I said, 'you were the D who blackmailed Derek into joining your scheme to sell fake art.'

'I'll come back to all that,' she said and turned her head to look directly at Maria Headlam. 'First of all let's return to my Home Office days, I was doing quite well, I had a very bright future, as my colleagues and superiors emphasised. And then I made a mistake. I became pregnant.'

She stopped and looked bleakly at the table. 'This was the early 'seventies, remember, and I could have arranged an abortion, but I didn't want to do that. I felt it was wrong.' We were all silent, although Mrs Headlam nodded her agreement to the last comment. 'So, I arranged a leave of absence and swore the people who needed to know about my pregnancy to silence.'

'And you had enough inside information about some of those colleagues to ensure they remained silent.'

'Yes, Chris. My word, you are well-informed, aren't you?' She smiled. 'And in due course when I returned to work, I changed my name and insisted on being moved to another department. But it was made plain to me that the heights to which I had once aspired would no longer be accessible to me. The dreaded word "unsound" was attached to me.'

'That's appalling,' Mrs Headlam muttered.

'Extraordinary, really,' Tim said. 'I thought that the 'sixties had changed all that, had made Britain swing, had liberated us sexually.'

'Not in the Civil Service, it didn't,' Wheeler said ruefully.

'Who adopted your child?' I asked. 'And by the way, who was its father?'

'You're very direct, aren't you, Chris. You don't exactly tread lightly on bruised memories.'

I shrugged. 'You are here to help us, Diana, or so you said. Was the father, by any chance, a member of the CIA? Codename S, and your partner in the fake art scam?'

'Yes,' she replied calmly, 'and that's another reason why I was termed unsound, for consorting with a member of the CIA. Even though they were our allies, there was a lot of rivalry between the two secret services. And it's another reason why I cannot reveal his name. He has become a prominent figure in the American secret service hierarchy. These days he's very close to the President.'

'And the baby?' Tim asked. 'What happened to him or her?'

'I saw him once,' Wheeler replied with great sadness, 'and then he was whisked away.'

I decided that there was no point in holding back and said, 'I learnt recently that the adoption was arranged through the good offices of Anthony Blunt and you were able to ensure that your name and the father's name did not appear on the birth certificate.'

'Yes, that's correct.'

'Oh, but that's impossible,' Mrs Headlam interrupted fiercely, 'the normal bureaucratic procedures must always be observed.'

'Not when you are sitting on confidential information about one of the top officials in the Home Office, eh, Diana?' She nodded sadly. 'Diana found out that this person was feeding highly sensitive information to the Soviet Union and was being paid for it.'

We all waited for Wheeler to speak and there was a tense silence until she spoke. 'Chris is correct and I persuaded this traitor to our country to make sure that the birth certificate was made out in the names of the adoptive parents.'

Once again a heavy silence pervaded the room. 'And that is why you're here, isn't it, Diana?' Mrs Headlam said harshly. With her head down, she continued. 'I'm sorry, Tim, that your father and I never told you about our secret. And we did of course impose a vow of silence on family and friends. We didn't want you to know about the subterfuges of your adoption to be known. I'm so sorry.'

Though clearly shaken, Tim looked steadily at his two mothers. 'I began to wonder about it all a few years ago,' he said calmly. 'It seemed strange that I was built on a much bigger scale than you and Dad. And the hair, too. Mine is jet-black, but Dad's was fair and yours used to be a sort of auburn colour. It seemed odd, and you'll remember, Ma, that some time ago I asked to see my birth certificate. And it all seemed above board. How on earth was it all arranged?'

'Very easily,' Wheeler said. 'I had to tell Blunt that I was going into hibernation and why and he mentioned it to Derek. He knew that his brother was keen to adopt a child. And the deal was done.'

Mrs Headlam was weeping quietly in her chair and Tim limped over to her and put his arms around her. 'Mother, don't cry. I had a lovely time growing up with you both. Dad was a fine father and you were an equally good mother. A little severe at times, though.' He grinned at me.

He then went over to Wheeler, hugged her and kissed her on both cheeks. 'Hello, Mother,' he said quietly. 'I'm so glad that you knew Uncle Derek.'

I felt like an interloper at this family reunion, waited for a while and then said, 'Diana, you're here to save your natural son from any more harm, so can you tell us who this mysterious billionaire is who is willing to go to extreme lengths to protect his investment in works of art, that are not what they seem.'

She sighed. 'I wish I could, but, apart from a couple of works we sold at auction, most of the collection was sold privately to one person through an agent and we were not told who he or she was.'

'And such transactions are swathed in secrecy,' I said. 'But can we assume that it was some billionaire or other from Russia, or the Middle East, or the Far East?'

'Undoubtedly.'

'And you had no qualms about defrauding him?' Tim asked.

'Why should I?' Wheeler replied vehemently. 'These mega-rich philistines buy works of art by the ton, just as they buy leather-bound books by the yard for their so-called libraries. They have no aesthetic sense at all. It's just another way of investing their filthy ill-gotten money.'

She looked at Tim. 'And they will, as Tim knows to his cost, do anything to protect their investment. From extreme violence to murder. It's said that fifty per cent of paintings are fakes, so why should we worry?'

'That's a rather elastic, not to say warped form of morality, isn't it, Diana?' I said.

'Yes, and if you'd worked for the Home Office and the Secret Service you would realize how easy it is to become entirely amoral.'

'And it didn't worry you when you blackmailed Uncle Derek into becoming a part of your scam?' Tim asked.

Wheeler looked thoughtfully out of the window and said, 'That aspect of it did trouble me. I liked Derek in many ways, and once he began, he played his part with great gusto. Of course, he also made a lot of money. And he had a great deal of fun, too.'

I wanted to get things back on track and asked Wheeler who was the agent for the buyer.

'Pearson Brothers in North Audley Street.'

'Are they still there?'

'No. They were investigated by the Art and Antiques Squad over some dodgy dealings. . .'

'Yours presumably?' I said.

'No. Other matters, years later. They were accused of money laundering. And there is someone from the Art and Antiques Squad who might be able to help us. I knew him well, once,' Wheeler finished with a half-smile.

'Are you thinking of Mark Preston? The man who helped you to set up Derek Headlam.'

'Well, well, you have done your research, haven't you, Chris.' Wheeler said.

I nodded complacently. 'He was partly involved with shadowing Blunt, I believe. But why didn't you insist on knowing the name of the buyer? Almost for reasons of self-defence, in a way.'

'We just took the money and ran. We'd had enough. And as you know, these billionaires are morbidly secretive about their purchases. They don't want anyone to know what they own or where it's located. Many of the great works of art are never put on display, they're kept locked away in impregnable vaults.'

'That rather negates the reason for owning them, doesn't it?' I said.

'One other thing,' Tim said, 'who do you think killed Uncle Derek?'

Wheeler shook her head. 'I don't know. It was reported as a hit-and-run accident in a back-street in Rome. Derek had been drinking in his favourite bar, it was after midnight, and he may have staggered into the road and been killed.'

'I don't buy that,' Tim replied quickly. 'Derek left a note for my father, and Chris has seen it, warning my Dad that his life was under threat.'

'Threat from whom?'

'He didn't say, but let's speculate. Top of the bill would be a group of art dealers who had heard that Derek's memoirs would lift the lid on the hundreds of fakes he'd foisted on collectors. That would put the market into free-fall, so they had him murdered.'

'I think it's much more likely to have been this billionaire who had acquired so many of his Old Master fakes,' Wheeler said.

'What about the mother of Headlam's boyfriend, Jason?' I asked. 'Do you remember the sequence in the book, Tim? After the lad died of a drug overdose, she sought Derek out in Rome.'

'Yes, it was an unnerving account in the book. She sounded like a very cold-hearted and angry woman.'

For Wheeler's benefit, I said, 'She told Derek that if her husband, the boy's father, were still alive, he would've killed Derek. So, it's conceivable that she took the law into her own hands.'

'That's a bit far-fetched, isn't it?' Wheeler said.

'Lots of things in the story seem far-fetched,' I replied, 'but nevertheless they're true.'

Tim spoke directly to Wheeler. 'I'll send you a copy of the manuscript. Maybe it will trigger something in your memory. But only on condition that you buy lots of copies when it's finally published.'

Wheeler grinned. 'I'll certainly do that.'

'And I hope that the damned book never sees the light of day,' Maria Headlam said bitterly.

CHAPTER 31

Two days later Jack Mason came to see me and, with his agreement, Toby joined us.

As I served coffee, Toby looked at his watch and said grumpily, 'Well, I suppose it is a little early for a drink, but only just.'

Jack laughed. 'It's just gone eleven o'clock. Still, I suppose you journos work to a different time-scale to the rest of us.'

We chatted about the golfing scene for a few minutes and then I asked Jack about his meeting with the betting syndicate.

'Outwardly it seems a respectable set-up. Smart offices in Marylebone and they're called International Gaming. According to the man I met, Charles Brandon, they have offices all over the world and are involved in all the sports you can name.'

'Especially golf,' said Toby.

'Yes, because the man who owns the company is from Hong Kong and is obsessed with the game.'

'His name?' I asked.

'He wouldn't say because the owner is highly secretive and conducts his business through a network of companies.'

'Many of which are in places like the Bahamas, the Virgin Islands, Liechtenstein and so on,' Toby said.

'Correct,' Jack replied. 'Anyway, the proposition to me was simple enough. I can earn lots of money by dropping shots at specific holes in a tournament. Especially on the final day, of course, when interest is at its strongest. Brandon made the point that if I happened to be in contention to win the tournament, I wouldn't be expected to jeopardise my chances – only if I was in the pack.'

'So, it's the same principle as spot-fixing in cricket,' Toby said. 'A bowler will guarantee to bowl a no-ball with, say, the fourth delivery of a given over and all those in the know will have placed their money with the bookies.'

'Exactly,' Jack continued. 'So I make sure that I have a double-bogey at a nominated hole, the easiest to handle being a short hole, for instance.'

'And the punters who are in the know back you to do that,' I said.

Jack nodded. 'And the alternative is to manipulate my score over nine holes, for example, or even over five holes. I make sure I'm a certain number of strokes over par.'

Toby looked puzzled. 'But surely the bookies would smell a rat? Such an unusual betting pattern would show up.'

'No,' Jack replied, 'because around the world millions of punters are laying billions of pounds on all sorts of wagers. It simply doesn't show up. The levels of betting in the Far East are insane, they'll bet on which raindrop will hit the bottom of a window pane first, they're so obsessed.'

I shook my head. 'It's hard to imagine, isn't it? And what do you get out of it, Jack?'

'First of all, they will give me back the amount of prize money I've lost. They'll subtract the two or three strokes I sacrificed and work out how much prize money should be reimbursed to me. Even better, they'll make some substantial bets on my behalf.'

'How substantial?' Toby asked.

'Oh, so that I make at least a hundred grand a time.'

Toby gasped and I looked in disbelief at my old friend. 'So what are you going to do?'

'I'm playing in next week's tournament in France and I'm going to look out for any suspicious scoring patterns and I'll make a note of them. You'll be there, Toby, so you can do the same.' Toby nodded his agreement. 'And Chris, you can keep an eye on the television coverage, too. But I'll really set things up for the PGA Championship in the following week. I'll tell them that's when I want to get involved.'

'And then what?' Toby asked. 'You're not going to play their game, surely?'

'No, I'm not. I'm going to let the officials of the European Tour know what's going on and I'll inform the police, the fraud squad.'

'You're putting yourself in the firing line, aren't you, Jack?' Toby said in a low voice.

'Yes, and I'll certainly need you, Chris, and Max to help me out. And you, too, Toby.' Jack laughed.

'Well, it'll make a great story,' Toby replied.

'One other thing,' Jack continued. 'This fellow Brandon mentioned in passing that there was a well-known agent who was involved in this scheme, as he called it.'

'Someone who is up to his eyeballs in debt?' I asked.

'That's him,' Jack said. 'Our lofty friend. Mister Lazenby.'

On the following morning Diana Wheeler telephoned me to say that she was meeting Mark Preston that evening for a drink. 'I realize that it's Friday, Chris, and that you're probably busy, but can you make it at six o'clock?'

I had arranged to have dinner with Jane but would warn her that I might be a little later than planned. This was too good an opportunity to spurn. I assured Wheeler that I would join them and said, 'Is he likely to give us any useful information?'

'Who knows? He will if it suits him. Mark is unpredictable.'

We met at a large hotel in the Cromwell Road. It was part of a chain and the bar was featureless, though well-populated with tourists. Wheeler and Preston were already ensconced at a corner table when I arrived and I noted how relaxed they seemed to be; they displayed an easy familiarity with each other's company.

Preston rose to his feet and we shook hands. 'I don't have to introduce you, do I?' Wheeler said with a smile that enhanced her attractive features.

I decided to have a glass of white wine and, when we had wished each other good health, Preston said, 'You seem to have made progress, Mister Ludlow, even though I tried hard to put you off when we met at my shop.'

I shrugged. 'Thanks to Diana, since she doesn't want her adopted son, Tim, to be beaten up, or worse, again.'

'Yes, she told me. And you want my help in identifying the man behind the attack?'

'It seems logical, Mark,' Wheeler said, 'since you were the person who investigated Pearson Brothers. They were after all the dodgy agents who bought the Headlam collection, if I may put it that way, from me and Derek.'

'And from your very close friend in the CIA,' Preston said with what amounted to a sneer. 'What was he called? S, wasn't it?'

Wheeler nodded and Preston continued, 'What you must realize is that the Pearson company was at the centre of a morass of illegal dealings. Money was flooding in from off-shore accounts and then pouring out to other off-shore accounts. So, I have no idea of who bought what from whom.'

'Even though you played a significant part in setting up Derek Headlam so that he would join Diana's scheme,' I said firmly.

Mark finished his glass of wine and waved at a waiter. 'We might as well have a bottle,' he said. 'And I take your point, without admitting any collusion with Diana.' He looked at her fondly. 'We were very good friends and I wanted to help. But, as I said, money came into the Pearson coffers and then went out, and the original source couldn't be traced.'

'We're not really going anywhere with this, are we?' I said irritably.

Preston poured the drinks and turned to Wheeler. 'The best I can do is point you at three particular collectors that we managed to identify. There are two Russian oligarchs, Andrej Petrov and Fyodor Sokolov. The third is a man called Adrian Carras.'

'Two Russians and a Greek,' Wheeler summed up.

'Not quite. Carras is an Aussie, of Greek origin of course.'

'And they all have houses in the most sought-after parts of London no doubt,' I said.

'Several houses. Because the United Kingdom authorities have very little interest in trying to regulate money laundering and all the business and property violations that go with it,' Preston stated. 'We are disgracefully lax in that area. More so than any other country.'

'And our Government doesn't give a damn,' Wheeler added sharply.

I asked how I would find the information I needed about these billionaires and Diana Wheeler volunteered her help. 'I still have friends in the Home Office and other useful governmental areas, and I will find addresses for these people, where they dine, where they entertain their acquaintances and so on. And I'll do it quickly, I promise.'

I thanked them both, explained that I had a date for dinner and headed for the exit. I looked quickly back and saw that their heads were quite close together. Clearly they had plans for the evening, too.

Diana Wheeler was as good as her word and by midday on Monday had faxed some relevant information about all three of the billionaires. Both Russians had benefited from Boris Yeltsin's insane generosity when he became President in 1991. His aim had been to put Russian industry into private hands as quickly as possible. And he sold off the country's assets at knock-down prices, thus making people like Petrov and Sokolov into multibillionaires. No doubt Stalin was spinning in his grave.

The curriculum vitae of Adrian Carras was even more intriguing. He came from a well-established criminal family, originally based in Sydney. His parents had emigrated from Greece just after the Second World War and he was the second of three sons. Diana Wheeler pointed out that the sons had started out as small-time operators in Sydney; they distributed drugs, ran a few brothels, and were involved in various protection rackets. Their big break came when Adrian Carras had come across a large tract of land on Sydney's north shore. It was classified as land to remain undeveloped, a green belt area, but he bought it from its unsuspecting owners and distributed enough cash amongst various members of the city's governing body to ensure that a change of use was granted.

The deal had been the springboard for Carras's ascent to billionaire status. He acquired property all over Sydney, Melbourne and the other major Australian cities and his two brothers, while not abandoning their interests in illegal drugs and prostitution, diversified into casinos and other forms of gambling, one of the best ways by which to launder large sums of money, as was their purchase of an Australian Rules football club.

Adrian Carras owned one of the biggest private yachts in the world and had houses all over Australia, in California and New York, the Bahamas, Switzerland and Paris. His London home was in Kensington and apparently contained thirty bedrooms. He was a prolific collector of art.

The Russian oligarchs, Andrej Petrov and Fyodor Sokolov, were also flagged as art connoisseurs (and that description made me smirk); one lived in Mayfair and the other in Knightsbridge.

Diana Wheeler had provided the London addresses of all three men.

CHAPTER 32

Saturday is usually a day I devote to golf. My preference is to play the game, but watching it is an acceptable substitute for the real thing.

However, the information that Diana Wheeler had provided about the three mega-rich 'art connoisseurs' was so intriguing that I decided to spend some of the day in looking at their main London residences.

If only I possessed a trench-coat and a homburg hat, I thought, but fortunately it was a warm day and I set out for Kensington in light, casual clothes. Having made my way to the High Street, I paused for a cup of coffee and, since I had no need to hurry, I decided to begin my research at the northern end of the exclusive road in which Adrian Carras had his house.

It was agreeable to stroll past the expansive blocks of apartments and lavish houses that distinguish this part of London and, after a short stretch of the Bayswater Road, I found the entrance to 'billionaires' row', as it is termed.

I turned into the broad avenue and paused to take in the grandiloquent buildings which stretched before me. I had done a little research and had learned that they dated from the middle of the 19th century, and many had been designed by notable architects such as Decimus Burton and Sir James Barrie.

The immediate outlook, however, was somewhat impaired by an ugly block of apartments on one side and a large hut in the middle of the road. I became aware that a policeman was studying me and he then walked towards me. His one hand rested warily on his gun in its holster.

'Do you have business in the road, sir?' His voice was gruff and the 'sir' grudging.

I wished him good morning and replied, 'No, Officer, I'm just going to walk down the road to Ken High Street. I'm interested in architecture and this is a fascinating street.'

The policeman looked me up and down and didn't try to hide his irritation. 'Well, don't linger, will you. There are several embassies in the road for a start and the other residents value their privacy.' He pointed at the notice board on the wall of the hut. 'And, like it says, no photos allowed. Okay?'

I nodded to him and set off down the broad avenue, lined with its lovely plane trees. Several of the larger buildings had indeed become embassies and heavily-armed men loitered in their gardens and by their imposing front doors.

All the private houses seemed huge, with the benefit of sprawling gardens and I wondered what was the market price for these elaborate residences. Undoubtedly way beyond the financial capacity of ordinary mortals. The smell of dirty money was almost tangible in my nostrils.

About halfway down the road I found Carras's house and looked at it with both envy and wonderment. It was as expansive as any of its neighbours and, if it had thirty bedrooms, there was certainly space for each of them to have a bathroom. There were four floors and a basement and the top of the white-painted building was crenellated. Outbuildings ran along one side and a glass-roofed balcony stretched along the other. A variety of trees adorned the gardens and I noticed how many surveillance cameras had been installed, especially near the imposing iron gates which guarded the property.

About fifty yards up the drive there was a substantial one-storey brick building, which was clearly some sort of guard-house and four large black limousines were parked nearby. Several black-suited chauffeurs, all with the obligatory dark glasses, were lounging near the cars. I wondered how many cars were needed by Carras and his family.

As I continued to stare through the gaps in the gates, a man, also dressed in black but of a more informal cut, left the guard-house and looked hard in my direction. He was tall and heavily-built and seemed familiar. Then I saw his tattoos; you could not miss them, primarily red and black in colour and flaring up his neck.

He turned on his heel and disappeared into the guard-room. I spotted the nearest camera and looked steadily at it, so that the thug who had recently invaded my home would realize that I had found the territory that he occupied and, above all, that I knew where his boss lived, and his name.

The thug re-appeared from the confines of the hut with reinforcements; he was the slightly smaller 'heavy' who had accompanied him on his visit to my apartment. They seemed just as formidable as before and I looked down the road towards Kensington High Street, my means of escape if matters got out of hand. I was confident that I could out-run the two giants.

They stopped on their side of the gates and, ready as I was to make a run for it, I was relieved. The bigger one, a theatrical smile etched on his mouth, said, 'What the fuck are you doing here?'

'Having a stroll and admiring this lovely house.'

'Don't waste your time, little man. You're not welcome here.' His hand strayed to his jacket pocket, as if seeking reassurance and I could see the tell-tale bulge of his gun.

I gestured at where his hand rested and said, 'The boss was good enough to provide you with another gun, was he? Another Glock?'

He started towards the gate, but his partner put a restraining hand on his arm. 'Leave it, Vlad, that piece of shit isn't worth it.'

I grinned at them both. 'Vlad, I would like to make an appointment to see your boss. Mister Carras.' I felt in my trouser pocket and slowly removed my wallet, aware that a sudden movement might provoke a violent reaction. I pulled a business card from the wallet and balanced it on the top rung of the gate.

'There's my card. I'm sure that Mister Carras will want to meet me.'

The smaller thug reached out for the card and tore it into several pieces and threw them at my face.

I looked at the scraps of paper on the ground. 'We don't like people littering our beautiful city,' I said. 'I think I'll have to inform one of the policemen up the road about you.' I grinned at the perpetrator.

'Some good that'll do you, little man,' he replied. 'The boss looks after all those bastards on the gates.'

'I still want to see Mister Carras,' I insisted. 'You'll let him know that I called, won't you.'

'Get lost,' number two thug snarled. 'Cause any trouble and we'll sort you out. Remember, we know where you live.'

'And I know where Mister Carras lives,' I replied cheerily.

I was about to continue my walk when a young-ish man, clad in bright blue shorts and a yellow T-shirt, walked around the corner of the house. Broad-shouldered and swarthy, he had thick black hair and a scrubby beard.

'Hey, Vlad,' he said in a noticeable Australian accent, 'get my car out, will ya.' It was an order, not a request; he was obviously one of Carras's sons.

'Right away, Mister Shane,' Vlad replied and hurried away.

Mister Shane frowned at me and said, 'Who are you and what do you want? The tradesman's entrance is round the side.' He laughed.

I produced another business card and offered it to him through the bars of the gate. He looked at it and I said, 'I'd like to meet Mister Carras. Your father, I assume.'

'Yeah. There are thousands of people who want to meet Dad, so you'd better get in the queue.' He glanced at my card. 'A book agent, this says. Well, as far as I know, the old man isn't planning on writing any books. So you're wasting your time, mate.'

'I'm sure you're right, but I want to discuss a book by an art faker called Derek Headlam and I'm sure your father would like to meet me. I want to talk to him about his art collection, and how the revelations in the book will affect its value.'

'What do you mean? Why should a sodding book affect the value of Dad's pictures? They're worth hundreds of millions of pounds.'

'Not if many of them are fraudulent. And it's highly probable that many of them were copies. Fakes produced by Headlam.'

Shane sneered at me. 'So, you're after some hush money, are you?'

'Not at all. What I want to tell your father is to stop trying to prevent the publication of the book. He has used threats and violence and it's got to stop. The book will be published, whatever he does.'

Shane shook his head, as if in sorrow. 'You don't know who you're up against, Ludlow, do you?'

'Neither does your father,' I replied. 'Anyway, would you please give him my card and ask if we can arrange to meet.'

Shane shrugged and turned away as Vlad rolled his car up next to the gates. It was a bright yellow Lamborghini.

As Shane spoke in low tones to Vlad, I decided to head for the High Street. I had walked no more than a hundred yards down the road when I heard the clang of the gates at the Carras residence and the strident noise of the Lamborghini's powerful engine. It screamed even louder as it sped towards me. I stayed well away from the road, but the car slowed as it drew level with me. The Carras son gave me a disdainful look and what began as a languid wave became the traditional two-fingered gesture.

Then he roared off. Obviously, no expense was spared for the children of Adrian Carras.

CHAPTER 33

I walked briskly down to the High Street and then headed for a pleasant pub that I knew in a side-road. It was buzzing with shoppers and people who, like me, fancied a lunchtime drink. I bought myself a pint of bitter, headed for the courtyard garden and found a seat in the shade. I began to wonder how quickly Carras and his cohorts would react to my unexpected visit. I was already uneasily aware of his capacity for extreme violence, though I did question whether he would have been ruthless enough to arrange the murder of the unfortunate publisher, Grant Jezzard.

On the other hand, Carras was a dyed-in-the-wool crook, who had constructed an extensive criminal empire in his native Australia. He was, therefore, capable of the kind of infamy that a normal person would find hard to imagine.

I was enjoying the ambience of the pub and toyed with the idea of drinking another pint of the very tasty beer, but discretion prevailed and I headed for home on a bus.

A modest cheese and tomato sandwich sufficed for my lunch and I settled in an armchair to watch the coverage of the Perrier Trophy, which was being fought out on a course just outside Paris and close to Versailles.

The coverage was sparse, but I saw that Jack Mason, with a few holes to play, was within five shots of the leader, an American import called Phil Jackson, who was no doubt being paid several hundred thousand dollars in appearance money.

Several of the leading European players were clustered behind Jackson, but I was surprised to see no sign of Gary Peters, whose form in recent weeks had been outstanding; even when the list of players was scrolled down the screen his name did not appear.

I toyed with the idea of calling Toby, who was covering the event for *The News*, but knew that he was unlikely to answer his mobile phone, 'that instrument of the devil'. I decided to try Jack Mason later in the day. It would be interesting to know if he had spotted any unusual patterns of behaviour relating to the illegal gambling which was being organised at tournaments.

An evening with Jane had been arranged and I met her in a pub on the river not far from her apartment. A rowing event had taken place during the afternoon and the pub and its surroundings were crowded with burly men in blazers and scarves of many colours. They were well into their cups, but their ebullience was tempered by good humour. Many an appraising glance was directed at Jane, and she was of course worth a good look.

Eventually I ducked and weaved my way to the bar and secured our drinks, another pint of bitter for me and a large glass of chardonnay for Jane. We stood by the wall alongside the river and the hubbub made it difficult to think, let alone hear what Jane was saying, but she was wearing her serious look, so I bent close to her and tried to listen.

'The restraining order has been served on Hugo. He mustn't come within eight hundred yards of me or my apartment.' She smiled. 'So, that's all good, isn't it?'

I nodded enthusiastically and Jane continued. 'And divorce proceedings have been started, so soon, darling Chris, you and I can think about a much closer relationship, can we not?'

Startled, I played for time by saying that I couldn't really hear her and could we discuss the matter later.

Jane did not return to the subject until we had eaten our main courses at a nearby vegetarian restaurant. I dreaded to think what Toby would say if he learned that my Saturday evening had culminated in a vegetarian meal.

As we shared a plate of cheese and tucked into glasses of shiraz, Jane said, 'You're not your usual relaxed self, Chris. In fact, you seem distinctly uneasy.' She grinned. 'I thought you'd be deliriously happy at the prospect of my being freed from Hugo and able to make myself wholly available to you.'

I guessed that whatever was my response, it would be the wrong one and merely said, 'Of course I'm delighted, Jane. Especially that we can spend more time together without worrying about your loony husband intervening.'

Jane speared a piece of cheese and chewed it, with her gaze focused steadily on me. 'I was hoping for something more tangible than that, more of a commitment actually.'

I played for time by swigging a mouthful of wine and saying, 'This is a really good drop, isn't it? As it should be from McClaren Vale.'

'You worked in the City for quite a long time, didn't you?' I nodded and Jane continued. 'And is that why you are so elusive, perhaps.'

'I wouldn't say that, Jane. You know that I'm very fond of you.'

'Fond. That's such an anodyne word, Chris.'

I shrugged and drank some more wine. 'I enjoy being with you, that is, when you're not being too serious. But, please, Jane, I beg you, let's allow things to settle, and then we can decide what to do.'

When I got home on the following morning, I found a brown envelope sitting on the mat inside my front door. It was from 'The Carras Corporation' and summoned me to a meeting on the following Tuesday at an office in Regent Street.

I grimaced at the idea of meeting Carras on his home turf, so to speak. He would undoubtedly have several of his thugs available to press home his wishes, probably with violent consequences for me. There was an email address on the letter and I decided to propose that the meeting take place on neutral territory at an hotel near the Carras residence in Kensington.

I also decided that I needed to take some back-up with me, a witness, and pondered who that should best be. Max would be ideal, but Tuesday was probably short notice for him. Perhaps Tim Headlam would be the right person.

Next on my mind was Jack Mason. I looked in the newspaper and found the starting times for the final round of the Perrier Trophy. Jack was four shots behind the leader and due to tee off at just before one o'clock.

It wasn't too late to call him, since Jack's warm-ups before a round were not exhaustive. As he said, 'It doesn't take long to warm up a Rolls Royce.' I smiled at the mental image of his effortless, rhythmic swing.

After a few rings, Jack answered his mobile phone and I apologised for calling him before an important round of golf. 'Not at all, Chris, I've got plenty of time. I can guess why you're calling.'

'Er, yes. Any signs of the betting scam being in operation yet? Any unusual scoring by any of the players?'

'Not yet. But it usually happens during the final round.'

'What about Gary Peters?'

'Gary. Yes, he missed the cut.'

'A bit odd, don't you think?'

'Well, even I've missed a cut, in my time. And he did play rubbish apparently.'

'Nevertheless, Jack,' I replied, 'I read that although his second round wasn't going all that well, he only needed a bogey down the eighteenth hole to qualify for the final two rounds. It's not a difficult hole, either, is it?'

'Not really. A drive and a mid-iron is usually sufficient.'

'And Peters hit his drive out of bounds and then took three putts.'

There was a silence on the other end of the line. 'That doesn't look good, Chris, I must say. The bookies would lay very long odds against Peters doing that. Not only missing the halfway cut, but also making a double-bogey on the last hole.'

'Do you think Lazenby put the bite on him to such an extent?'

'I find it very hard to believe that Peters would compromise his season in such a way. There are Order of Merit and Ryder Cup points at stake. Christ Almighty.'

I heard Jack sigh in frustration, or maybe misery. 'Remember,' I said, 'that Peters and Lazenby are inextricably linked, they're like twins joined at the hip. Our lofty friend is up to his neck in debt and owes Peters hundreds of thousands of pounds in fees for his endorsements. But Peters dare not do a bloody thing about it because he's broken the rules by using performance-enhancing drugs, and his agent could shop him to golf's powers-that-be.'

Jack was silent again and then replied. 'It's difficult to believe, isn't it? When this comes out, it will shake golf to its foundations. But I'm bloody determined to shine a very harsh light on it at next week's tournament. I'll see you there, Chris, I trust?'

'I'll be there. And good luck today. Play well.'

CHAPTER 34

Sunday dragged by as I carried out a variety of domestic tasks. They were necessary, and I lessened the tedium by making a few telephone calls. First of all to Tim, who was more than willing to join me at the meeting with Adrian Carras. I warned him that intimidation would probably be Carras's main objective.

'I look forward to it,' he said with a laugh. 'After all, I've got you to look after me.'

Later I managed to contact Max and, to my surprise, he agreed with great enthusiasm to join us at the meeting. I gave him a resumé of how, with Diana Wheeler's help, we had fingered Carras as the person likely to be the biggest loser as a result of Derek Headlam's revelations about art fraud; and as the man behind the attacks on us and on Tim.

'Do you think he had Jezzard murdered?' Max asked.

'Possibly.'

'To state the obvious, Carras is clearly a ruthless and unprincipled bastard. I've heard of him, of course. He's become fabulously rich and is a crook through and through. The authorities, both here and in Australia, have signally failed to prevent his illicit activities, especially all the ways in which he launders his filthy money.'

'So, what's new?' I replied cynically.

'I'll try to do some more research on his business activities before we meet. See you on

I was delighted that Max would be there to formidable support.

Towards the end of the afternoon I tuned in television coverage of the tournament in France saw that Jack Mason had finished in a very credita tenth place; and that the American import, Phil Jackso had won the event. I wondered whether there had bee any more deliberate misadventures by golfers involved with Lazenby in the betting scam. I resolved to call Toby on the following day.

Mrs Bradshaw had not been much in evidence in the last few days and, feeling guilty about neglecting her, I invited her to join me for a glass of wine at around six o'clock that evening.

Her injured arm had almost recovered and she was in an ebullient mood. She looked around my apartment and said, 'I'll start keeping your flat in order again soon, Chris. Maybe in a couple of weeks or so. The sooner the better, eh?' Her smile tempered the implied criticism.

Obviously, my efforts at house-keeping did not meet her high standards. I told her that she must not tire herself out and changed the subject by asking about her relatives and their efforts to take over her life, or more to the point, her finances.

Mrs Bradshaw smiled contentedly. 'I think they've given up. They still make their tiresome phone calls, but I think the fight has gone out of them.'

'I'm not surprised,' I said and grinned at her. 'No more visits from the social services, I hope.'

'No, thank heavens. Anyway, what about you? How are you getting on with the lovely Jane?'

I told her how Jane had dealt with the odious Hugo and tried to answer her question. 'I'm not sure, Mrs B, how we're really faring. Let's say we are now going through a period of re-adjustment and I have no idea how it will turn out.'

Mrs Bradshaw looked at me sympathetically. 'You could do worse, you know. Oh dear, that's very rude. Sorry, Chris, you know that I have your best interests at heart.' I nodded and she continued. 'But I just wonder if the time has come for you to settle down with a pleasant and intelligent woman like Jane, have children, and so on. The usual clichéd stuff.'

'Maybe. But I may not be ready for all that quite yet.'

We left the topic there and I re-filled our glasses.

Toby had a favourite hotel near the Luxembourg Gardens and I guessed that I would be able to find him there at around ten o'clock on Monday morning.

His voice sounded more than usually hoarse when he greeted me.

'I hope you had some top-notch French cuisine last night, Toby.'

He grunted. 'A rather unremarkable cassoulet, actually. But the Burgundy wine made up for it. I dined with Jack Mason among others.'

'Oh, good, and did he mention our suspicions about Gary Peters and his premature exit from the tournament?'

'He did and I tend to agree with your suspicions.'

'Any other peculiar patterns of play yesterday?'

Toby paused. 'Well, it did strike me as odd that two players in succession, Mark Delaney and Sven Ericsson, took three putts on the final green. It's by no means a tricky green, not devilish like some of those at Augusta or St Andrews. The interesting thing is that if Ericsson had taken two putts, and he was well-placed to do so, he would have finished on the same score as Delaney. So, young Chris, what does that suggest to you?'

'I'm not sure. Tell me.'

'There could be another angle to this betting scam. Two players set out together on their final round on level terms, but the gamblers who are on the inside back one of them to finish the round with a lower score than the other golfer. And, of course, both players have been bribed to ensure the result that the scamsters want.'

I thought about Toby's theory and it seemed plausible. 'What did Jack think about it all?'

'He was livid at the idea of such corruption despoiling our great game.'

'I should warn you, Toby, that Jack wants to bring the matter to a head this week, at the Players' Championship.'

'I'll be there, with my pen poised,' Toby said with relish. 'What a story this could make.'

I was a few minutes late for a meeting at the offices of Gold Medal Management and Dan Fairfax gave me his trademark glare and told me that a meeting at eleven o'clock meant exactly that and not ten minutes later.

He then hit his stride as he summarised how various projects were progressing. 'The Cyprus golf resort was nearly dead in the water until I got five hundred grand out of that bar and restaurant owner, Ronnie Mansell.

He thinks he's a hard nut. What a wally. I've forgotten more about negotiating than he'll ever know.'

I looked at Simon and Lindy and saw the tiniest glimmer of smiles on their lips. They knew what was coming as well as I did.

Fairfax continued on his well-trodden verbal path. 'I'll remind you what one of my old guv'nors in the City told me long ago: "Always negotiate as if you've got fuck-you money and you can't go far wrong". That's what I do. Remember that, my children.'

As if we could forget.

The meeting ended about an hour later and, as the other two left, I asked for a few minutes of Fairfax's time.

I shut the door and got straight to the point. 'Are you doing much business with Lofty Lazenby?'

Fairfax studied the papers which were stacked on his desk and said, 'Yeah. We do some bits and pieces. But what's it got to do with you?'

'I just want to warn you that he's almost certainly involved in a number of illegal activities. Gambling on golf, for instance.'

A glare disfigured the Fairfax face. 'So, Lofty likes a flutter. On the horses, in the casinos, and on the golf course too. There's bugger-all wrong with that, is there?'

'Yes, there's plenty wrong, Dan. For a start, he's up to his ears in debt and is using his clients' money to fuel his gambling addiction. He owes Gary Peters a small fortune.'

'That's bullshit, Chris. He's investing Peters's money, which is something that many of the top agents do for their clients.'

'Well, they shouldn't. An agent's job is to negotiate contracts for his clients and pass on the money within seven days of receipt.'

Fairfax shrugged. 'I suppose you've got all this bloody nonsense from that journo mate of yours, Greenslade. But he'd better be careful or he won't have a job at *The News* for much longer. And Lazenby's lawyers will be after his blood.' He paused and looked steadily at me. 'And that goes for you, too, Chris. If you stir things up unnecessarily, your job here will end. Am I coming over loud and clear?'

'Understood, Dan. But I hope you won't get too involved with Lazenby. He hasn't promised any investment in the Cyprus venture, has he?' Fairfax shook his head and I continued. 'Good, because he could find himself in deep trouble before he's much older.'

Fairfax grunted. 'He is involved in a different way. You already know that Peters is pencilled in to endorse the resort.'

'Not a good idea, Dan, because Peters could be just as tainted as his agent.'

I headed for the door before Fairfax could say anything more.

CHAPTER 35

The meeting with Adrian Carras was scheduled for 11 o'clock on Tuesday morning at an up-market hotel overlooking Kensington Gardens.

Max arrived at my apartment at around 9 o'clock and Tim Headlam about an hour later. We speculated about the tactics which Carras might employ at the meeting and came to no conclusions beyond guessing that threats and bribes would be on the agenda.

We arrived a few minutes ahead of the agreed time and were intercepted by one of receptionists. 'Are you meeting Mister Carras?' he enquired. We nodded and he ushered us to a corner of the opulent lounge where Carras was waiting.

In my mind's eye I had pictured him as being an older version of his son, Shane, a man clearly from a Mediterranean locale. But he was slight of frame and, despite his suntan he was comparatively light-skinned. Carras had neatly-parted grey hair and below his broad forehead his eyes were notably dark, almost black in colour. He wore an expensive suit that would not have looked out of place in the City, and a striped tie.

He rose to his feet and took my hand in a firm grip. 'Good to meet you, Mister Ludlow. And I see you've brought some associates with you.' His voice had the lightest of Australian undertones, unlike the broad Aussie twang of his son, Shane.

I introduced Tim as the editor of his uncle's book and Max as a director of my agency. Carras nodded briefly at them and said, 'I've reserved one of the hotel's conference rooms for our meeting. Just over there.' He gestured at a door a few yards away.

His son and the odious Vlad were waiting inside and Carras said, 'You know both of these gentlemen. Vlad, one of my assistants and my son, Shane.'

I nodded to them and received a scowl from the thug and a smirk from the son. Vlad was dressed in a navy-blue track suit and had soiled white trainers on his feet. It was hardly the garb for a smart London hotel, but was a distinct improvement on Shane's ripped jeans and wrinkled T-shirt. The inevitable tattoos crawled up his arms.

We all accepted the offer of coffee from Carras and Max said brightly, 'We certainly know your so-called assistant over there. He held me and my brother up at the point of a gun a few weeks ago.'

Carras sipped at his coffee, grimaced at its taste, and replied. 'Apologies for that. A misunderstanding. My men went over the top. They merely wanted to talk the matter of the book over with you, not threaten you.'

I shook my head in disbelief and grinned at Max. Just to rile Carras, I said, 'Why is this book so important to you?'

He shrugged. 'It's not that important. I have no doubts about the provenance of my many works of art. Sure, there may be the odd questionable attribution, but the efforts of a two-bit dauber like Headlam wouldn't have got past the experts who advise me.'

'That two-bit dauber, as you call him,' Tim said emphatically, 'was good enough to have one his drawings in the style of Poussin accepted as authentic by Anthony Blunt, who was the leading expert on his work. And I emphasise that my Uncle Derek never claimed it was by Poussin. Blunt made the attribution off his own bat.'

Max intervened. 'If you have every confidence in your art advisers and agents, what's the problem? You've threatened us and used violence against young Tim here. Were you perhaps also behind the death of Grant Jezzard, the original publisher of the book?'

Carras's eyes widened and seemed to glow even darker. He slammed his hand violently on to the table and his coffee cup jumped in its saucer. 'Is your brother crazy, Mister Ludlow?' he shouted. 'I've never heard of this Jezzard fellow. No, my concern is with the wider art market, with its integrity, and Headlam's book could possibly destabilise it.'

'So, it's all about your altruism, is it?' Max asked, the cynicism clear in his voice. 'It's remarkable how altruism like yours is used to disguise other motives.'

'That's a very unpleasant remark. But I will admit that there's a grain of truth in it. Of course, I am concerned that the book, however ridiculous are the claims made in it by Headlam, might affect the value of my collection. It's unlikely, but it could happen and I want to prevent it.'

'Hey, Dad,' said Shane, 'let's get on with it. Make them an offer they can't refuse.' He grinned at us across the table.

Carras looked at Tim. 'How much has the new publisher offered you up front?'

Before Tim could answer, I said, 'Twenty-five thousand pounds and he's about to make the first payment.' The advance from James Trimby at Purple Patch

Publishing was only ten thousand pounds, but to Tim's credit his expression did not change.

Carras studied his hands, which were splayed across the table, for a moment and then said, 'This is my proposal. I'll pay you fifty grand, in cash if you like, Tim, for the rights in the book. You must guarantee to hand over all copies of it. They will be destroyed.' He half-rose to his feet and extended his right hand towards Tim. 'Do we have a deal?'

Tim looked at me and then steadily at Carras. 'You don't get it, do you, Mister Carras? The one thing I want is to see my uncle's story in print. It's the story of an artist's life, of a man with a remarkable, if unfulfilled, talent. In my view, he was a genius and I want the world to know it.'

Max patted Tim on the shoulder. 'Well said, Tim.'

'Bloody stupidly said,' Carras growled. 'I'll double the offer, OK? A hundred grand. A young fella like you could buy yourself a nice little flat with a hundred big ones. A great start to your adult life.'

Tim rose slowly to his feet. 'Come on, Chris, Max. I've got nothing more to say to this person. Except that my uncle's wonderful book will be published.'

We all walked towards the door and heard Carras say, 'You'll regret turning me down, you really will. All of you.' There was a coldness and a certainty in Carras's voice that made me quiver inwardly. It was obvious that he meant what he said.

Shane piped up as we opened the door, 'No more Mister Nice Guys.'

We decided to have some coffee and a snack and were tempted into a nearby café by the array of cakes and pastries in its window. We all succumbed to temptation with great ease. As Max said, 'To hell with the calorie counting.'

We both congratulated Tim on his eloquent rejection of Carras's offer and he said, 'These mega-rich bastards think they can buy anyone, don't they,'

'That's because they usually can', Max replied.

With a worried frown, Tim asked how serious were the Carras threats. 'I mean, he didn't seem to be a violent person, not a real hoodlum.'

'That's because he has many of his so-called assistants, like Vlad, to do his dirty work,' I said.

'Yes,' Max agreed, 'the days when he went out on the streets of Sydney or Melbourne to collect his protection money or do a bit of enforcing are long gone.'

'Don't be deceived, Tim,' I added as I finished a last delicious slice of lemon drizzle cake, 'Carras has a past which was saturated in violence. In the late sixties Melbourne's underworld was largely run by a mafia, not so much from Italy, but from Malta. Carras took them on, killed most of the bosses and took over their rackets. Illegal gaming, brothels, all sorts of extortion, and so on.'

'And then he went legitimate,' Max said with a laugh. 'He bribed the politicians to favour his various schemes, especially in property, and set up money laundering facilities on a world-wide basis.'

Tim laughed. 'Maybe I should take the money and run.'

'Nobody would blame you,' I said. 'But what you must do is proceed with caution. There will be reprisals against all of us, so the first thing you should do is leave your digs in Oxford.

'I suppose I could move in with Mandy for a while.'

'Not a good idea. She works for James Trimby, your publisher, doesn't she?' Tim nodded. 'And they'll no doubt have their beady eyes on him. But they are unlikely to do to him what they did to Jezzard. That would look very suspicious.'

Tim was silent and then said, 'I have a godmother who lives in Epsom. Auntie Maud. She's got loads of room and we get on well.'

'Sounds good,' Max said, 'but move in discreetly. I tell you what, I'll take you in my car, when you're ready. But, for safety's sake, let's make it today,'

'But maybe they'll tail you,' Tim objected.

'No,' I said, 'Max won't be tailed.'

Tim looked carefully at Max, 'Why not? What are you? One of Smiley's people?'

Max laughed. 'Not at all. Just careful. Incidentally, I have a thought about Carras and his merry men. I think we should take the fight to him.'

'Are you sure?' I exclaimed. My brother was still able to startle me.

'Well, Chris, do you want to hang around, waiting for one of his thugs to knock seven bells out of you or worse, or do you want to knock him off his balance?'

'If I could, I would.'

'Everyone has a weakness. What's his, do you think?'

'His family,' Tim said eagerly.

'Exactly. And in particular that self-satisfied bugger, his son, Shane.'

'But we don't know much about him,' I protested, 'except that he has appalling dress sense and drives a Lamborghini.'

'True,' Max replied. 'We'll have to put Toby to work, scanning the gossip columns. Young Shane is bound to have form in the scandal pages. Is he a party-goer, interested in sport, a gambler, a dabbler in drugs, fond of the ladies? Let's find out.'

I had an immediate thought: that Larry Steinman, who wrote bits and pieces about the social scene for a local London newspaper, might be able to help us.

CHAPTER 36

When I reached home, I found a message to call Toby. He answered his telephone almost immediately and suggested that we met for 'a quick drink' that evening. I was cautious, since a quick drink with Toby has the opposite meaning. 'It's about Jack Mason and the betting business and it's important,' he insisted. We agreed to meet in a wine bar in Fulham.

I asked him if the name Shane Carras meant anything to him and it didn't. He agreed that Larry Steinmann was likely to be the best source of information, and I wasted no time in calling him.

'Ah, the spectacularly opulent Carras family,' Steinmann said with a laugh. 'I assume this is in connection with the Headlam book.'

'You've got it in one, Larry. And I'm looking in particular for information about the son, Shane. What are his interests, or more to the point, what are his weaknesses? Sex, drugs, booze, girls, boys?'

'All those and many more, I would imagine. Why set any limits when your father is mega-rich?'

'Oh lucky man,' I said.

'Maybe not,' Steinmann replied. 'But I'll do some digging for you. Give me a day or two.'

I thanked him and then began to wonder about my own safety. My apartment, located on the ground floor of the house, was hardly a fortress and Carras's thugs were capable of anything.

A few weeks ago, Jane would no doubt have welcomed me into her flat with open arms, but when we last met she had not seemed as uxorious as usual. Anyway, I did not want to compromise her safety. However, I knew that several of her neighbours used their apartments more as *pieds-a-terre* than homes and they were often vacant. She was on good terms with some of the various owners and perhaps she could borrow a property for my temporary use.

Although it was mid-afternoon, a time when Jane was often out and about, seeing a film, visiting an art gallery, window shopping or dropping in on friends, she picked up her phone.

Her greeting was hardly warm; the right word would probably be non-committal, but I explained my problem without being too specific about the reasons for needing alternative accommodation.

There was a pause and Jane said, 'What's up, Chris, are you avoiding another avenging husband? Are the bailiffs after you?'

I decided to tell her a part of the story. 'You will recall the problem with the Derek Headlam book. Well, the very rich man who wants to prevent its publication may well send the heavies along once again to intimidate me.'

'I see. I am of course flattered that you don't want to endanger me, so I'll contact Caroline. Her flat is two floors above mine and she is currently in the Dordogne for several weeks with her latest paramour. I'll ask her permission to move you in for a few days. I have a key.'

A couple of hours later I entered the wine bar which Toby had nominated. It was in a side-street off the Fulham Road and Toby favoured it because it was relatively quiet, had an air of shabby comfort and, above all, because the prices were reasonable.

A bottle of champagne was sitting in its ice-bucket on Toby's table, so all was right with the world. For the time being, that is. He poured me a measure and we clinked glasses.

'How did you get on with dear old Larry Steinmann?' Toby asked.

'He's doing some digging for me and will get back to me soon.'

'This Shane Carras, what's the story?'

I explained that we had discovered that his father had been behind all the efforts to bury the Headlam book, and how our plan was to try to attack his weakest point: his son Shane.

Toby shook his head doubtfully. 'For heaven's sake, Chris, be very careful. Carras has already shown what a ruthless bastard he is, and he won't stop now.'

'That's why we want to hit him where it really hurts, show him that he doesn't scare us. Anyway, tell me how Jack is getting on.'

'He's as stubborn and hard-nosed as you. Ostensibly he will take part in that betting scam on the final day of the Players' Championship. He won't of course do anything crooked, but he's determined to nail the people involved.'

'How will he do it?'

'He doesn't know yet. He'll be given his instructions in the next few days. As you know the real action is always on the final day, so, assuming that Jack makes the cut for the final two rounds, he will then be set up.'

'Am I right to suppose that those instructions, where and when to drop shots, will be passed on to Jack by telephone? They'd want to avoid any personal contact at that stage, wouldn't they?' Toby nodded and drank a generous measure of fizz. 'We'll have to help Jack to get some solid evidence. Maybe he could record the conversation.'

Toby waved at one of the barmen, who nodded eagerly and soon appeared with another bottle of champagne. 'That's no use if we can't identify the caller,' Toby said. 'And, of course, his telephone number will be concealed.'

I shook my head in despair. 'Our problem is that we must establish a direct link between that gaming company and Lazenby.'

I felt uneasy for the rest of the evening, aware that Carras's thugs might be lurking nearby. I made sure that the front door was securely locked and all the windows bolted. My meal was scant, since my appetite was predictably poor. As the light faded, I pulled the sturdy shutters across my windows and settled down to watch some television.

A series about a private detective in Brighton was succeeded by a sit-com, which was unsubtle to the point of being patronising. It caused me to wonder if Dan Fairfax was making any progress in selling the allotment sit-com to one of the TV companies. Would 'From the Ground Up' appeal to any of them?

Midnight approached and I tried to settle down to sleep, but every creak and groan of the building jerked me awake. I took some comfort from having the old truncheon, with which Hugo had tried to attack me, near at hand on my bedside table. Several times I got out of bed and patrolled my apartment in the darkness.

Sleep finally claimed me in the early hours and it was deep and dreamless.

In the morning I called Jane and she confirmed that her friend Caroline's apartment was available from that morning for several weeks. I packed a bag with a few necessities and prepared to leave.

I needed to keep Mrs Bradshaw in the picture, knocked on her door and explained that I would be away from my home for a few days. I told her the reasons for my absence and she agreed to phone me if she noticed any suspicious men in the vicinity; in particular, large men with tattoos.

Less than an hour later I had taken possession of my temporary accommodation. Caroline's apartment was spacious, had two bedrooms and a view of the Thames. It was almost obsessively neat and tidy, and I was conscious that I must keep it that way.

'Caroline is very house-proud,' Jane said in a rather pointed way, before suggesting that we met for coffee in her flat in half an hour.

As she closed the door my mobile phone buzzed and Larry Steinmann was the caller. After the usual preliminaries he said, 'This Shane Carras. I'm afraid that there's not much I can tell you about him. Just a rich spoiled kid who does the things rich spoiled kids do.'

'Sex and drugs and rock 'n' roll.'

'Exactly. But not so much the drugs. Apparently his father is vehemently against the use of recreational drugs. Anything more than the occasional puff of marijuana and he hits the roof.'

'Even though he's made stacks of money from drugs.'

'Because of that, I would imagine,' Steinmann replied. 'He's seen at close quarters what harm they can do.'

'Girlfriends?'

'Oh yes, he plays the field. Nobody special as far as I could establish.'

'Not even a top model, with long legs, blonde hair and a pouty face?'

Steinmann chuckled. 'You're becoming as cynical as your chum, Toby. Anyway, Shane frequents all the expected up-market restaurants and clubs. There are lots of overseas excursions, mostly travelling in Daddy's yacht or in his private jet. Often to one of his father's many houses around the world.'

'Oh dear, what a life, Larry,' I said with feeling and he laughed. 'In summary, Shane is just a very lucky, laid-back hedonist.'

'That's about it. Oh, and he likes fast cars.'

'Yes, I've seen his Lamborghini.'

'He has several other cars. He belongs to a group of petrol-heads who like to show off their motors – Ferraris, Porsches, Lamborghinis and so on – around Chelsea and Knightsbridge. They race them down the roads at dead of night, do stunts like hand-brake turns in them, rev their engines up to deafening crescendos and generally make some of the other residents' lives a misery.'

'Why don't the police stop them?'

'Probably too difficult for them. Anyway, what can they do? A fine is nothing to these blokes.'

I thanked Steinmann and was about to bid him farewell, when he said, 'I'm sure that Toby will have an inside track on this, but I heard that there's a big story about to break concerning the illegal use of drugs in sport.'

'Tell me more.' I tried hard to still the excitement I felt.

'A freelance writer called Steve Allen has been investigating the problem for years and apparently he infiltrated the records of a group of dodgy medics in and around Harley Street, don't ask me how, and he's got the names of the sportsmen, what they've been taking, and for how long.'

'This is dynamite, Larry. And it presumably includes the names of golfers.'

'Of course. Along with the usual suspects, the athletes, the cyclists, the tennis players, and so on.'

'But I imagine that he'll want loads of money to share this information, won't he?'

'Maybe not. It seems that Allen is a bit of a moral crusader. His plan is to go to the ruling bodies of the various sports, show them the evidence, and tell them to take all the steps necessary to stop the abuse.'

CHAPTER 37

Enthused by the information provided by Larry Steinmann, I made a call to Toby. I assumed he would still be at home; he rarely arrived at a course on a practice day before lunchtime.

'Ah, Chris,' he said, 'I was about to call you with some interesting news. From Jack Mason.'

'And I've got some interesting news from Larry Steinmann.' Toby asked me to go ahead and I told him about the startling discoveries that had been made by Steve Allen.

'Heavens above, so Steve Allen's come out of the woodwork again. He's been gnawing at the drugs problem for years. In his time he's put many an athlete in the dock, so to speak, not that it's too difficult to do that. Their arrogance, or probably it's just plain stupidity, is sickening. And so is the incompetence of the sport's ruling bodies.'

'Is Allen to be trusted?'

'Yes. He's a very good journalist, hard-nosed and, as Larry told you, a bit of a moral crusader. I did some work with him many years ago. Some magazine articles.'

'It's a tantalising thought,' I said, 'that if he were willing to give us chapter and verse about the golfers using these illegal drugs, we might be able to put Lazenby out for the count.'

'Agreed. I'll get in touch with Steve. He owes me a favour or two and he might help us. However, he may have a much more ambitious plan in mind. Anyway, Jack is very keen to talk to us about the betting scam. He sounded very up-beat, as if he's stumbled upon something of importance.'

'So, let's go and talk to him. He usually finishes his practice by the middle of the afternoon. I'll pick you up in an hour.'

The Players' Championship was held at a different course each year and, on this occasion, the venue was a traditional and very picturesque parkland course about twenty miles west of London. Critics had questioned its suitability for a major professional tournament, on the grounds that its length at just over seven thousand yards wasn't severe enough to test the leading players. But, in the opinion of many people, the subtleties of its design, by one of the best British golf architects of the early 20th century, more than compensated for its lack of length.

Although the day was overcast and threatened rain, a good crowd of spectators had gathered behind the practice area, and some curious glances were directed at us as Toby waved his press pass at one of the stewards and we walked on to the range and greeted Jack Mason, who was clearly coming towards the end of his practice session.

He hit a few more drives, showing off by alternating a fade with a draw, and told us how pleased he was to see us. He turned to his caddie and asked the time. Marlon, his head encased in an over-large cap, replied and Jack said, 'I've got to take a call on my mobile in a couple of minutes.' He turned to me and Toby and said,

'You two know what it's about, and so does Marlon, because I had to keep my caddie in the picture.'

Marlon was studying the ground, his features creased with worry and Jack continued. 'As a result, we've got some good news because Marlon has a mate called Ronnie Martin and he, as you probably know, is caddying for Gary Peters these days. And he's got something of great relevance to tell us. That's right, Marlon, isn't it?'

Marlon, his head down, muttered his agreement.

'So, this is the plan. Obviously, Ronnie can't be seen with us, so we'll meet at around five o'clock at a pub down the road. The Black Swan, it's about five miles away. I expect you know it, Toby.'

'Yes,' Toby replied. 'It's a bit rough, as I recall.'

'Anyway,' Jack continued, 'Marlon and Ronnie will make their separate ways there on their motor-bikes. OK? Right, I'm off to take that call.'

Jack made his way, behind the golfers at practice, towards the far side of the range. He stood with his back to the players and spectators and out of their hearing. I saw him press his mobile phone to his ear.

The conversation didn't last long and Jack waved at us to join him. Marlon shouldered the golf bag and told us that he was off to put it in Jack's car. Having taken the keys from Jack he told us that he would see us in the players' tearoom.

Jack spoke quietly to us as we threaded our way through the spectators. As always, he was punctilious in acknowledging their good wishes and, if requested, in signing his autograph.

'It's just as I anticipated,' he said. 'Assuming that I make the halfway cut, these bastards will give me an instruction for the closing holes of the final round. To drop a shot or shots, presumably, at a specific hole.'

'Did you recognise the voice?' I asked.

'No chance. A standard outer London accent.'

'And what will you do?' Toby asked.

'Try to get a birdie or an eagle, and then give the whole sordid story to the Tour officials.'

'To Jeremy Foote, the chief exec, presumably,' I said.

'Yes, and we'll have a lot more ammunition after we've talked to Marlon's mate, Ronnie.'

We walked past the handsome clubhouse. A veranda, crowded with members, some taking tea and others more powerful drinks, ran along its full length. The players' lounge was at the side of the clubhouse, next to the sponsor's tent. Inevitably, Toby professed a need 'to show his face to the sponsors'.

Jack said, 'Don't drink too much of their fizz, Toby, we've got work to do soon.'

We settled down with a pot of tea in the other lounge and Marlon soon returned with the keys to Jack's car and a promise to see us in the pub in less than an hour.

The Black Swan was housed in an unprepossessing red-brick building on the edge of a village which seemed to consist of just one street with a scattering of shops, modest two-storey houses, a long row of alms-houses and a small church.

Toby, as was his wont, headed for the bar and asked the young barmaid for a wine list. With a bemused air, she told him that they had some white wine and some red.

'Champagne?' Toby asked.

'Oh,' the barmaid replied, 'I'll have to check with the guv'nor.'

I could see the man, who presumably was 'the guv'nor' several yards down the bar. A portly figure, as befits a landlord, he was deep in conversation with a group of men, all with pints of beer in front of them. He turned slowly in response to the barmaid's shrill request for help.

'What's the problem, Jen?' he asked with a scowl in Toby's direction.

'This gentleman wants to know if we've got any champagne.'

'No. All we've got is some Spanish cava. In the fridge in the other bar.' He turned and rejoined his mates along the bar.

'Cava?' Toby said, a note of incredulity in his voice. 'Well, there's a first time for everything, eh, Jen? A bottle, please.'

Jack and I grinned at each other and, since we had to drive our cars later, ordered half pints of bitter.

As Toby looked suspiciously at the label on the bottle of cava and gave out one of his trademark harrumphs, Marlon entered the pub with Peters's caddie, Ronnie Martin. They both asked for a pint of lager and then we all gathered around a table near the door.

I had only caught fleeting glimpses of Ronnie Martin on television as he carried out his caddying duties for Peters, and had expected him to be roughly the same age as Marlon. But he looked at least ten years older, in his mid-thirties, I guessed. He was stocky, with a thick mane of black hair and designer stubble across his cheeks. Another surprise was the gold stud in one of his ears.

I noticed that he seemed to be nervous; he kept fingering the strap of his crash-helmet as we settled down to talk. But Toby has that effect on some people.

Jack Mason didn't waste any time in opening the discussion. After thanking Martin for passing on the information about Lazenby's involvement in the betting scam, he explained why Toby and I were present: that we were helping him out with the problem.

Martin looked at each of us in turn and then said, in a pleasant low-pitched voice, 'Marlon's my mate, Jack, as you know, and he told me, in the strictest confidence, what you've decided to do.'

He took a good gulp of his lager and continued. 'It made something I heard the other day seem much more important. There'd been talk amongst us caddies for some time about some sort of betting ring. That's right, isn't it, Marlon?'

'Yeah, there'd been lots of rumours over the last few weeks, before the boss got involved.'

'So, what did you hear, Ronnie, that surprised you?' Toby asked.

'Well, I was over at Lazenby's house on Monday. He's got an office there and I wanted to collect some money, some expenses and some of the fees I've earned. I had to wait to see them and Mrs Lazenby fixed me up with a cup of tea. She told me to make myself at home, to sit on the terrace in the back garden.'

He took another swig of his lager. 'Lazenby's office is just by the side of the house and I could hear him and Gary talking. One of the windows was open, see, it was a warm day.' Ronnie paused for effect. 'Then a bloody great row started. I saw Gary stand up and he started yelling at Lazenby. It was all about the money Lazenby owed him and how Gary was going to get his lawyers on to him and so on.'

'And then I hear that it got really interesting,' Jack said.

'Yeah. Gary said that if Lazenby ever thought he'd pull another stunt like the one in Paris, deliberately missing the cut in the tournament, then he could think again. He told the bastard that he wanted all the money due to him within the next two weeks or he'd go to Jeremy Foote with the whole story.'

I jumped in at this point and said, 'What did Lazenby say to that?'

'He said that he had all the details of the illegal drugs that Gary had taken over the last year and that he'd also reveal how he'd taken part in the betting scam at the Paris event. Lazenby didn't lose his temper, didn't even raise his voice. It was really scary. He just told Gary that he'd drop him as deep in the shit as he could. They could drown in it together, as far as he was concerned.'

There was a heavy silence around the table, until Toby said, 'What a hell of a story, albeit a horrible tale of deceit and dishonesty. So, what happened next?'

'I thought it best to get the hell out of there, so I told Mrs Lazenby that I couldn't wait any longer, got on my bike and headed for home.'

'I wonder what Lazenby will do next?' Toby said quietly. 'He would have recouped some of his losses by backing Peters to miss the cut, but it wouldn't come close to covering what he owes to Peters and his other clients and, most of all, to the bookies.'

'I think it's time we took the initiative,' I said firmly. 'Let's try to get that information about drugs from Steve Allen, and put the whole package together. We won't give Lazenby a chance to react, we'll just screw him to the wall by Sunday evening, when the Players' Championship finishes.'

Jack Mason grinned at me. 'That's what I like to hear. The whole sorry mess needs to be exposed to view.' He nodded at the two caddies and said, 'And you two lads must keep a low profile. We'll keep you in the frame, because Lazenby is bad news. Ruthless, unpredictable. You'll remember what happened to Peters's previous caddie, Andy Massey.'

Martin nodded. 'Bloody horrible. But I heard he's down in Kent now, working as a greenkeeper.'

With a grimace, Toby finished his glass of cava and said, 'What motivated you, Ronnie, to get involved in such a direct way?'

'Gary's a decent bloke, he doesn't say much, but I like him. OK, he's used illegal drugs and that is wrong, but he's only one of dozens of pros who've done that. And he's a great golfer, he's got a chance of winning a major one day. And I don't want him to be messed up by that shit, Lazenby.'

Jack Mason nodded approvingly and I decided that a note of caution was needed. 'You realize, I hope, that when all this comes out, Peters will be tarred with the same brush as Lazenby.'

'He's likely to receive a lengthy suspension from the game,' Toby said.

'It depends on what Steve Allen is willing to tell us,' I said. 'As Ronnie has said, quite a number of the pros could be implicated and their suspensions will have serious repercussions for the professional game.'

'Sponsors will take flight, for instance,' Jack said.

'Perhaps the powers-that-be will see fit to be lenient. Light penalties in return for full disclosures by the guilty parties,' I said.

'In view of that, Ronnie,' said Jack, 'do you think that Gary will help us? You can tell him that one way or the other I'm going to expose this betting ring and, with the help of Chris and Toby, the use of illegal drugs. So, why doesn't he come in with us, join the good guys?'

Martin nodded. 'I'll put it to him. I think he'd do whatever he can to screw Lazenby.'

'Yes, he's the real target,' Toby growled. 'What an idiot that man is. He had a good business, and he's ruined it all by an addiction to gambling.' He shook his head sorrowfully. 'Why are men so bloody stupid?'

I smiled at Toby. 'What a great title for a book. "Why Are Men So Bloody Stupid?" It's bound to be a best-seller.'

Jack guffawed. 'And Toby is just the man to write it.'

CHAPTER 38

I had passed a peaceful night in my borrowed apartment, though with a slight hangover, since Toby had insisted on 'a couple of sharpeners' before we went our separate ways.

Sitting by one of the front windows of my temporary abode, I sipped my first coffee of the day and absorbed myself in the tranquillity of the Thames below me and the tree-lined shore beyond. And then my mobile phone buzzed and broke the spell.

Mrs Bradshaw, sounding a little flustered, said, 'Chris, sorry to disturb you, but there's something wrong at your flat.'

I was on the alert at once, fearing what one of Carris's thugs might have done. 'What's the problem?'

'I was going out to the shops, and thought I'd just take a look at your place, make sure all was well. Some misbegotten person has sprayed petrol on to your doorstep and, I think, through your letter box. I didn't want to go in and check, for obvious reasons. But you'd better come over.'

I thanked Mrs Bradshaw and was about to leave the apartment when the accursed phone rang again. It was Tim Headlam. 'Chris, I've just had a call from Mandy. Her boss, James Trimby, has been threatened.'

'In what way?'

'He found a note this morning at the office. The gist of it was that if he published my book he'd regret it and so would his family, and his employees.'

'And what was his reaction?'

'He's considering his position.'

'Well, we know what that means.'

I told him about the problem at my apartment and said, 'This is of course the work of Adrian Carras. We'll have to hit back, and hard. I think we should get together soon and work out what to do. You and I, and Max too, if possible.'

'And Diana Wheeler. She still has a lot of useful contacts.'

With trepidation I parked my car and walked to the front door of my apartment. The smell of petrol was at once apparent. Random splashes of it lay on the doorstep and I opened my door with great care.

The perpetrators had emptied a quantity through the letter box and the smell was unpleasant enough to make me gag. It wasn't a time to light a cigarette, I thought. Then I spotted an envelope and with great circumspection I picked it up and took it outside.

Printed in crude capitals on a piece of lined paper the message read: 'Next time we light the fire.'

I put the note in my pocket, found a bucket and a mop with difficulty and cleaned up the mess as best I could. I then went upstairs to reassure Mrs Bradshaw that all was well and, under her persistent questioning, eventually told her who I suspected was behind the act of intimidation.

She urged me to go to the police and I replied, 'What can I tell them? I have no evidence against Carris. But we have a plan, well, the beginnings of one and we'll give him some of his own medicine.'

Mrs Bradshaw shook her head resignedly. 'Do be careful, Chris, I beg you.'

The day went by in a whirl of activity as I was informed by Toby that Gary Peters had talked at length to Jack Mason and had agreed to 'turn Queen's evidence', as he put it. He also emphasized his loathing for his erstwhile agent, Lofty Lazenby. Toby also told me that we were to meet Steve Allen that evening in a Mayfair restaurant.

It was a popular haunt for media people, but Toby had secured a table in an alcove at the far end of the dining room.

Steve Allen arrived shortly after the appointed time and apologised profusely. He was tall and cadaverous, with a beaky nose and bright eyes which seemed to have a smile implanted in them. He was probably about Toby's age.

He ate and drank sparingly, but Toby more than made up for his friend's meagre appetite.

As we tackled a generous cheese-board and a very tasty red wine from Italy, Toby broached the subject we had met to discuss. 'Steve, you're a journalist like me, so I will understand if you don't want to reveal anything you've discovered about this vexed subject of performance-enhancing drugs in sport. But Chris and I are on the track of it in golf and it's Jack Mason's intention to blow the whistle this weekend. Possibly with the help of Gary Peters. And I'm intrigued to know how you found an inside track on it all.'

'Well, Toby, you know how long I've been involved with this age-old problem, which has plagued sport for umpteen decades. I was about to say "I've got a little list", but it's rather more than that.' Allen smiled. 'Ron Rigby, the runner, sparked me off again recently. He's notorious and he spilled his guts to me several months ago. He actually gave me copies of his prescriptions, all signed.'

'By a certain Doctor Cockburn, perhaps?' I asked. I then explained how I'd taken Max to see the same doctor.

'That's Cockburn all over,' Allen said.

'And he's also supplied Gary Peters,' Toby said.

'Oh yes, and many other pro golfers. Rigby gave me the names. Here's a list, and it's not exactly little.' Allen handed a sheet of paper to Toby.

'Did you confront Cockburn with this?'

'Yes, and he told me that all the prescriptions were to cover legitimate physical problems that these sportsmen had to resolve. And if I published anything adverse about his activities, he would sue me.'

I looked at Allen, who had speared a modest slice of cheese and was now chewing it appreciatively. 'Will you allow us to use this information?'

'Of course. Do whatever you like with it. If it helps Jack Mason in his crusade, all the better. And by the way, I've heard from a colleague of mine in America that a big exposé is about to break over there, too. And Cockburn and other medics in and around Harley Street will be implicated.'

Toby smiled and said, 'I think this calls for a very good bottle of champagne.'

CHAPTER 39

During Thursday and Friday I had to attend several meetings at Gold Medal Management. Dan Fairfax's hard-nosed brand of management-speak did not disguise the fact that several of his projects were not just promising, but likely to come to fruition and make profits. He had unearthed some more money for the Cyprus golf resort (and still wished to use Gary Peters as one of its 'ambassadors'); the golf clothing offshoot was showing some good returns; and the pilot episode of 'From the Ground Up' had been well-received at the BBC. It was now being viewed by various focus groups, and would then be analysed by one of their comedy teams. As Fairfax said, 'The whole bloody process will probably only take a year or two, while the so-called comedy team do so many re-writes that the original script will be unrecognizable.' A cynical remark, but accurate in describing the plodding bureaucratic procedures of the BBC.

Despite these essential activities, I managed to organise a meeting on Saturday with Tim Headlam, Max and Diana Wheeler to discuss what we should do to combat Carras's various acts of violence and intimidation.

I was encouraged to see that Jack Mason made the halfway cut in the Players' Championship. He was only five shots off the lead and Peters was even closer, just three shots adrift. With some anxiety, I wondered how Jack would set about exposing Lazenby as the crook he undoubtedly was. I hoped he would exercise some discretion, and resolved to be on the spot at the finale of the tournament. Toby would be there, his pen and tape-recorder poised, and I hoped that Max would also lend his support.

Diana Wheeler invited us all to gather at her home in Chelsea. Max and I arrived at the appointed time of midday and we stopped briefly to admire Diana's house, which was in a quiet road off Sloane Street. It was unusual, in that though relatively small, it was detached and had a garage, an invaluable asset in that area of London.

Just as Diana opened the door and welcomed us, Tim coasted to a halt on his motor-bike. We all went into a surprisingly spacious living room, beyond which was a dining room and then a kitchen, with glass doors on to a small paved garden. Some food was laid out on the dining table: smoked salmon, cold meats, cheese and salad.

We all made the right admiring noises about Diana's house and she produced some white wine from her refrigerator. 'Beer for me, if possible,' said Tim. 'Because of the bike.'

Diana suggested that we had a drink and some food before 'getting down to business' and we gathered around the dining table and sampled some of the cold collation.

We then moved into the sitting room for our discussion and settled into some comfortable and roomy chairs. A number of drawings and oil paintings were displayed on her walls and I said, 'All originals, Diana, or by Derek Headlam?'

'That would be telling, wouldn't it,' she replied with a wide smile. 'Maybe Tim can give us an educated opinion.'

'All originals,' he replied, as he returned her smile.

'To get straight to the point,' I said, 'did Carras take the whole collection that you and Derek and your CIA friend, S, put together?'

'I'm not sure,' Diana replied. 'We had to deal through an agent and he was under no obligation to give us a name. And, anyway, most buyers insist on anonymity. But it became fairly obvious that it was Carras.'

'How?'

'Because people were indiscreet: the agent himself and, of course, dear old Derek. It doesn't take long in the enclosed world of art for rumour to become fact.'

'But they weren't all fakes, were they?' Max said. 'There was the incident in Berlin with the Stasi gentlemen. A genuine Monet was acquired, admittedly at gunpoint.' Max laughed. 'It scared the living daylights out of Derek.'

'Yes,' Diana replied. 'There were a few genuine paintings, in addition to the Monet, and several Old Master drawings, but the rest were fakes.'

'But fakes by a genius,' Tim said.

'I'm going to play devil's advocate,' Max said.

I grinned and said, 'So, what's new?'

'Thank you, brother dear. Why should Carras worry? Derek's copies are hardly likely to be identified as such. And everyone in the art business is well aware that at least half of the Old Masters that are in circulation are fraudulent. There are several thousand Renoirs in the

United States alone that have been authenticated. What a meaningless joke. And how many Picasso and Dali fakes are there? Tens of thousands.'

'I think, in the case of Carras,' Diana said, 'it's a matter of pride. He doesn't care if the Russian oligarch down the road has been conned, as he undoubtedly has, but he's beside himself with indignation at the thought that he himself has been taken for a ride. And the idea that people might find out and take the mickey is anathema to him.'

'Which is why he's become so dangerous,' Tim said.

'So, what should we do?' I asked. 'Max and I are agreed that we should take the fight to him. But how? It's no use thinking we can infiltrate his home and dish out to him what he's dished out to hundreds of his enemies.'

'Including me,' said Tim plaintively.

Diana patted him soothingly on the arm and kissed his cheek. A true mother, even if she had assumed the role both late and unexpectedly.

'I wonder if we could find out more about his money laundering activities?' Max suggested. 'Perhaps there's a chink in his armour there. If we could find enough evidence of financial malfeasance we could threaten to shop him to the authorities here in Britain, unless, that is, he stops trying to scupper Tim's book.'

'That would take ages,' Diana said, 'even if we were lucky enough to uncover any evidence. No, we must act with great speed. I think we are all agreed that Carras has an obvious weak point, his son Shane.'

'The abominable Shane.' I said. 'I did get some background on him from a journalist friend, Larry Steinmann. All the usual stuff, girls, booze, gambling, fast cars.'

'Lucky bugger,' said Max and Tim in unison.

Diana re-filled our glasses and fetched another beer for Tim. 'Perhaps we could set up a good old honey trap for the boy Shane,' she said, with a fleeting smile. 'The girl would accuse him of rape and we then use that to threaten his father. I think I could organise that, with a bit of help from some old friends.'

'What about fitting him up with a drug dealing rap?' Tim suggested.

'Yes,' I said, 'that's more up your street, isn't it, Diana.' She grimaced and I smiled in apology.

'Two reasonable ideas,' Max said. 'And what else have we got? Fast cars. Anything there?'

I sipped some of my wine, a lovely tipple from Burgundy, and a thought struck me. 'Apparently, Shane is one of a band of rich kids who race their cars around Belgravia and Chelsea at dead of night. I wonder if we could interrupt him, frighten him in some way.'

'That's an intriguing idea,' Max said, 'and I might be able to take it a bit further.'

We all looked expectantly at my brother and he continued, 'When I was doing my research in Ireland, I got to know a bloke who worked in some capacity or other for the British government.'

'A spy?' Tim asked eagerly.

'Heavens above, no. But he told me once about how British under-cover people used to stop some of the Irish extremists in a very simple and effective way. They'd use what's called a stinger to stop their cars. It's a steel mat, in effect, with rows of spikes and it halts the car in its tracks. And as a result the driver is usually in shock, which helps.'

Diana looked at him closely. 'So, you worked for Department Zero over there, did you, Max?'

'No, of course not. I've never heard of Department Zero. I was doing my research for the Ministry of Agriculture. I only knew Fergus on a social level. Nice guy, liked a drink.'

The look Diana gave Max was scepticism personified. 'Ah, Fergus. He's quite an operator. We used him occasionally for Home Office purposes. Are you still in touch with him?' Max nodded briefly.

'Well, this all sounds great fun,' I said. 'But once we've stopped young Shane, what do we do? Tell him he's a naughty boy and that we'll ask his father to gate him for a month?'

'No,' Max replied. 'We'll kidnap him. We'll sedate him, put him in the back of a van and keep him in a safe-house until Carras sees sense and does a deal with us. You can find us a safe-house, Diana, I expect.'

She nodded.

'All this is very exciting,' said Tim quietly. 'I'm suddenly in an alien world which I've only read about or seen on the telly.'

I was suddenly assailed by severe doubts about the scheme. Tim was right; the plan was too fanciful. 'Aren't we making this too complicated? I asked. 'Why go to such lengths as stopping Shane's car and so on. We're not making a James Bond movie. Why not simply shadow Shane one evening when he's out on the town and grab him when the time is right?'

Diana spoke up. 'I agree with Chris. The simpler the plan the better. And Fergus can call upon plenty of people to help him.'

'And we'll only hold Shane in the safe-house until Carras agrees a deal and he'll certainly move fast. Shane will be our bargaining chip and an immensely powerful one,' I said.

'It still sounds very dodgy,' Tim said. 'Illegal, to put it mildly.'

'Nevertheless, you must remember what Carras has done,' Max said. 'For a start, he was probably responsible for the murder of Grant Jezzard.'

'My publisher to be,' Tim muttered sadly. 'And the police haven't managed to find the culprits.'

'I talked to one of the detectives a couple of weeks ago,' I said, 'and they've made no progress whatsoever.'

Max intervened. 'We are agreed, then, to take Shane into custody, as soon as possible?' We all nodded our assent. 'Good. I'll get in touch with Fergus.'

'And I'll set up the safe-house,' Diana said.

'Let's do it as early as possible next week,' Max said decisively.

'One more thing,' Diana said, 'I've something to show you. It should be of interest. Give me a moment.'

She returned within minutes, clutching what was obviously a painting, wrapped in part of an old blanket. It was rectangular, just over two feet in length and a little less in width. With a flourish Diana withdrew the wrapping and said, 'Behold, Raphael's "Portrait of a Young Man".'

Tim was first to break the silence. 'I can't believe my eyes. It's fantastic. Ma, where did you get it? It's been lost since the end of the war.'

'That's right, Tim. It was in Krakow for the duration of the war, in the hands of that mass-murderer, Hans Frank. He was supposed to be taking it back to Berlin for Hitler's own art collection. But it disappeared, and has never been seen since.'

Ever the realist, Max asked how much it was worth. 'Well over fifty million dollars,' replied Diana. She grinned at us. 'Except that it's not. Derek faked it.' She turned the picture over and the word 'Fake' was inscribed in deep black paint on the back of the canvas.

'But it's a supreme work of art,' Tim said forcefully.

'Your uncle said it was the best work he'd ever done,' Diana said in agreement.

'So, why didn't you sell it with the rest of the pictures?' I asked.

'We decided it was too grandiose an idea. Such a famous work would have attracted so much attention, not to mention a really severe forensic investigation.'

'But Derek would've got all the details right,' argued Tim. 'A canvas from the right period, paints made from the correct materials, he was a genius.'

'Yes,' Diana agreed, 'but he didn't want to risk it in view of the grander scheme of things.'

'What will you do with it?' I asked. 'Keep it hidden away? Surely it deserves to be seen.'

'I'm going to offer it to Carras. As a fake. But he might blow a nice sum of money on it. A hundred thousand, perhaps.'

It was time to go and we confirmed that we would put our plan into action as soon as possible in the coming week.

CHAPTER 40

The final day of the Players' Championship dawned bright, but with blustery winds, conditions which can disconcert even the best of golfers. But I was sure that Jack Mason, a master of the art of improvisation on the course, would find the right shot at the right time and fare well in the finale of the tournament. He was only five shots behind the leader and Gary Peters was one better.

Max and I, using the press passes provided by Toby, were able to park in comfort close to the clubhouse and were well in time to meet Jack, who was due to begin his round at just after one o'clock; Gary Peters was in the group behind him.

My brother and I could not resist a visit to the tent where all the main equipment manufacturers were displaying their wares. It was entertaining to see the exaggerated claims made for clubs and balls and the other products on display, and hear them repeated by the eager salesmen.

As Max said with a laugh, 'If we spend a few hundred pounds on up-to-date clubs, the newest balls, and the best golf shoes, we should improve our handicaps dramatically. Perhaps we can qualify for the Open.'

'What we must do,' I replied, 'is make sure that we play more golf.' I was determined to do so, since I had played so rarely in the last few weeks and missed all aspects of the game.

We threaded our way through the throngs of spectators, expectant and excited by the idea of watching some of the world's best golfers. I was equally buoyed up by the atmosphere, one in which I had been absorbed for so many years.

After we had watched the practice routines of some of the players, it was nearly time to meet Jack Mason and Toby and we headed for the players' lounge. We ordered some coffee and spotted Toby and Jack in a corner of the tent. To my surprise, Gary Peters was sitting with them.

I knew that Toby had made Jack aware of Steve Allen's revelations, and had given him a copy of the list of the golfers who were guilty of using illegal drugs and I assumed that Jack, in his turn, had put Gary Peters in the picture.

Clutching our cups of coffee, we greeted the others and at once Jack said, 'I'm grateful for that list from Steve Allen. Gary knows he's on it and that I'm going to use the information.'

His face grim, Peters nodded his agreement and Jack, in a low voice, continued. 'To pass swiftly on from illegal drugs to illegal betting, I've been given my orders. I'm to drop a shot on the sixteenth hole, which is a par three, as you know.'

'That could happen to anyone,' I said.

Jack nodded. 'Sure, but then I must contrive a double-bogey on the final hole.'

'That would attract long odds,' Toby growled. 'Especially if you're in one of the leading places. So what are you going to do?'

'I certainly hope I can make at least a par at the sixteenth. And since the eighteenth hole is a par five, I'll do my very best to get a birdie.'

'An eagle would be fun,' said Gary Peters, with a smile. It was the first time I could recall seeing him show any animation.

'I take it that Lazenby or one of his fixers hasn't been in touch with you, Gary?' I asked.

'No fear.'

'But Gary was able to put a name to the bastard who gave me my instructions,' said Jack.

'Yeah. I spotted him. Henry Lomax. Lazenby calls him his financial adviser, but he's just a fixer, up to all sorts of fiddles. He's worked for Lofty for years.'

Jack put his hand in his pocket and produced a miniature tape-recorder. He smiled grimly. 'By the way, I've got Lomax on tape, telling me what to do.'

I looked at Peters. 'And you will give your full support to Jack?'

'You bet. Whatever the consequences and, as you can guess, they could be severe for me. But it's a huge relief to me. I'm sick to death of the whole business. Lazenby owes me a helluva lot of money. And then he blackmailed me into cheating in a tournament. I've had enough.

'But how will you break the story?' Toby asked Jack.

'I'm going to get hold of our esteemed chief executive, Jeremy Foote, and take him through all the evidence we've collected. The illegal betting and the illegal drugs. I'll ask him to deal with both matters. To warn Lazenby off and to institute proper tests, random blood tests in other words, to prevent drug abuse.'

'And if he refuses?' Max asked.

'I'm going to give him until Tuesday to deal with the problems. If he doesn't, I'll call a press conference for Wednesday morning just before the tournament in Ireland. Gary will be there, and we'll tell the world of golf what we know.'

There was silence. Then Peters said that he must begin his warm-up on the practice ground, and Jack said that he was overdue to do the same thing.

'We live in stirring times,' Max said facetiously, as the players left.

'We certainly do,' agreed Toby. 'Gary Peters could, in golfing terms, lose everything. A long-term ban at the very least.'

'He's fronting up, with great courage,' I said. 'Let's hope it all turns out well for the good guys.'

While Toby headed for the sponsor's tent to 'do my bit for the people who make professional golf possible', in other words to deplete their supplies of champagne, Max and I walked some of the opening holes. They all posed different problems for the golfer and rewarded touch and intelligence rather than power and unthinking aggression.

After a good walk, and a glass of beer and a pork pie at one of the many bars, we walked back towards the clubhouse and the first tee in order to watch Jack Mason's opening drive. Once again I felt a surge of pleasure at being a part of the golfing milieu. The spectators were lively, but never too boisterous, and they were clearly there to enjoy the occasion to the full.

Fifteen minutes before Jack was due to begin his round, I expected him to be having a few putts on the practice green. Marlon was there, but I saw no sign of Jack. I asked the caddie where his boss was and he gestured towards the clubhouse. By the side of the building and out of earshot of the members on the verandah, he was talking to Jeremy Foote and, judging by the latter's body language, it was not an amicable conversation.

'Come on,' I said to Max, 'let's give Jack our support.'

As we reached the two men, I heard Foote say, 'I've never heard such nonsense. I'm surprised at you, Jack, I thought your feet were firmly on the ground.'

We stopped by Jack's side and he said, 'You know Chris, my old caddie, and this is his brother, Max. They have both been of great help in nailing down this betting conspiracy. Chris will also confirm that I have a list of most of the golfers on the Tour who've been using illegal drugs to enhance their strength and stamina.'

Foote's face was reddening as his temper got the better of him. 'Stuff and nonsense, Mason, and why should I give any credence to what a caddie has to say? Our drug tests have never revealed any problems.'

'They wouldn't, would they?' Max said drily, 'because they are urine tests. What are needed are blood tests. And by the way, my brother is a literary agent these days. Maybe he could handle your memoirs one day.'

Jack laughed. 'That's a book whose sales might just get into double figures.'

Foote glared at Max and then spoke directly to Jack. 'I'll give you some time to explain yourself after the tournament's over. The evidence for your ludicrous claims, if you have any, had better be good.'

'It will be and Gary Peters, who is on the list of drug users, or abusers I should say, will have plenty to say, too. Particularly about your good friend, Lofty Lazenby.'

Foote started to turn away, but Jack continued. 'One thing you ought to bear in mind, Mister Foote, is that I will take whatever actions are necessary to protect the reputation of our great game.'

Without another word, Foote turned and strode off towards the main entrance of the clubhouse.

'What a prick that man is,' Jack muttered.

'Never mind, Jack,' I said. 'You're on the tee in a few minutes. Concentrate on your golf and forget Foote and the rest of it.'

He nodded and walked purposefully towards the first tee, where Marlon was waiting.

I knew from my years as his caddie, that Jack Mason had a strong mind and great powers of concentration. Nevertheless, it was noticeable that he was not his usual efficient self over the opening holes. Max and I joined Toby in the sponsor's tent and watched on television as Jack dropped three shots in the first six holes. On the final day, that was sufficient to send him spinning out of contention for a high finish. In contrast, Gary Peters made two birdies in the first four holes and moved higher up the field.

We joined Toby at the buffet table and told him about the confrontation between Jack and Jeremy Foote. 'I actually think that Foote is stupid enough to think he can either bully Jack into silence, or ignore what he has to say,' Toby stated.

We tended to agree with him and, after our pleasantly informal lunch, noticed that Jack had made up some ground with three birdies. He was lying just outside the top twenty, whereas Peters was in the top ten. Ahead of him were two Spaniards, a German, a Swede and a couple of British players. It was an apt reflection of the cosmopolitan nature of professional golf in Europe.

We lingered over some coffee and Armagnac for a while longer and then decided to make our way to the final holes. Would Jack make his birdie on the sixteenth and his eagle on the eighteenth, and thus confound Lazenby and his crooked betting syndicate?

CHAPTER 41

Well in time to see Jack Mason play the short 16th hole, Max and I took some seats in the grandstand which had been erected behind the large green. The hole was nearly two hundred yards in length, not excessive for professional golfers, but its difficulties lay in the subtle slopes of the putting surface.

We watched two groups play the hole and then Jack's imposing figure appeared on the tee. His two playing companions hit reasonable shots on to the green and then it was Jack's turn. One of his great merits has always been his speed of play: he teed up his ball, took a look at the flag, waggled his club once, and then hit his shot. His ball soared high into the air, dropped a few feet behind the flag and then spun backwards to within a few inches of the hole.

The applause and yells of delight were deafening. Max grinned at me and shouted in my ear, 'Nearly a bloody hole in one. That'll put the cat among the betting pigeons.'

'Yes, but those bastards will still be hoping that he'll have a double-bogey on the eighteenth. That's where the big money is to be made.'

There was renewed clapping and cheering as Jack marked his ball. The other two players putted out for their pars, and then Jack tapped his ball home for a birdie.

Because of the dense crowds we decided to walk straight to the 17th green, so that we would be in a good position to watch Jack play the final hole. We watched him record an efficient par four and then edged our way close to the rope guarding the 18th tee.

I looked down the fairway at the formidable final hole. It is a par five of over five hundred and fifty yards, and the fairway dog-legs left about halfway along its length. Bunkers encroach on to the fairway where a professional would aim to put his drive; and then there is a long slog uphill to a two-tiered green. A bunker lies in wait about thirty yards short of the green, and four more bunkers guard the green itself.

As Jack approached the tee, I was amazed to see Toby alongside him; he is a golf writer who prefers the comforts of the media centre to the uncertain demands of the course itself.

'Good luck, Jack,' Max called out and Jack looked our way and waved us over.

A steward lifted the rope and, as we ducked under it so did a man in dark-blue trousers and a bright yellow sweater. He hustled his way past us, went straight up to Jack and whispered something in his ear.

'Rather odd behaviour,' Max said.

'Yes, and I think I know who he is,' I replied.

Jack was due to play first, but, instead of preparing to do so, he took a few paces forward and turned to face the spectators crowded around the tee. 'My apologies, ladies and gentlemen, for holding up play. But I have just been threatened by that man over there, in the yellow sweater. He's called Henry Lomax.'

There were shouts of surprise and an outburst of chatter from the crowd. Lomax moved rapidly towards the rope on the other side of the tee and Jack yelled, 'Chris, Max, grab him.'

A steward stood four-square in front of Lomax and we both approached him. 'Don't you dare touch me,' he said, in a rather patrician voice.

'I wouldn't want to defile myself,' said Max, 'but you'd do well to listen to what Jack has to say.' There was a murmur of approval from the crowd, and one of them shouted, 'Let's de-bag the bastard.' That caused a burst of laughter.

I noticed that Toby, true to his journalistic craft, was scribbling rapidly into his notebook.

Jack continued. 'I'll be brief because there's an important tournament to finish. Lomax is a fixer for an illegal betting syndicate. They place huge bets on golfers to drop shots on certain holes and then bribe them to do it. I've been stringing them along and I am supposed to drop two shots on this hole. I'll be doing my level best not to, and then I'm going to expose these people to the authorities.'

There was a stunned silence and then the applause began. When it ended Jack asked me and Max to allow Lomax to leave and he dodged his way through the spectators and headed for safety, but not without hearing many forthright remarks about his parentage.

Jack took a few more moments to compose himself and then hit his drive down the right side of the fairway, in order to give himself the best angle for his second shot into the green. His ball seemed destined for one of the bunkers over there, but he was fortunate when the ball bounced firmly, hit the back of the bunker and rolled into the semi-rough beyond. He winked at me and said, 'Let's hope my luck holds.'

It did. When we reached his ball, it was sitting reasonably well in the grass. He conferred with Marlon about which club to use.

'Five-wood, boss,' said Marlon.

'No,' Jack replied, 'give me that twenty-degree hybrid.'

Marlon sucked in his breath and I sympathised with him since it was a long carry for a hybrid club, even in the hands of a powerful hitter like Jack.

We need not have worried. With his long and rhythmic swing, Jack deposited the ball on to the middle of the green.

Once again, a huge burst of applause erupted and lasted all the way up to the green. I felt sorry for the other two golfers, who had become bit-part actors in a greater drama. Wisely, when they reached the green, they both putted out and left Jack to take centre-stage.

Several thousand people were silent, as if holding their collective breath. Jack's ball was about fifteen feet from the hole. He peered along the line of the putt, made one practice swing with his putter, and settled above the ball.

The tension was extreme. Several people in the crowd around me had covered their eyes, as if afraid of what might or might not happen. With his smooth delivery, Jack sent his ball on its way. There was a break from right to left near the hole on a slight downward slope and his ball seemed to be travelling too fast. But Jack's luck held; his ball hit the back of the hole, jumped into the air and subsided into the cup with a rattle. He had made his eagle.

The crowd went wild and the stewards could hardly contain them. Jack was grinning widely and Max and I managed to get close enough to give him the thumbs-up salute.

With so many spectators clamouring to shake his hand or just pat him on the back, Jack made his slow progress towards the scorer's hut and, no doubt with great relief, he disappeared inside to register his score.

By the time we reached the hut, we found Toby nearby and in conversation with Jeremy Foote. We decided not to interfere, but to wait for our journalist friend to give us the gist of the discussion. After a few minutes Toby nodded briskly to Foote and joined us.

'Time for a bloody good drink before I send off my story to *The News*. And what a story.'

When the bottle of Veuve Cliquot had been procured, courtesy of the sponsor, Toby began. 'I told that loathsome globule of vomit, Foote, what had happened out there on the course. How Jack had dealt with Lomax.'

'What was his reaction?' I asked.

'He realizes, at last, that he's in serious trouble and is obliged to meet Jack and Gary Peters to sort things out.'

'And they will need someone there as a witness,' Max said, 'because Foote is not to be trusted.'

'Unfortunately, it can't be me,' Toby said wistfully, 'since I'm a member of the Fourth Estate and, by definition, tainted.' He laughed. 'I think you're the man for the job, Chris.'

CHAPTER 42

Jack Mason, anxious to resolve the various problems that confronted him, had agreed to attend a meeting with Jeremy Foote at midday on Monday. I promised to lend my support, such as it was.

Before I left for the meeting, I bought a copy of *The News* and read Toby's terse but amusing account of Jack's confrontation with Henry Lomax; he did not name him, but referred to 'a nondescript fellow in a vulgar yellow sweater'. However, Toby ended his article with a clarion call to Jeremy Foote and his ranks of golfing bureaucrats to expose and punish all those involved in the betting scam and any other instances of corruption that were besmirching the good name of golf.

We convened at the headquarters of the European Tour, which occupied several rooms at the rear of a rather grandiose golf club to the west of London.

As I explained to Toby when I met him later that evening at one of his favourite wine bars, the atmosphere was unpleasant from the outset. Foote was seated in a comfortable armchair behind a large and ornate desk and was flanked by two of his so-called executive officers. Jack and I sat on uncomfortable dining-chairs in front of them. I supposed that the idea was to emphasise their importance in the world of golf and our comparative insignificance. But Jack was not a person to be affected by such a petty display of points-scoring.

The meeting lasted less than an hour. As usual, Foote would not admit that there was any problem with illegal drugs in golf, but even he could not reject the evidence which Jack laid before him. In addition, he produced a written confession from Gary Peters that he had used anabolic steroids and other performance-enhancing drugs during the past two years. Peters also confirmed that other golfers, and they were on Jack's list, had used the same doctor to procure their supplies of drugs.

The equally thorny problem of illegal betting on golf was dealt with swiftly by Jack. He told them how he had infiltrated the conspirators, played back the tape of the original conversation in which Lomax had issued him with his instructions for the final two holes of the Players' Championship; and made a point of emphasising that Lomax was a close associate of Lofty Lazenby. By this time, Foote and his colleagues had lapsed into an uneasy silence.

'So, Jack had those miserable time-servers by the short and curlies,' Toby said, with a satisfied smirk. He swallowed some of the fizz in his glass and asked what Jack's demands had been.

'Very straight-forward. First, that random blood tests be instituted at the beginning of next season. Secondly, that Lazenby is barred from any involvement in golf at any level.'

'But what about all the money he owes to Peters? And what about the golfers who've been doing drugs, and the others who've been involved in the betting conspiracy? If they are all disciplined, as they should be, the European Tour will look pretty drab, won't it?'

'Very true, and that meant that some sort of compromise was crucial. The three Tour officials were stony-faced, to put it mildly, when Jack finished. They muttered among themselves in a corner and then asked us to give them a little time to consider matters. They looked even more put-out when Jack said that we'd go to the bar and have a bit of lunch and he hoped an hour would suffice.'

Toby laughed. 'Jack's a tough bugger, isn't he, in every way.'

I nodded. 'As you pointed out, Toby, Foote was over a barrel. He had to ensure that the Tour retained its appeal, to the fans of course, but above all to the sponsors.'

'An amnesty was proposed, I imagine,' said Toby disdainfully.

'Yes, both for the dopers and the betting scamsters. But, any future transgressions will bring a lifetime ban.'

'And what about Gary Peters's money?'

'This is where Jack was really clever. He knows that the Tour has a substantial reserve of money in case a sponsor defaults.'

Toby nodded. 'Yes, I remember when that department store group went bust a couple of years ago and the Tour stepped in and financed the event.'

'And Jack really put the screws on Foote by emphasising on several occasions how close his ties were with Lazenby. The upshot is that Peters's losses, because of Lazenby's crookery, will be covered by the Tour.'

'And they all lived happily ever after,' Toby said.

'Maybe. One other interesting thing is that Gary Peters is going to take what he calls a voluntary leave of absence from professional golf. For three months.'

'To sort himself out, presumably.'

'Yes,' I confirmed, 'and he's lucky enough to have Jack Mason to help him.'

'When can I write the story?' Toby asked brightly.

'When you get the press release from the European Tour.'

'Thanks a million,' Toby muttered sarcastically.

CHAPTER 43

I was greatly heartened by the way in which Jack Mason had prevailed over Jeremy Foote; the forces of good had certainly triumphed over evil in the form of Lofty Lazenby.

Unfortunately, my mood of optimism was later dissipated by Jane. I admit that I was late for our dinner date, since Toby's 'one for the swing of the door' effortlessly became several. But, from the start of our evening together, Jane was in a waspish frame of mind. She spent most of the meal criticising my way of life, my lack of commitment to her and the many other failings which she saw in me. When we reached her apartment, it was obvious that her favours were unlikely to be offered to me and, without hesitation, I ascended the stairs to my borrowed accommodation.

Jane's parting shot was: 'Caroline is back on Friday, so you'd better move out in a day or two.'

Still cocooned by the enjoyment of Jack's successful campaign against Jeremy Foote, I slept deeply and was only awakened by the buzzing of my mobile phone at just after eight o'clock. Only half-conscious, I mumbled my name and then heard Diana Wheeler's agreeable, low-toned voice. 'Wake up, Chris, I have some news for you.'

'Er, yes, sorry Diana. What's up?'

'We've got the Aussie kid. Fergus lifted him last night. No bother at all and he's in the safe-house.'

'Bloody hell, so we're on our way. I'll contact Carras.'

'Not yet, Chris. Let him sweat for a while. He should be in a rare old panic by lunchtime, when the kid hasn't turned up. Leave it until the early afternoon and then set up a meeting.'

'You'll be there, I trust?'

'Yes, and Tim of course. And I suggest your brother, Max, would be helpful. There's something about him, he has an aura, a sort of latent strength.'

'You don't know the half of it, Diana. And maybe Toby? He can be there as Tim's literary mentor. He'd like that description.'

Diana laughed. 'Let me know when and where we'll meet Carras. I'll warn Tim.'

I composed myself by drinking some coffee, while gazing out of the window at the always enticing riverscape: 'The thrilling-sweet and rotten, unforgettable, unforgotten river-smell', as Rupert Brooke wrote of another stretch of water.

I called Max an hour or so later and he told me that he would leave for London before lunchtime. 'So, Fergus has done his stuff,' he said, with relish. 'He's a hell of an operator, always has been.'

I knew that there was no point in contacting Toby before eleven o'clock at the earliest, by which time his system might have returned to some sort of equilibrium after the previous evening's entertainment. I explained the circumstances and that we would be negotiating a deal with Carras.

'Negotiating from a position of strength, I'm glad to see.'

'Yes. The boy Shane is one of the most important things in his life.'

'I hope you're right. And I'll be there. Whatever happens it should make for an interesting page or two in my memoirs one day.'

At just after two o'clock, I sent a cursory message by e-mail to Adrian Carras. I guessed that he and his henchmen would be looking constantly for some sort of communication either from or about Shane. I merely suggested a meeting, as soon as possible, to discuss his son.

Within minutes my mobile phone rang and Carras said, 'I don't know what you're up to, Ludlow, but if you harm Shane in any way, you will regret it for the few days of life left to you.' I noticed how strong his Australian accent seemed to be.

'Your son is safe and secure and unharmed,' I replied. 'When you in your turn guarantee our safety and security, and when we've agreed how to proceed with Tim Headlam's book about his uncle, we'll release your son.'

'You don't know who you're dealing with, Ludlow, that's obvious.'

'Yes, I do. And we are making sure you know that our resources are the equal of yours. Anyway, let's cut to the chase. When can we meet?'

'As soon as you like,' Carras replied. 'In an hour?'

'No. Let's say at six o'clock this evening. In the same hotel as before.'

'I'll be there.' Carras's telephone was slammed down.

We all gathered at the coffee shop we had used after the first meeting with Carras. I noticed that Diana Wheeler was carrying what was clearly a painting. She caught my eye and nodded. 'Yes, it's the Raphael. Well, the fake Raphael. It may come in handy in the bargaining process.'

Max then spoke. 'I'm sure we all want to be clear about our objectives at this meeting. Chris, can you please summarise them for us?'

'Two things,' I replied. 'To ensure that Carras never again attempts to intimidate any of us, and to force him to accept that the Headlam memoirs will be published.'

'Then Shane will be released,' Diana added. 'As soon as I give the word to Fergus, he'll be delivered back to his father.'

'And I think you should put some extra pressure on Carras,' Max said to Diana. 'With your Home Office background, perhaps you can imply that if he doesn't behave himself you'll put his finances under the microscope, and especially all the money-laundering schemes in which he's been involved.'

Diana nodded her agreement and it was time to go.

We were directed to the room we had occupied at the previous meeting and Carras was waiting, accompanied again by the menacing figure of Vlad, who was sitting to one side of his boss. On the other side there was a slender man with a bald head; he was attired in a well-cut, dark suit and an open-necked shirt.

Carras looked askance at the five of us and said sharply, 'Who the hell are all these other people, Ludlow? I didn't realize you were bringing a delegation.'

I introduced Diana Wheeler, who said quietly, 'I am Tim's mother and I'm here partly to look after his interests, and partly to do the same for the Home Office. You should know that my main role was investigating the activities of money-launderers. And who is your colleague?'

The dapper man next to Carras rose to his feet and told us that his name was Jason Flynn and that he was one of Carras's legal executives.

'Let's get on with it,' Carras said sharply. 'I want my son back, and pronto. What do you lot want?'

At this point there was a knock on the door and Vlad leapt up and opened it. A young girl in a smart black outfit was allowed to enter and she put a large tray on the table. To Toby's clear disappointment only coffee and tea were being offered.

I decided to take the initiative. 'Mister Carras, we are all well aware of your more than colourful past, and we've seen at first hand that violence and intimidation underpin your way of doing business. That thug sitting just behind your right shoulder threatened me and my brother with a gun. Tim was attacked and I was the recent recipient of a petrol bomb warning. So, first of all, we want your solemn promise that none of us will be harmed in any way in the future. Diana has already told you of her influence at the Home Office and she won't hesitate to use it against you.'

Carras glared at me, dropped his gaze to the table in front of him, and was silent.

'I think we've made our point,' Max said, 'that we have enough friends in the murkier corners of the British Civil Service to make life very uncomfortable for you.' He looked straight at Flynn. 'Would you agree, Mister Flynn?'

Flynn looked quickly at Max and then turned and spoke quietly into Carras's right ear. 'He takes your point, Mister Ludlow,' Flynn said.

'I'm glad we understand each other,' Diana Wheeler said in the tones of a school-mistress. 'Now let's discuss the book. I believe that Tim has already dismissed your offer, Mister Carras, well, your bribe, of a hundred thousand pounds to abandon the project. That should tell you that he is determined to have it published, whatever it costs him.'

Carras replied quietly and in an almost placatory tone. 'I understand and it does your son credit. I just hope that we can reach a compromise.'

'No compromises,' Tim said heatedly. 'The book will be published.'

His mother patted his hand to calm him. 'Let's listen to what Mister Carras has to say, darling.'

Carras continued, his tone still mild. 'The first thing to say is that I have an interest in a publisher in Australia, and the company has a branch here in London. They would certainly take the book on. But with certain changes.'

I saw Tim stiffen in his seat and his mother patted his hand again. 'Listen, Tim, please,' she said.

'Would you consider writing the book as a novel? All the material is there, and you can make it clear that it's based on an unfinished memoir left by your Uncle Derek. But it's fiction.'

'You mean it will masquerade as fiction,' Toby said.

Carras nodded. 'If you say so. But I will stick to my original offer. A hundred grand up front for Tim.'

My group was silent, until I said, 'We'll have to talk this over. If you don't mind, we'll sit outside in the lounge for a few minutes.'

We trouped out and settled in a corner of the spacious room, now filling up with residents and people craving a drink in agreeable surroundings. Our discussion did not last long since all of us, except Tim, felt that Carras's offer was a fair one.

'But I've never tried to write any fiction,' Tim said querously.

'All the material is there, in your uncle's book,' I said, 'and you'll have Toby to help you.'

'Toby's an expert,' said Max, with a laugh. 'Most of his golf reports are fiction.'

'But how do we know that Carras won't renege on his agreement?' Toby asked.

I pointed at Diana. 'Because he's already accepted the fact that Diana has enough influence at the Home Office to ruin him.'

Tim rose to his feet and shrugged his shoulders resignedly. 'Let's go back in there and tell the bastard that he's got a deal.'

Carras instructed Flynn to put a contract for the book into my hands on the following day; and added that the whole advance would be paid at once, rather than in the customary three instalments.

In return, Diana promised that Shane would be returned to the Carras home in Kensington within two hours.

As we all rose and shook hands in perfunctory fashion, Diana said to Carras that she had a painting that might be of interest to him. With a theatrical flourish she unwrapped the fake Raphael and showed it to Carras.

Wide-eyed, he stared at the painting. 'My God, the missing Raphael. Portrait of a Young Man. It's worth millions. Where on earth did you find it?'

Diana smiled broadly. 'It's actually a genuine Derek Headlam, the finest forgery he ever created. Would you like to make me an offer for it?'

Carras spoke very quietly to Flynn and then said, 'It's a wonderful work, even if it is a fake. Would you accept two hundred grand?'

'Yes, as long as you never try to sell it as the real thing. Because I would blow the whistle. Anyway, as you see, the word Fake had been embedded in the back of the canvas.'

'All I will do with the painting is hang it prominently in one of my homes. If anyone asks me how I came by it, I'll say it was bought in great secrecy from a shady gentleman in Switzerland. Now, Mrs Wheeler, if you will give your bank details to Flynn here, you will receive the money tomorrow.

As we left the hotel, Diana told us that she would call Fergus and tell him to release Shane immediately. 'For obvious reasons he won't actually show him out of the front door of the safe-house. He'll sedate him, take him in a cab to his home and prop him up against the front gates. He'll recover his wits, such as they are, within half an hour or so.'

'I've done the same for you, Toby, many a time,' I said.

'Very funny,' he growled. 'Now, let's all meet later for a small celebration.' He named a bistro in Fulham and, with great enthusiasm, we all agreed to be there.

With Max in tow, I gathered up the few belongings I had taken to Caroline's apartment, posted the keys through Jane's door and headed, with great relief, for my own home.

Within minutes of our arrival Mrs Bradshaw knocked on the door to welcome me back. 'I hope that everything is back to normal,' she said and I assured her that the various problems had been resolved.

'Well, it must have been nice to be so close to Jane for a few days,' she said.

'Er, yes,' I replied vaguely, 'but I was too busy to spend much time with her.'

'I see, Chris.' She gave me one of her knowing looks and said she would catch up with all the news on the following day.

We took a taxi to the bistro in Fulham and on the way there, Max said that he had a great idea for an entry for the Turner Prize. 'It will involve Toby,' he said enthusiastically, 'and the work will be entitled "Writer's Block".'

'But he can't paint,' I objected.

'Not needed. It will be a video.'

When we had all settled at our table, Diana told us that we were her guests and took on the role of hostess with aplomb. She asked Toby to select the champagne, and not to spare the expense. He needed no encouragement to spend her money and ordered two bottles of Pol Roger. 'If it was good enough for the great Winston, it's good enough for us,' he said with relish.

Diana confirmed that Shane had been successfully returned to the bosom of his family and we all raised our glasses to toast our various successes.

'Do you really think Carras will pay up as promised?' Tim asked. 'And, above all, leave us alone. You don't think he'll want his revenge?'

'He'll want revenge, but I doubt he'll attempt it,' I said. 'He'll know that it would be very unwise to cross your mother.'

'We also have the invaluable assistance of Fergus,' said Diana. 'Anyway, all will be clear tomorrow, when a contract arrives for you, Tim, and two hundred grand for me. Well, for you, Tim, because I want you to have the money.'

His jaw dropped, then he grinned and gave his mother a hug. The celebration went with a real swing thereafter and, when the coffees and liqueurs were on the table, Max delivered his idea for a Turner Prize entry.

'This is right up your street, Toby,' he began. 'A video called "Writer's Block". It starts with you on the practice range with your driver in your hand.'

'And you hit your usual shot,' I said. 'You block the ball way to the right, about fifty yards off target.'

'And you do it several times,' Max continued, 'as is your wont.'

'Very funny,' Toby boomed, as he lowered half a glass of Armagnac. 'Then what?'

'We cut to you, sitting at your desk. You're typing a story. The floor around you is littered with torn-up sheets of paper. The camera looks over your shoulder and you type: "Once upon a time". Then you stop, put your head in your hands, tear the sheet out of the typewriter and throw it on the floor. You insert some more paper and start typing. "Once upon a time".'

'You've got writer's block,' I said.

Tim and Diana were giggling loudly by this time and I said, 'Do you think Toby can win the Turner Prize with such a work?'

'It's ridiculous enough to stand a great chance,' said Diana.

'It's a certainty,' Tim said.